PERMUTED PRESS

NEEDS YOU TO HELP

SPREAD THE INFECTION

FOLLOW US!

 FACEBOOK.COM/PERMUTEDPRESS

 TWITTER.COM/PERMUTEDPRESS

REVIEW US!

         YOUR BLOG

GET INFECTED!

SIGN UP FOR OUR MAILING LIST AT **PERMUTEDPRESS.COM**

PERMUTED PRESS

BOOK 2 COMING SOON!

Keep up on this and all your other apocalyptic favorites at

PERMUTEDPRESS.COM

PERMUTED PRESS

ZOMBIE ATTACK!
RISE OF THE HORDE

DEVAN SAGLIANI

A PERMUTED PRESS book

Trade Paper ISBN: 978-1-61868-116-4
eBook ISBN: 978-1-61868-117-1

Zombie Attack! copyright © 2011, 2013
by Devan Sagliani.
All Rights Reserved.
Cover art by Roy Migabon.

This book is a work of fiction. People, places, events, and situations are the product of the author's imagination. Any resemblance to actual persons, living or dead, or historical events, is purely coincidental.

No part of this book may be reproduced, stored in a retrieval system, or transmitted by any means without the written permission of the author and publisher.

CHAPTER ONE

If I can survive this day, just this one day . . . my crazy thoughts raced as the monstrous hordes closed in on me . . . *then I can survive anything this world throws at me.* Where did it all begin? How did I even get to this place in my life?

The last words my brother said to me were, "Don't leave this place, no matter what happens." But there was no way he could have known when he said it that one day zombies would form into wild hordes large enough to take out a military stronghold—especially one as large as Vandenberg Air Force Base. We were a small band of survivors, in the end mostly made up of military families, staying together in a big huddle at the back of the barracks where we watched as, one by one, the monsters picked off the soldiers protecting us. We'd made a break-out toward an abandoned elementary school at the edge of the base and taken refuge there.

For a while we were all safe. No one said much. We'd piled up all the furniture against the windows to make sure the ravenous creatures wouldn't just break the glass and flood in. It's not like the living dead feel pain. They never get tired either. Once they got the urge to kill and eat you that was pretty much it. They just kept coming until you were dead. You couldn't plead with them; they had no feelings. Crying wouldn't do any good.

The creepiest thing I've ever seen in my whole life was

one of those monsters that used to be a man, all tangled up in barbed wire and broken glass, frantically chewing its own arm off to get loose and join the feed.

We were herded together with no will of our own, desperately trying to survive this madness all around us.

This isn't going to work, I thought. *We're going to need a better plan, fast.*

Mostly we just listened to the fighting outside — the gun fire and the yelling and that terrible low moaning that sucks the very life out of you when you hear it. We learned it was smart to stay away from the windows. Eventually there were less and less of the piercing popping noises and terrified cries. One final living soldier let out a gut wrenching shriek as he ran out of ammunition and they tore him apart, advancing on him from all sides. A cold streak ran down my spine, leaving me shivering in mindless fear as his sobs faded off into echoes of wet, slurping sounds. Then there was nothing but the infinite chorus of low moans and the lifeless shuffling of feet outside. Their massive meal kept them satisfied for about an hour — probably the longest hour of my life. But then their heads came up one by one as they started smelling the air, recognizing that we were there, packed like trapped rats quivering in our own stinky fear.

Time's up, I thought.

No one made a sound that hour. Honestly, there wasn't anything to say. I guess we were just praying in our heart of hearts that they might lose interest and leave, but knowing beyond all hope that it wasn't going to happen. Eventually they'd be coming for us again.

I'd made friends at the base with this younger kid named Benji Jones. He was twelve years old, quiet, choosing not to talk with others and keeping mostly to himself. We all developed ways to block out what was happening, trying to keep our sanity intact in what had become an impossibly insane world.

For me that meant an endless series of martial arts practice and training sessions. I'd go over the top five my brother had taught me in succession, like a loop, often warming up with Tai Chi and ending with high kicks. I used the common grounds area between the buildings and spent hours each day going over the different karate forms until I was literally exhausted. It had become the only way I could sleep at night. When my body was tired, my mind would keep going, but eventually the darkness would pull me under.

There wasn't a whole lot to do at the base most of the time. They'd assigned jobs to the adults, but for the rest of us, the kids, the days were long and boring. Outside of the base the world as we knew it was burning away, and we were sitting around twiddling our thumbs waiting for someone else to handle the problem for us. It didn't make any sense at all.

A couple of times, other kids around my age would come up and watch my routine respectfully from a distance. Once a red headed kid asked if he could train with me, but he quit after a day and went back to hanging at the perimeter of the base with the tough looking kids—smoking cigarettes they'd pilfered from their parents and trying to act cool. I hate to say this but he was one of the first I saw go down when they overran us. One minute he was behind us as we fled for our lives and the next I saw him buried alive under a mass of dead, squirming, biting corpses.

Poor bastard, I thought. *He didn't deserve that. None of us deserves this.*

For Benji, sanity meant losing himself in comic books. He'd brought a sizable stash with him from his house in Santa Cruz. *Captain America. X-Men. Fantastic Four. Justice League. Avengers. Witchblade.* A whole bunch of *Spiderman*. He even had a couple of *Walking Dead* comics, ironically enough. After a few weeks he got to swapping them with other kids for other comics. People got to know him as the Comic Kid. They'd see him coming and hide, knowing if they started talking with him they'd never get him to shut up. What they didn't know was that Benji didn't have anyone else in his life—that he looked forward to having someone to chat up. The stories he kept rambling on about were the only things keeping him from sinking into a deep, dark depression. He'd lost both of his parents on Z-Day—right before his eyes.

By the time the government started acknowledging that there was a real problem, it was already too late to save the civilian population at large. I guess they tried to contain whatever caused the outbreak of people going nuts and eating each other in the streets, and they failed badly. That's when they officially declared Zombie Day, or Z-Day for short. Talking heads in newsrooms interrupted every channel to tell people that they needed to evacuate their homes and drive to a safe zone, generally a military base or installation. There, they would be quarantined, then set up in internment camps to wait out the worst of it.

Sadly, at that point, there weren't a whole lot of people who didn't already know how screwed they were. Most of the major American cities were already crawling with the hungry dead. It wasn't safe to stick your head outside your house much less drive around like a big, fat target. Let's just say a lot of good folks didn't make it.

Benji's parents told him to wait in the car while they grabbed the last of their valuables before heading to the base. The street had been swarming with zoms by that point. Benji locked the doors and hunkered down. Horrified, from the backseat of his parents' minivan, he'd seen them devour his family on the front lawn—mom, dad, and little sister. Benji hadn't been able to make a move to save them.

He must have gone into a state of total shock. He said it was like watching a really scary horror movie on pay-per-view. He hadn't even thought about what he was doing as he climbed into the front seat and started the van with the keys they'd left in the ignition. Before he knew it, he was calmly driving over bodies in the street. Some were alive and fighting to survive, but most were the living dead. He said he turned on the Frank Sinatra CD his parents had in the van and cranked the volume. The last thing he saw was one of his neighbor's houses going up in a fireball while Ol' Blue Eyes crooned "I did it my way . . ."

When he got to the base they took the minivan and all his possessions, except the comic books, and sent him into quarantine. The military needed all the supplies they could get to help take care of all the civilians they'd taken in. Originally they were only supposed to be able to care for about two thousand, but within days of the outbreak the base had about ten thousand people—all hungry, all scared, all pushed to the edge of their sanity by what they had seen and done to get there. A lot of amazing stories will probably never get told.

Some of those people wandered off on their own after a month or so had passed. They were willing to take their chances outside rather than stay on the base and starve while being told what to do all the time. Some wandered out of the safe zone and got picked off by stray zombies. Others volunteered to risk being moved to another safe zone. Some enlisted. By the end of two months we were down to a thousand or less survivors and things were much more manageable—until the horde came, that is.

I met Benji one day when I was heading back after a practice that involved taking out multiple attackers with my beloved katana. It was a gift from my big brother and had turned out to be the most important thing I owned. When the outbreak first started, I didn't bother to take anything with me other than my sword.

"It's better than a gun," my brother had said. "It's quiet, so it doesn't draw a lot of attention. And you never have to reload it. All you have to do is keep it clean." As usual, he was dead right.

I turned a corner and found several boys, eighteen or nineteen years old at least, shoving Benji around between them. His right eye was already swollen up and bruised. No doubt from one of their balled up fists.

"It's no use fighting us, Benji," said the biggest of the

gang—a greasy haired bully they called Weasel. "We're going to get them and there's nothing you can do to stop it. You might as well just give up and put this behind you. Get in line like the others. What's the point in getting roughed up when you can't win?"

Just what the world needs, I thought. *A philosophy-spouting hooligan.*

My fingers twitched slightly with anticipation as I began to remove the blade from its casing. To my surprise, Benji managed to wriggle loose from his captor's hold. He dropped to the ground, red faced from being choked, and thrust his fist straight out with all the might he could muster, connecting hard with Weasel's groin. Weasel let out a high pitched squeal like a girl and fell over, frantically clutching himself. The others looked on in shock. Benji used the distraction to grab up his comics and dash toward me.

As fast as he was, it still wasn't fast enough. Another one of the boys stuck out his leg and tripped him. Benji went down face first, his arms letting go of the comics and thrusting out in front of him to break his fall. A blur of paper showered over me for a minute as comic books rained down and landed at my feet. It was the first that they'd noticed me, but right away I could see from the looks in their eyes that they knew the balance of power had just dramatically shifted.

"What's going on, Weasel?" I asked.

"This doesn't concern you, Xander," he huffed, still winded from getting his family jewels rocked. "Just walk away."

Despite being only sixteen, I usually got a lot of respect because I knew how to handle myself and I never backed down from a fight. People knew that I was a Macnamara-- the equivalent of military royalty because of my brother. Breaking a grown man's arm when he had tried to steal my samurai sword the first week we were here hadn't been so bad for my reputation either. Word got around fast after that not to cross me. Since then I'd kept to myself and usually the only time anyone saw me outside was when I was training. To be honest, I was surprised Weasel had challenged me in the first place. As far as I could figure, he must not have wanted to lose face in front of his pathetic gang of long haired thugs.

"That's not gonna happen," I said. I thought I heard Weasel let out a small groan as he righted himself back to full standing position. He still looked a little green from the punch to his privates. "In fact, I think you owe young Benji here an apology."

Weasel smiled at the suggestion, flashing a crooked row of teeth the color of melted butter.

"Is that a fact?" Weasel scoffed.

"For the last two weeks I've watched your little gang prey on younger kids on the base," I said. "I've heard stories about you stealing everything from food to family heirlooms. I'd be only too happy to teach you some manners."

"You got proof to back up those accusations?" Weasel challenged me.

His boys began to fan out in an attempt to circle us. I helped Benji up, pushing him behind me while never taking my eyes off Weasel. A fight was definitely going to happen now. There was no doubt about that. All the talking was just to distract me while he gathered up his courage. I smiled at the thought of having a chance to practice my skills on real life volunteers. I began regulating my breathing, slow and steady.

"I don't care who your brother is," Weasel said, spitting on the ground and wiping his mouth with the back of his dirty hand. "I'm not afraid of you, Xander."

"Well, you should be," I said in a low voice, more of a promise than a threat.

"No one is going to save you. Out here it's just you and us."

"If you're not afraid of me why don't you take me on yourself?" I asked as the first of his guys slipped past my peripheral vision.

Weasel smiled wide, looking just like a jack-o-lantern. "You must think I'm stupid."

"Oh, I do," I assured him.

"Look out!"

I felt the first blow coming toward the back of my head even before Benji cried out. By the time his warning reached me I'd already ducked under a wide right hook, setting down my sword and reaching up to trap his arm. I grabbed onto it with both hands as I lifted up and jammed my shoulder into his armpit, immobilizing him.

With the slightest amount of downward pressure I could have easily shattered his arm in several places, but I knew I'd catch a lot of heat if I did. Being trained to fight came with certain responsibilities, including knowing when to show some restraint. As good as it would have felt to teach this coward a lesson he wouldn't forget for trying to sucker punch me in the back of the head, I'd be tying up some limited hospital resources in the process. I'd gotten away with it once before, but the circumstances were radically different. Doing it twice in a row would raise a lot of red flags and bring heat down on me and my brother as well. I couldn't let him down like that. I locked eyes with Weasel and smiled as I held his minion in place while he hopelessly squirmed to get free. All the color drained from his face.

"Let him go," Weasel demanded.

The third guy puffed his chest up, gathering all his courage to do something foolish, and then he lunged toward me. With barely a pivot I turned and threw his buddy at him head first, causing his outstretched fist to collide dead on with his pal's unsuspecting face, knocking him out cold. The weight of his unconscious body pushed the assailant to the ground and pinned him there, helpless.

"Okay then," I said calmly. "What now?"

"This isn't over," Weasel warned me in a low growl. "One of these nights, when your guard is down, I'm gonna pay you back for this."

I glared at him, all traces of my smile vanishing at the sound of his words.

"Did you just threaten me?"

I knelt down and swooped up my sword, unsheathing the blade and letting the sunlight dance across it. Weasel turned in his crud-covered Converse high tops and ran away as fast as his feet would carry him. I never had a problem with him again. If he had been planning some kind of surprise attack on me, it might have been foiled by the amassing zombie horde, but I doubt it.

I helped Benji gather up his comics and cautiously walked back to the barracks, avoiding making eye contact with soldiers along the way. Military royalty or not, I could be in as much trouble as Weasel if word got out I was fighting civilian kids on the base. I didn't feel like having to explain myself so I shushed Benji until we were back in his room. After that, there was no keeping him quiet—and he's been with me ever since, like my shadow.

Suddenly, a loud, inhuman grunt coming from outside the barracks tore through the silence and shook me out of my little trip down memory lane. It was a cold-blooded sound and caused one of the smaller kids to wet himself in fear. The smell of his urine, salty and metallic, harshly permeated the tiny room. No one said a word. I knew we were all thinking the same thing—if we just held our breath long enough the zombie horde would move on and we'd be left alive. No such luck. The sinking feeling in the pit of my stomach told me it wasn't going to end well for most of us in that room.

Sure enough, within less than five minutes the zombies had sniffed us out. *For dead things who can't feel pain or show emotion, they sure have a fantastic sense of smell*, I thought. Soon they were beating their dead fists on the doors and windows. The sound of the hammering echoed down the empty hallways of the elementary school, ringing off locked windows and unoccupied metal lockers.

A couple of the adults got up and blindly bolted out the

back door, no doubt thinking they could escape down that long hallway. I knew better than to even try. The way the school was laid out meant that they were heading into a dead end with a high block wall down at the perimeter—originally intended to keep predators out and kids protected from wandering off into traffic unsupervised. Once the zombies got inside, those adults would be trapped like rats in a sinking ship with only one way out—through a maze of undead former human beings, all trying to eat them alive.

The pounding grew louder and more determined. Once those monsters got it into their heads to get into a room, nothing could stop them. It was just a matter of time until they broke down one of the doors and came flooding in. So far as anyone could tell, zombies were driven by an insatiable hunger. It's not just brains they were after—they would literally eat anything they could get their hands on, so long as it's got a heartbeat.

No one knows why, or even where they came from. It's not like there are any experts on the subject. It all happened so fast, no one had time to ask. Anyone who stopped and asked questions was bound to get eaten.

Benji squeezed my hand and gave me a concerned look.

"I'm working on it," I said in response to his tense stare. "But you're probably not gonna like it."

He swallowed hard, bracing himself for action we both knew was coming. In times like these you had to think fast or you were literally dead meat. I was just working out the finer points of my plan to throw open the front door and make a mad dash out past them, straight through the courtyard, when a loud crash shook the building.

Two of the windows popped, showering us with shards of broken glass and drawing loud, terrified screams from several adults. The hinges on the door began to creak under the unstoppable weight of the bodies trying to force their way in. We had only seconds left. I turned back to Benji, unsheathing my blade as I spoke.

"Stay right on my heels," I said. He nodded back to me in

reply. "And no matter what happens, *do not fall down.*"

I'd barely finished speaking when the metal door flew off its hinges and the putrid stench of the living dead filled the air. Their rank smell overpowered the senses as they poured into the room like demons racing up from the bowels of hell for an all-you-can-eat smorgasbord.

CHAPTER TWO

My first instinct was to spring out and start slashing through them as they came rushing in. Benji and I were crouched so close to the door that it only made sense they would go for us first, piling on top and pinning us down before ripping out and devouring our insides like a piping hot Extra Value Meal at McDonalds.

Only they didn't. Zombies were attracted to noise and movement first. They rely on their sense of smell when they've got nothing else to work with. Benji and I sat as still as the grave these monsters should be rotting in, while the rest of the adults in the room began running around, waving their arms, and screaming at the top of their lungs in fear. They didn't stand a chance. The zombies were on them before most could make it out the back door to the rat trap.

I'm not gonna lie. There was a part of me that wanted to jump in and fight too, wanted to help the other people in the room as much as I wanted some kind of payback for what was happening to our world. It wasn't fear that held me back. At that point, I knew I couldn't save them and jumping in and getting myself killed wasn't going to change anything. I could feel Benji holding on to the back of my shirt, tugging on it as if he was asking me what my plan was.

I turned back to see his eyes bulging wide with fear as he watched three ghoulish, full grown zombie chew right through a man's leg. Blood squirted almost to the ceiling as the man endlessly shrieked in agony and despair.

The doorway was clear. Most of the living dead were already in the room with us, snacking on anything that moved or chasing the helpless leftovers down the long corridor.

It's now or never, I thought.

Taking a deep breath and nodding at Benji, I stood up and bolted forward, sword in hand, ready to slice through anything that got in my way, living or dead. Instantly several sets of jaundiced yellow eyes turned toward us. The zombie with a chunk of a man's leg in his mouth spit it out and roared in anger as we cleared the door. I didn't bother to look back. I was certain he was right behind us. I sprinted out into the courtyard, taking in the insane view of the utter carnage as I went. Every few feet, a headless zombie corpse lay twitching. Every few feet, the mangled body of a dead soldier lay ripped to shreds, camouflage stained red and black with blood and ooze.

A zombie woman with long, stringy brown hair and scarlet blood covering her mouth crawled mindlessly toward us. Cut in half by gunfire, she pulled her upper torso along by scratching at the asphalt with long fingers that ended in blood red nails. I had no doubt that if she reached us she would be just as dangerous as all the other reanimated corpses. A sense of dread crept over me as I watched her for a brief moment.

How can we win if cutting them in half doesn't even stop them? I wondered to myself.

"He's gaining on us. Which way do we go?" Benji shouted, snapping me out of my horror induced stupor.

A quick glance backward confirmed his words. A single zombie had followed us out of the classroom and was making good time across the gore-strewn grounds in our direction. Whatever intelligence drove these creatures sent him our way to finish off the massacre.

"Hurry!" Benji screamed, fear grossly twisting the

features of his face.

Scanning the yard, I saw the route between the far eastern side buildings was wide open. I'd spent countless hours getting the lay of the land when I first arrived and I knew that across the field was Cabrillo Highway, leading south to Lompoc. The sun was already starting to set. Walking in the dark was maybe the dumbest thing we could do, but we had two things going for us. The first was that zombies tended to slow down some at night. Like it or not, they still had human eyes so that meant their visibility went down after dark. The other thing working in our favor was the isolated area we'd be crossing through. Zombies tended to congregate in highly populated areas, as far as anyone knew. That was probably what had driven them to overrun the base in the first place. We weren't likely to find many of them in the relatively empty space between the base and town. It wasn't like we had many options at that point, anyway. Either way, we were going to be moving at night.

Better than being trapped inside a small building and surrounded by another horde, I thought.

I pointed toward the buildings to the east.

"We're heading that way," I said as calmly as I could, trying to sound like I was in control of myself. I could feel my hand shaking as I pointed, so I dropped it back to my side.

"Watch where you're stepping," I cautioned, gesturing toward the ground, "so you don't slip on the blood and guts, or trip over a body, or get dragged down by a partial zom crawler like that woman."

The zombie chasing us stopped and let out a loud shriek, sounding like a war cry. He was less than a hundred feet away. Benji and I both stopped and stared at him. Within seconds several other zombies came out from the school, sniffing the air. They turned toward us and began lumbering in our direction, the evidence of their ghastly last meal still staining their fronts.

"No time to waste," I said. We both took off at a full run,

giving it everything we had. I still had my sword in my hand. As we passed the female half zombie, she reached up toward me and bared her teeth. I brought down my katana and decapitated her with a single swipe of the blade. Benji kept glancing back as he ran, trying to see where our pursuers were.

I yelled out and caught his attention, fire burning in my lungs. "Don't look back. Just keep running!"

By the time we were halfway to the buildings, the carnage beneath our feet had disappeared. The majority of the fighting happened in the open area near the school, as soldiers sacrificed their lives for us.

Most of them died in vain, I thought. *What if that had been my brother?*

I didn't have to imagine what it would have been like to know them because I had been on a first name basis with most of the enlisted men since I had arrived. I recognized too many faces on our sprint to freedom, faces frozen in death, twisted by pain and anger. So many people had already died. With a small gang of the undead still chasing us, I knew I didn't have time to mourn these fallen heroes, but I made a mental note that if I made it out alive I would honor them. They deserved that mark of respect for all they had done, all they had given.

We were less than twenty feet from the buildings when I saw something moving in the shadows. My heart skipped a beat and I felt the familiar sour sensation rising up in my guts. We were racing as fast as we could go, straight into a zombie trap. A million horrible thoughts all went through my head at once. Maybe there was a swarm of them in there, faces peeled off, nothing but teeth and sharpened bones. Like insects working together they'd used their *hive mind*, their animal intelligence, to force us into a monstrous feeding pit. How many people were already dead in there, having been torn to bits by these disgusting monsters?

Rapidly I glanced around for a way out even as my legs carried us forward. I knew that if I tried to change course too suddenly, chances were I would trip and roll right into whatever demon was hiding in the shadows waiting for us. And even if I did make it, there was no way Benji would.

If I am going to die this way then I'll clear a path for him, I thought as I gripped the handle of my sword tighter. It was the only answer that made sense. I raised the sword in front of me and let out a loud battle cry as I charged forward toward the terrible darkness that awaited us. Before I could cross the threshold, two teenage boys stepped out of the alley and faced us. It was the Parker twins, Joel and Tom. They were covered from head-to-toe in dried blood.

What is that in their hands? I thought as they raised their arms chest high and pointed black steel at us. Guns. I'd seen them before. Not just any guns—an MK-13 and a grenade launcher. I slowed down just enough to let Benji get in front of me and then tackled him to the ground with all my might, holding him down as he squirmed and fought. The grenade flew past us a split second later.

"Cover your ears!" I yelled.

Benji stopped fighting and stuffed his fingers deep into his ears as if they were foam plugs. I barely got mine in when the explosion went off. The ground we were sitting on rippled from the force of the fiery blast.

I looked back to see pieces of the foul zombies flying apart. The ones who had joined the chase were now down for the count, but our main attacker was still in hot pursuit. He was less than twenty feet away. We were screwed. With my sword over ten feet away, I didn't stand a chance of retrieving it before he reached us. I was going to have to use hand-to-hand combat, knowing a single bite would transform me into one of them.

"Stay down!" Tom Parker yelled.

The next thing I knew a hail of bullets came ripping out of the MK-13, penetrating the soft flesh of the hell spawn and cutting him in half before our eyes. Strips of gray flesh, black muck, and oily red contaminated blood showered us. I did my best to cover Benji from the cascading flow of filth. It felt like the gunfire went on forever but in reality it was probably less than a minute.

Tom walked over to the bullet riddled zombie and kicked him over with his foot. Despite taking so much lead and being sawed in half, the thing was still moving its mouth, flexing its neck muscles as it lunged at Tom with its teeth.

"Suck on this," Tom said, sticking the barrel of his automatic weapon into the creature's snapping mouth and blowing its blackened brains all over the asphalt.

"Where the hell did you two come from?" I asked, sitting up and wiping the mess from my clothes the best I could.

So far as anyone knew, you couldn't get infected with the zombie virus by coming into contact with their blood or guts. The disease was spread by being bitten, the saliva transmitting the virus directly to the blood stream. You could bathe in a pool of undead guts and not get it, not that anyone I knew wanted to test that theory. Nothing smells as bad as the living dead. Words just can't begin to describe the disgusting stench.

"A simple *thank you* will suffice," Tom said, extending his hand to help me up.

I took it and got to my feet. Joel had set down his grenade launcher and was turning my blade over in his hands, mesmerized by its perfection. It made me uncomfortable to see him with it. A katana is not a toy to be played with. It's a delicate flower and a deadly instrument of justice. My blade was like my secret girlfriend and I didn't appreciate him causally putting his paws all over her.

"Thanks," I said, turning my back to him and walking over to Joel.

"Don't mention it," Tom said with a note of mild sarcasm.

"I believe that belongs to me," I said, with just a hint of force in my voice. He looked up into my eyes.

"Right you are," Joel said, immediately handing it over. Instantly I felt the muscles in my neck relaxing. "Just taking a look. No harm done."

"How did you two survive?" Benji asked. I was glad for a reason to change the topic. "And where did you get those amazing guns?"

"We were in the mess hall when the order came to evacuate," Joel said.

"We were way back in the kitchen, um, liberating some grub for those late night snacking fits," Tom added, looking sheepish. "Our candy supplies were running dangerously low."

"Right," Joel said, taking back the conversation. "So we hear all this earsplitting screaming, chairs scraping, people stampeding out the door, just general mayhem. We pop our heads out just in time to see a soldier shut and lock the door."

"Why would they take the time to lock the door?" The words were out of my mouth before I realized I was speaking.

"That's exactly what we said when it happened," Tom chimed in.

"So we creep up and take a peek out the window," Joel said, taking back the narrative. "You gotta realize at this point we have no clue what's going on. It could be a drill for all we know."

"I was hoping we were being evacuated to new housing, to be honest," Tom said. "There's a big spot above my bed that I am pretty sure is the start of black mold."

"It was unreal," Joel said, waving his arms to make his point. "First I see all the people on the base running toward the old elementary school. There are flashes of green as the soldiers run behind them, forming something like a human shield. There's a lot of screaming..."

"But it's like someone screaming *orders*," Tom interrupted.

"Exactly," Joel said. "Then the screaming started getting louder and blending together more. That's when we saw the first wave of zombies attack."

"I didn't know they could move that fast," Tom said. "I've only ever seen them kinda moping along. Sure they're lethal, because they don't ever let up once they catch a whiff of you."

"We never imagined they could move like that," Joel said. "It must have been the extreme hunger or something."

Get to the damn point, I thought. Just as I was getting ready to lose my patience, Benji prodded them for the rest of their long, drawn out tale.

"So how did you escape?"

"We cracked a window and slipped out," Tom said. Joel shot him a look that seemed to say thanks for ruining the story.

"I've done some research," Joel said. "Zombies are attracted to noise and movement."

Everybody knows that, I thought, rolling my eyes and fighting back an exasperated sigh. Joel pretended not to notice.

"They were too busy going after the cluster of screaming adults and fighting soldiers to notice us. So we slowly walked over to where the fighting had started. There were three dead soldiers just ripped to shreds lying there."

"It was ugly stuff, man," Tom said, looking at the ground.

"That's when we saw the second wave coming over the west wall," Joel said dramatically.

"Zombies can't climb walls, man," I said.

"They didn't have to *climb it*," Joel countered. "They lined up against it and just pushed it over like a human tsunami. They climbed over the rubble. They were coming right for us."

"What did you do?" Benji's eyes were wide with fear and anticipation as he listened, totally absorbed in the twin's story.

"We hid," Tom said. "Under the bodies."

"No way," I blurted out.

"It's true," Joel said, not sounding so cocky anymore.

"We didn't have much of a choice, did we? The zombies were heading toward us so we got on the ground and pulled the dead bodies over us for cover, hoping it would distract them."

"It did," Tom said defiantly, puffing out his chest. "They went right past us and toward the fighting. I remember thinking I must have wet myself out of fear and not even known. Only when I got up I saw it wasn't urine—it was blood coming out of the soldier I'd pulled over me, leaking out what was left in his body. It was still warm."

"Soaked right through our clothes," Joel said. "We grabbed these guns and broke out as fast as we could, using the buildings for cover."

"Why did you follow them to the school?" I asked.

"I dunno," Tom said. "I guess we just had to know what happened."

"I kept wishing there was some way to stop them," Joel said. "Instead, we were as helpless as babies and couldn't do a damn thing."

He looked upset with himself for not doing more to help. I understood the feeling. A wave of guilt crashed over me as I thought about all the people we'd left behind. I swallowed it back. There would be time for self-pity and wallowing later. For now, we needed to keep it together if we were gonna make it out of this alive.

"So you've never shot that thing until just now when we arrived?" I was having a hard time wrapping my head around it all. The MK-13 was a fierce piece of machinery. Tom had handled it like it was an Xbox 360 accessory.

"Our dad is a marine who saw action in Iraq," Joel said proudly, the grin returning to his dirty face. "Between us, we've pretty much practiced shooting on every kind of automatic weapon imaginable."

"Let's just say we've had a colorful childhood," Tom added.

"Where is your dad now?"

"We don't really know," Tom admitted. "He left us here

right after Z-Day."

"Haven't seen him since." Joel worriedly shrugged.

"Thank you for saving our lives," Benji said with shiny eyes that fought back tears of gratitude.

"Yeah," I added lamely, feeling like a moron. "Thanks."

"You're welcome," Tom said with an easy smile.

"We were just working on a plan to leave when we saw you hauling ass this way," Joel said. "I think we should give the kitchen another once over for supplies before heading out. Tom thinks it's too risky."

"Tom's right," I said. "It's not safe to stay here with the horde on the loose. It's just a matter of minutes until they eat their way through the school and start looking for fresh victims."

"So you've got a better plan?" Joel gave me a menacing look.

Everyone got real quiet and looked at me. I felt my throat going dry but pushed through it.

"If we take the 1 south past the housing, we'll literally walk right into town. I'm hoping we can grab an abandoned car along the way, maybe gas up in town, then head south to Hueneme. My brother is stationed there. He'll know what to do."

No one said a word. I felt my skin crawl as they stared at me. I didn't know if they thought it was the most brilliant plan ever or the dumbest.

"You're old enough to make your own decisions," I stumbled on, trying to come off more casual than I really felt, "but we are heading south. You're welcome to come with us."

"What makes you think it's any better down south?" Joel asked, fire still burning in his eyes. "How do you know we'll be safe there?"

"I don't," I shrugged. "All I know is we can't stay here anymore."

Joel and Tom stared at each other a long time, as if they were communicating by telepathy. Tom nodded and Joel shook his head. Benji watched on, fascinated. They turned back to us at the same time.

"Okay," they said in unison.

"Okay what?" I asked.

"We'll go with you," Joel said. "On one condition."

"What's that?"

"You let us do the shooting," Tom said gleefully.

"Fine by me. I've got a condition of my own."

"Oh yeah?" Joel said. "What's that?"

"The minute we find a place that's stocked up and safe, you two shower and change into clean clothes," I said, pointing at them with the end of my katana. "You look like something out of one of his more screwed up comic books."

"I think they look kinda cool," Benji said.

Tom smiled at him and messed his hair up.

"I knew you were gonna say that," I replied, walking past them and through the field that led out to the blacktop.

CHAPTER THREE

"Who would TiVo the *Jersey Shore*?" Benji had settled into the couch and was flipping through channels as if he didn't have a care in the world. He had his dirty, crud-crusted Nike's up on the table. Not one station was broadcasting, not even the armed service network emergency warning that used to go out on every channel, so he had switched over to recorded programs. He was scrolling through *Nitro Circus, Wipeout, American Ninja*, and *Jackass*.

"Someone who liked the show, I guess," I shot back, trying to hide my annoyance.

The truth was, I just didn't feel safe and I wanted to get moving as soon as we could. I peeked out the front window at the empty suburban street. There was no sign of the zombie horde. It was quiet—too quiet. The sun would be going down in just over an hour. I wanted to be sure we were on the road by then. Out there in the dark, the only thing worse than getting surrounded on foot by walking corpses would be getting trapped in a house with no escape.

I wish Moto was here, I thought. *He would know exactly what to do. He always knows.*

On our way down the street, we walked through a typical cluster of track homes. It was starting to get late and I didn't think it was safe to stop, but Joel reminded me of my taunt for the twins to get cleaned up and I eventually relented.

Tom picked the house he liked best then we made a full sweep of it, coming up empty. The fridge was stocked to maximum capacity. The electricity was still on. The AC hummed. Everything was about as perfect as you could ask for until we reached the upstairs bedrooms.

The master bedroom was fine. Nothing under the bed. Nothing in the closets. Then we swung open the second bedroom door. With stuffed animals, nursery toys, a child's bed, and a crib in the corner it was obviously the kid's room. No big surprise there. What we hadn't expected was all the blood. The whole room was covered in dried streaks of blood from floor to ceiling. It looked like something out of a Halloween horror house, like someone had taken buckets of blood and just flung them in every direction, painting everything.

There should be flies swarming all over this room, I thought, *like in the Exorcist.*

If a single window had been cracked, there would have been. My guess was that they kept the place air tight so they didn't waste money on air conditioning. The air smelled like dull rust. I was surprised it didn't smell like the zombies did, like death and decay.

We turned over every inch of the room but didn't find any trace of body parts. No bones. No bloody weapons. No fingerprints or bloody smudges. Nothing that would tell us what nightmarish, unthinkable thing had happened in that place. There weren't any signs of struggle or clean up going into or coming out of the room either. How it all happened remained a mystery to us. Nobody said a word. We backed out of the room and shut the door, lost in our own thoughts.

Joel and Tom raided the guy's closet for clean clothes and stayed upstairs to shower. Benji and I set up shop downstairs, tearing into the soda and snacks to fuel up on carbs before our big walk south. We were supposed to keep watch and let them know if any zombies showed up so we could bolt over the back wall and down the street. They had already been showering over a half an hour. I knew they had at least a gallon of blood each poured over them, but it was starting to get ridiculous how long they were taking. This was the zombie apocalypse, not a damn fashion show. Who were they trying to impress?

If they don't hurry up I might just grab Benji and go, I thought. I didn't have anything against the Parker twins. Like I said, waiting there like that was making my skin crawl.

"Yeah but MTV plays the show over and over on a loop," Benji protested, bringing me back to his present gripe about *The Jersey Shore*. "If you ever missed an episode all you have to do is just wait for it to start over." He dug into the bag of Frito's he'd salvaged from the kitchen, washing them down with an ice cold Mountain Dew. In the background,, Snooki fell off a bar stool and flashed her crotch to the camera.

I took a swig of Coke from the two liter I'd grabbed. We'd bagged up a bunch of non-perishables to take with us, just in case. I can't tell you how happy I was that the previous tenant left two huge bags of high quality beef jerky. Light, easy to carry, tasty, and chock full of protein. The only downside was it made you thirsty as hell, but we'd cross that bridge when we came to it.

"Lucky for you that they liked it," I said sarcastically.

"How can you not like *Jersey Shore*?" Benji turned to me, genuinely surprised. "It's the most entertaining show I've ever seen. It's like watching a train wreck in slow motion."

I smirked to myself at his seriousness. *Wonder if he knows the meaning of the cliché he just used*, I thought. Everything seemed like the biggest deal on earth when you were twelve. Everything was new and exciting. A lot more of the buzz than I'd like to admit wore off each year. I was only sixteen and I had already learned that. *Maybe that's why people are so jaded*, I thought. *There's nothing new when you get older. Just more of the same old crap being repackaged and shoveled down your throat with a shiny new bow on top.*

"I don't have anything against the show," I said, feeling

bad for disturbing what was probably the only relaxing moment he'd had in the last twenty-four hours. "I guess it's just not my thing."

"You're not into reality shows?"

"I've seen my fair share," I said. "Dancing contests and sing-off's and dating shows. I guess I just prefer to spend my time reading or surfing the web over watching television."

"What about *Breaking Bad* and *Dexter*?" Benji asked.

"Yeah, I've seen those."

"*Sons of Anarchy*?"

"I was gonna get around to it," I answered reluctantly.

"Oh man, you missed out! Too bad they didn't TiVo that," Benji said, slipping back into a false sense of security. "We'd have to camp out here until you'd seen them all. If Netflix was still working you'd have to drag me out of here kicking and screaming."

"We'll have to look into that at some point," I said. "You know, when things slow down."

I flashed a weak smile. Benji gave me a look that suggested I'd given him a satisfying answer and he turned back to the television. He switched shows to some guy doing a back flip on a motorcycle over a monster truck. It's amazing how much comfort we all used to take in moving pictures. I'm not gonna lie. I loved television when I was younger, just like everyone else. Moto used to call it the "slave box" and make fun of my obsession for Saturday morning cartoons.

"You've got all the freedom in the world," he would taunt. "No school, all your chores done, and instead of running wild and exploring the whole neighborhood you're sitting in your footed jammies eating sugary cereal with your eyes glued to the screen while it kills the few brain cells you still have."

I used to think he was so weird, but I soon chalked it up to him being raised in a foreign country. I didn't know why he was giving me such a hard time. Japanese kids loved television even more than we did. Eventually he got under my skin and I bit the hook, letting him lure me in and feed me his philosophy. Less than a month later, he started my martial arts and weapons training. Given the circumstances, it turned out he did me the biggest favor of my life. If he hadn't taught me all that stuff back then, I wouldn't have made it through my first zombie night.

Loads of people didn't. They saw the monsters coming but their brains couldn't process what they were witnessing. They'd been taken care of their whole lives, protected from things like this by other people. I heard that tons of them just stood there blankly staring while the zombies knocked them over and ripped off their pound of flesh with their dull gray teeth.

Don't think about it, I told myself. *Stay focused on your goal. If you start thinking about it all now it will overwhelm you and weaken your will to survive. Your survival depends on your staying sharp. What did Moto teach you? Moto told me to stay put. There was more. Think! What did he say about being out in the open? Keep moving until you know you're safe. Never let your guard down until you are absolutely sure you're out of harm's way. This isn't a mistake you get to make twice.*

I turned back and scoured the street for signs of life, coming up empty again.

"I think it's time we get moving," I nervously said. A voice behind me made me jump.

"Not thinking of leaving without us, are you?" I turned to see Tom's smiling face.

He looked like a different person. He had on khaki's and a navy blue polo shirt. Joel was behind him, not smiling, wearing practically the same thing in a darker shade of green. In fact, the only way to tell them apart was by their radical personality differences.

"Wouldn't dream of it," I said.

"Good," retorted Joel, pushing past Tom and looking out the window. "I got an idea."

"I'm all ears."

Benji shut off the television and walked over to us

carrying the bag of kitchen loot we'd snatched while the twins were cleaning up.

"One of these houses has a car in the garage," Joel said. "I know it. I say we make a sweep and find which one it is then load the thing up and head out."

"You know how to hot wire a car by any chance?" I asked.

"People left everything when they deserted this area," Joel shot back. "They didn't have time to turn off their sprinklers or shut off appliances they wouldn't be using. That's why we have this beautiful air conditioning right? So it stands to reason that if they left all their valuables, they also left a set of car keys."

"I hate to argue with you . . ."

"Then don't," Joel interrupted, casting me an impatient look. I ignored him and continued on.

". . . but I think the reason we're not seeing cars on the street isn't because the people who own them left 'em in the garage. It's because they used them to flee."

Joel shook his head in disbelief. Tom looked down at the carpet. Benji awkwardly looked between Joel and me to see if we were going to escalate this argument into a full scale fight.

"The sun is setting soon and with a zombie horde just north of here, I'm not sure wasting more time is a good idea," I said as softly as I could.

"Fifteen minutes of searching could save us a long and dangerous night walk," Joel said. "Think about that."

Everyone turned and stared at me. It felt weird to have so much pressure on me all of a sudden. That was the last thing I had wanted.

"Okay then," I said, giving in and letting him have his way. There was no reason to keep having a power struggle. At the end of the day we wanted the same thing—to be safe and far, far away from that horde. "You lead the way."

Joel nodded. A hint of a smile creased his face as he charged out the front door, leaving it wide open for us. Benji was last out and he shut it, mostly out of habit I think. We went door-to-door like super aggressive Jehovah's Witnesses, yanking open garages only to find them empty. If we couldn't get the garage open, we went through the house. If the house was locked, we broke a window. Just as I had expected, there wasn't a car to be found. Joel's earlier swagger seemed seriously diminished by our inability to lay hands on a functioning vehicle. At one point we were all excited to find an old Mustang, only to have our hopes dashed when it didn't have an engine. With one house left at the end of the block, the odds were looking pretty slim on locating transportation.

"You wanna do the honors?" I asked, trying hard not to gloat.

"Naw," Joel said in a defeated, but much more congenial, tone. "The kid can take this one."

Benji looked glad to get a chance to participate. The only thing we'd let him do on our search so far was climb through a window to unlock a sliding door. He ran up the driveway and began trying to pull the heavy door up. It didn't look like he was making much progress but then he gave it a hard shove, getting the door over his shoulder and forcing it up.

"Guys! Hurry! Come quick!" Benji huffed, out of breath and sounding like Sean Astin without his inhaler in the *Goonies*.

We all turned and ran up, expecting to find a brand new SUV or maybe a stash of weapons. Instead we found a tiny looking kid, Samuel Thorn, curled up asleep in a pile of candy wrappers. My only guess as to why he hadn't heard the door open was that he had passed out from exhaustion. Tom nudged him with his foot and the little guy sat up straight and screamed at the top of his lungs like a cornered raccoon. He pulled a dull steak knife from his waistband and waved it at us.

"Stay away!" Sam threatened.

"That supposed to ward off the undead?" Tom taunted

him.

"Who are you people and what do you want?"

"It's me, Sam," Benji said stepping forward and pushing the knife aside. "It's Benji. Remember me? We used to trade comics back on the base."

"What are you doing here?" I didn't want to sound rude but we didn't have all night to sit around while the kid figured it out.

"I'm hiding from zombies," he said.

"Perfect," Joel said. "That's exactly the answer we were looking for. Bravo." Obviously he was as frustrated by this kid as I was.

"But how did you get here?" Benji patiently asked.

"I was in the school when they swarmed in. I ran down the long hallway to the back."

"That's a dead end," I shot back. "How did you get out?"

"You know the large oak tree in the yard? I climbed up to get away from the fighting. From there I managed to get on the roof and jump the back wall."

"Pretty resourceful little guy, aren't you?" Tom said.

"I didn't know where to go, but then I found these houses," Sam said. "They're just like my neighborhood back home in Sacramento. I didn't even know any of this was here. And I sure didn't realize how tired I was. I guess I just fell asleep."

"Looks like you did more than sleep," Joel said, kicking the empty candy wrappers. "Think you got enough sugar in your system?"

"Enough for what?" Sam looked confused as he turned back and forth from me to Joel.

"A long night's walk," I said, putting my hand on Joel's shoulder to console him.

CHAPTER FOUR

The sun set even faster than I expected. By the time we'd left suburbia, there were only faint traces of light left in the sky. Once we got down the road from the track homes, the landscape changed pretty dramatically just within minutes. Unruly weeds and brittle-looking scrub bushes covered the sides of the highway. All we could see were small, grass covered hills and patches of dry looking trees in every direction. Within half an hour of walking it felt like we were in the middle of nowhere. We could have been in a foreign country for all we knew. If we hadn't stuck to the road I would have been truly freaked over getting lost or being attacked by a wild animal — or worse.

We passed around the bag of goodies we'd grabbed at the house and soon the only sound was the crinkling of wrappers and the crunch of loose gravel between our shoes and the asphalt. I was glad to finally tear into that beef jerky. It was salty and sweet and spicy and surprisingly tender. I chewed it with great relish, enjoying every second of it. It lived up to every expectation I'd conjured up. It was filling, unlike the candy bars we'd grabbed which were mostly just sugar. I tucked away a Snickers bar for when I got tired later and needed the extra boost.

We naturally fell into two groups without really thinking about it. Benji and I walked a little farther ahead of the pack while the twins kept pace with Samuel and tried to keep him moving along. I could tell Joel was frustrated but didn't want to leave his brother's side, while Tom had just the right disposition to keep the little guy motivated.

"I'm tired," Sam whined.

"We just gotta keep moving," Tom replied.

"But my feet hurt," Sam groaned, letting out a loud sigh.

Joel fought back a growl of disapproval. He was more like me than I'd realized—which was probably why I felt threatened by him in the first place.

"That's nothing compared to what it will feel like when a wild pack of zombies rips you to shreds," I muttered under my breath, picking up my pace to try to distance myself from the annoying conversation behind me. Benji shot me a sympathetic glance.

I wasn't cut out to be a leader. Plain and simple. I didn't mind taking care of Benji because he never complained. He did what you asked and was always happy and grateful, always trying to make the best out of this insane situation.

"Try not to focus on them," I heard Tom say as Benji and I power walked farther out in front of them. "Maybe think about something that makes you happy for a bit. That always helps."

Benji must have heard Tom's advice and taken it to heart.

"It sure was great to be able to watch television again," Benji said shortly after. "Sitting there in that living room on a comfortable sofa, feeling the cool air on my skin and flipping through shows was like a small slice of heaven. It was like coming home after school before my parents got home and having the run of the place, like the way things used to be."

"Yeah."

"Do you think there might be a time in the future when all of this is behind us?"

"You mean the zombies?"

"Yes."

"Definitely," I answered. "It's just a matter of time until our military forces eradicate all the infected. All we have to do is survive until then."

Easier said than done, I thought.

"Sometimes I feel like it will never end," Benji said honestly.

"It just feels that way. It will end. You'll see."

"How long do you think that's gonna take?"

"It's hard to say." I shrugged. I think it was the first time I had admitted the truth to myself. "This thing is way more out of control than I ever imagined it would be. Then again, we might be closer than we think. It all depends on what the military has been able to accomplish. We have no way of knowing what they're working on, what their ultimate strategy is."

"Do you think it's gonna be months or even years until they have it under control?"

"Without radio or television news reports, it's all kind of a guessing game," I said. "Then again for all we know, we could wake up tomorrow and everything could be back to normal."

"Man I hope that happens." Benji gave a little laugh. "I'd love to go home. I never knew how much I could miss it."

I liked the way a little bit of hope had lifted his spirits, so I pressed on. "They're probably using all their energy to reclaim the cities."

"You think so?"

"Sure," I offered. "It's what I would do. Secure the bases then start spreading out slowly and taking back the land. The cities already have everything they need to support a population. There is food, shelter, water, the means to create electricity. The way I see it, all they have to do is quarantine off a major city then slowly move in, wiping out the biters as they go. Then they set up a detail to guard the perimeter and move on to the next city."

"That makes sense," Benji said. There was a noticeable skip in his step now.

"Eventually the only zombies left will be out in the wild."

He shot me a worried glance and I realized what I had said. *We* were out in the wild! My mind made the same connection his had just made. What if a horde of zombies was being flushed our way from Lompoc right now?

Smooth move, I thought. *Say something quick to make him feel better.*

"I'm pretty sure we're alone out here, so don't freak out and let your imagination get the best of you."

Benji didn't say anything. He just nodded and gulped. We walked along in silence for what felt like over an hour before he spoke again.

"So what's the deal with your brother?"

I was glad to have a reason to speak again.

"He's a corporal in the marines," I said proudly.

"So why didn't he stay with you at Vandenberg?"

"He's got too much work to do to stay in one place. Since Z-Day hit, he's been called to service up and down the coast."

"And he's in Hueneme now?"

"That's right. Like most military bases that are still active, they've combined all the different armed forces into one cohesive unit down there. He told me he was working on something big. Something that could change the course of this fight. Maybe end it all together."

"So why didn't he take you with him?" It was an innocent enough question. Benji hadn't said it with any malice in his voice, yet it felt like someone had socked me hard right in the gut when I heard it. He had a good point. I didn't know for sure why Moto hadn't taken me. There was a part of me that did feel abandoned. I'd trained hard, always done exactly what he said, but he still left me behind with the rest of the kids when they called him down. Didn't he realize I wasn't a child anymore? When was he going to stop treating me like one?

"He was coming back for me," I said, my voice cracking, "once he got things set up."

"Oh." Benji looked sorry he'd brought it up.

"He was just getting settled in. That's all."

"Right."

"Then once he had things under control he was going to set me up on the base," I said. "Until then he wanted to make sure I was safe."

"Well that worked out just great, didn't it?" I heard Joel say mockingly.

I jerked around to see the Parker twins and Sam staring at me. I hadn't realized they had caught up to us. My face burned with embarrassment.

"You don't know anything about it," I shot back self-consciously.

"How do you figure?" Joel yelled back.

"Guys," said Benji.

"You don't know the first thing about my brother."

"I know he didn't come back to save you when that horde of flesh eating demons overran the base," Joel spat.

"Yeah? And neither did your father!" I angrily shouted.

Fire flashed in Joel's eyes. I was instantly sorry I had said it, but not because I was afraid of Joel. It was a cheap shot and I knew it. We were all hurting. We were all scared. And now we were turning on each other like feral animals. Still I knew I couldn't back down an inch. If I didn't stay on top of Joel he would wrestle control of the group away from me. I wasn't about to let that happen. I needed to keep us on course.

"Take it back," Joel retorted in a low, threatening voice.

"Make me!" I said, my fists bunching up defensively.

"Guys!" Benji shouted again.

"What?" I said, turning to face him.

Joel was on me before I had time to register what was happening. I didn't think he had it in him. I was so used to most of the people at the base respecting my reputation as a fighter and staying clear of me. He knocked me off my feet and we rolled on the ground. He got in a quick punch to the right side of my head and then I blocked the next. I flipped him over and slapped him hard across the face. I pinned him to the ground as he fought to get up and a stream of curse words came out of him like he was possessed.

"Guys!" Benji shouted a third time, trying to get our attention. "Listen!"

Everyone stopped moving and listened. Off in the distance there was a loud rumbling sound that filled the pit of my stomach with churning fear.

Please don't let that be a zombie horde, I thought.

"What is that?" Joel asked. All the fight had left him. I got up and helped him to his feet. He jumped back away from me and dusted himself off.

"Quiet," Benji admonished.

The unexplained noise grew louder and louder. The closer it got, the more it sounded like some kind of big machine and less like the undead.

"Look," Sam shouted, pointing back in the direction we'd come from.

We all turned at once and stared in astonishment as a black military helicopter shot up over the ridge and passed over the top of us. It was so loud we couldn't hear anything else, but Joel and Tom waved their arms and yelled anyway. The helicopter was gone just as quickly as it had come, leaving us alone with our desperate thoughts.

"That's a good sign," I said.

"How do you figure?" Joel asked.

"Yeah, man, they left us out here," Tom loudly complained.

"It means we're still in control," I said confidently. "We've still got equipment and we're still fighting."

"Unless those were zombies," Sam said.

Everyone laughed at him.

"What?" He tried to cover up his embarrassment.

"Last time I checked, zoms can't fly helicopters," Tom said. "I think we're good."

"Oh," muttered Sam.

"Can you even begin to imagine how screwed we'd all be if that were the case?" Benji patted Sam on the shoulder and walked to my side.

Joel gave me a guarded look and I turned and walked on. Neither of us spoke about our scuffle but I knew I didn't plan on letting my guard down around him any time soon. He was faster than I had thought he would be. Sooner or later we were going to butt heads again. It was just a matter of time. I was seriously hoping we could go our separate ways once we got into the city. After all, there was no reason for him to follow us all the way to Hueneme. And he had Tom to keep him company.

The first chance I get, I've got to ditch him, I thought. *The sooner the better.*

We came to a fork in the road where the freeway became an overpass as it intersected another highway. A curl of fog wrapped over the bank, giving it an eerie feeling. There was something in the way up ahead, something big and still. It was way too large to be a zombie, but even from a distance I got the feeling it wasn't going to be good.

"What is it?" Benji whispered.

"Only one way to find out," I replied.

I unsheathed my sword and carefully sauntered forward. Joel followed close behind me, then Tom, Benji, and last, Sam. There was an orange street lamp overhead illuminating the object. The fog drifted away by the time I was ten feet from it to reveal a large deer laying on its side with its throat ripped out. Dark blood pooled onto the ground around it. Foot prints dragging through the blood led away into the dust on the side of the road.

"What did this to it?" Benji looked stumped.

"From the looks of those foot prints I'd say it was a zombie," I suggested.

"Nonsense," Joel chimed in. "There is no way a deer would let one of those undead things get this close to it, let alone stand there while it tore its throat out."

"It doesn't make any sense, man," Tom agreed, obviously trying to diffuse the tension between us.

"Maybe it was wounded," I said.

"Or sleeping," Benji added.

"It's a mystery," Tom agreed.

"First the helicopter and now this," Joel said, sounding exasperated. "What's next?"

Almost as if on cue, Sam let out a blood curdling scream that ripped through the night. We turned and saw that something had attached itself to his leg. It was a zombie that had been cut in half, a crawler. It had snuck up over the side of the embankment and taken him by surprise, wrapping its arms around Sam's tiny limb and pulling itself in for a bite. It all happened so fast there was nothing we could do. Sam wailed in pain like a siren.

Joel lunged toward him and kicked the twisted corpse off with his combat boot. It rolled helplessly on its back, trying to flip itself over. Blood covered its dark mouth as broken teeth snapped at the air like some kind of swamp creature straining for its last meal.

"It's getting back up," Tom yelled, shaking me out of my state of shock.

As quickly as I could, I ran over and cut its head off, separating the brain stem from the body. Instantly it went still, like a deadly toy with its battery removed. Sam fell on the ground and began examining his bite mark with shaking hands. We all gathered around him.

"That thing came out of nowhere," Benji said.

"Let's have a look at that wound," Joel said.

Sam had been pulling the skin to show the blood oozing out. He moved quickly to cover it up. "It's not that bad," he said.

"Does it hurt?" Tom asked.

"It stings a little bit. But I'll be fine."

For a kid who was crying about his feet being sore, he sure got tough all of a sudden, I thought.

The truth was that he wasn't going to be fine. He was infected and there was nothing in the world we could do about it. Every second that past brought him closer to his fate of transforming into a mindless killing machine with an insatiable appetite for living flesh.

No one said anything for a long time. We just exchanged looks and stood around Sam while he stared down at the concrete not blinking. It had to be setting in, what the bite meant. His life was over now. Nothing could bring it back. Ten minutes ago he had a future. Now all that existed were his last few moments.

Benji leaned down and hugged him and Tom sat by his other side. Joel gave me a glance that told me to meet him a little ways over toward the deer. We both quietly walked away and stood looking at the dead animal, not making eye contact.

"What do you think we should do?" Joel fidgeted.

"What can we do?" I asked. "He's a goner for sure."

"Yeah. That thing got a good chunk of him."

"The virus is definitely in there. No doubt about it." I turned and spit over the side of the bridge.

"How long do you think it's gonna take him to turn?"

"Hard to say." I looked back at Sam to see if he was watching us. He hadn't lifted his head. Benji was cooing words of encouragement in his ear. "From what I've seen, when someone gets bit good and deep like that it doesn't take long for them to go full zom. Especially someone that small."

"Yeah." Joel absentmindedly tapped the deer carcass with his boot. "I've noticed that too. So what do you think we should do with him?"

"I hate to say this," I started, "but there is no way we can take him with us now."

"No argument there," Joel said sternly.

"I hate to leave him out here. I'm not sure we have a choice now."

"He's gonna become one of those things soon," Joel said in a gentle tone. "When he does, he will be a danger to all of us. Plain and simple."

"What are you suggesting?"

"Isn't it obvious?" Joel looked up into my eyes. "The only

humane thing to do is to kill him."

He's right, a little voice in my head told me, even as I shook my head no.

"But he's just a kid," I feebly protested, "a small, helpless kid."

Joel looked sympathetic as I struggled with it. "He won't be for long. Think about it."

"No," I said in total shock, and yet it made sense what Joel was saying. Soon Sam would not only be a tiny, out-of-control monster but also a threat to each of us. "He's terrified. Look at him! We can't do that to him."

"We have no way of knowing what happens after someone turns," Joel argued. "We don't know if they die right away or if they are, you know, trapped in there, seeing everything they are doing but unable to control it. By not killing him we could be condemning him to a living hell beyond anything you or I ever imagined."

"So we just shoot him in the face and move on?" My voice cracked. "Would you do that to me if I was bitten? Or Benji?"

"If that's what it came down to, I would."

I'll bet, I thought. *He's probably wishing it was me that got bit in the first place so he could get me out of the way.*

"What if it was Tom?" I asked. Joel hesitated. I'd hit a nerve. "Would you be willing to casually blow your twin brother's head off because he was going to turn into a zombie?"

Good, I thought. *He does have some kind of moral center after all.*

"If it came down to that," he said, but it was clear the wind had gone out of his sails. He couldn't even look me in the eye anymore.

"Let's hope it never does," I said, turning and walking back over to Sam.

"We about ready to get going?" Sam asked, trying to sound calm. "I think I can walk on it as long as I don't put any pressure on it. Maybe I can get a tree branch and make some crutches out of it."

"You can't come with us anymore, Sam," I said. The others looked away as I spoke.

Sam looked crestfallen. "I'll be okay," he said, trying to change my mind. "It's not that bad."

"I'm so sorry buddy," I offered, leaning down and looking him in the eyes. Tears burst out and drooled down his face. "We can't take that risk. I wish there was another way, but there just isn't."

"You can't just leave me out here in the middle of nowhere all alone."

"I'm fairly certain you wouldn't appreciate the other suggestions floated for how to deal with this situation," I said.

Sam's young eyes filled with fear as the meaning of my statement settled over him in a chilling moment of realization. His eyes flashed from Joel to the gun he was carrying then back to me.

"Please don't kill me," he begged as a fresh round of tears burst out of him. It was taking everything I had in me not to lose it. A tiny spark of anger at Joel rose up in me but I held it in check.

"No one is going to kill you," I promised.

"What am I supposed to do? Sit out here and wait to die?" Sam wailed and Benji put a hand on his shoulder, comforting him.

"Listen, little man," I said, "this is what you're going to do. You're going to turn around and follow the road all the way back to that set of abandoned houses where we first found you. Got it?"

Sam didn't answer. He just nodded. I wasn't sure he entirely believed us. I glanced at Joel and burning hatred filled my guts. It was wrong to scare this poor kid in his final moments.

"Don't stop walking until you get back," I said, reaching into my pocket and handing over my emergency Snickers bar. "Pick a house you like, maybe something with a pool, and lock yourself in. Once we find help in Lompoc we'll come back for you."

"How will you know which house I'm in?"

"We'll search all of them until we find you," Tom said softly.

"What if I get attacked on my way back? I don't have a weapon to fight off the zombies."

"We can't leave him a weapon," Joel said. "It's a waste. Chances are we're going to need it far more than he is. By the time the sun comes up he won't even know who he is!"

Sam looked down, afraid to make eye contact with him. The rest of the group shot Joel dirty looks that shut him up.

Tom handed over his grenade launcher. "Here. Take this. It's only got one good shot left, but it's heavy enough to swing around and use as a club if you get jumped."

"You're going to be all right," Benji said.

"He's right," I lied. "There is less chance of being attacked during the night so you'd better hurry. You're going to want to get back before the sun comes up."

"Okay," Sam said, standing up with his new gun. He wiped his tears on the back of his hand.

"Good luck," Tom offered.

"See you later," Benji said sadly.

"Pick a good house," Tom added with a brave smile.

"We'll be back before you know it," I encouraged.

Joel looked away but the rest of us watched as the young boy limped off along the road in the direction we'd just come from, the direction we'd been fleeing due to a wild zombie horde. When we could no longer see him, we turned and continued on down the highway, the weight of everything that had happened making my feet feel like two blocks of heavy lead.

CHAPTER FIVE

We'd been walking in the pitch black for less than an hour when we saw headlights approaching in the distance. The sound of the truck buzzing along toward us reached us after we spotted what looked like an insect glowing in the darkness. I was starting to feel delirious after all the walking. It was the dead of night, the air was biting cold, and we'd been walking so long my feet were going numb. I was totally wiped out. A quick glance around showed me that the others were pretty much in the same state I was. The incident with Sam hadn't helped with morale either. Aside from the savage hunger and rotting skin, we weren't all that much different at that point than the creatures we were fleeing. It took a moment for it to sink in, but when it finally did I stopped dead in my tracks and just watched the truck heading our way.

"That thing is headed right for us," I mused.

"Thank God," Joel coughed. "I'm walking along like one of the zombies at this point. I feel dead on my feet."

"Careful," I cautioned. "We wouldn't want to have to shoot you."

He blasted a nasty look in my direction and I immediately returned his glare.

"Guys," Benji said, his voice weary and filled with dread. "What do we do?"

"What do you mean?" Joel wheeled around on him. "We

flag him down and ask for a ride, obviously."

"Benji's got a point," I said. "How do we know he's friendly?"

"Now just what is that supposed to mean?" Joel asked, the anger rising up in his voice.

"We're not on the base anymore," I continued. "Everyone we meet isn't just going to be nice and want to help us. It's a lawless zone out here. We have no way of knowing how the driver of that truck is going to react to us. Plus they're heading in the wrong direction, straight toward a zombie horde."

"All the more reason we should wave them over and warn them," Tom interjected, looking over to Joel who gave him a nod of solidarity.

"What if we take cover for now until we see what the driver looks like?" Benji offered. "If we feel safe once we've gotten a decent look at the truck, we can make our presence known and try to flag him down. If not, we haven't given ourselves away."

"Now that is good advice," I said. "Anyone have a better idea?"

I could see that Joel didn't but he still wanted to argue. After what happened with Sam I wasn't able to hide my disgust for him. As far as I was concerned, Joel was a bigger threat to our safety than any zombie ever would be. Zombies weren't accountable for their actions. They were victims just like the rest of us. Joel, on the other hand, was a bloodthirsty killer just waiting for an excuse to execute one of us. I felt like a monster for even thinking of hurting Sam. Joel had been ready to pull the trigger himself! If I hadn't been there to stop him he'd have walked the poor little guy off into the bushes like an old dog and shot him in the back of the head. The thought of it made ice flood through my veins, hardening my heart further against him.

"Fine," Joel said, relenting at last. He was trying his best to maintain the illusion that he was in some sort of control, but he was failing miserably.

We scurried off the road and into a cluster of bushes to wait. The sound of the truck grew closer and I grew more and more impatient. Hunger was starting to make me edgy. I wasn't sorry I'd given away my emergency candy bar as a last meal to a sad kid, but I sure wished I had another one. I continued to think about Sam despite the fact it was the last thing in the world I wanted to be pondering.

The mind has a way of playing tricks on you when you're tired. What if these people came across him walking back to Vandenberg and discovered that he had been bitten? Who knows what they would do? They might very well have the same reaction that Joel did. Then again, what if Sam hid his bite wound out of fear and got into the truck with them? They might be carrying the disease back to an area they thought was safe and spreading it. Under those circumstances, Joel would have been right to want to kill Sam. There was no way I was going to ever admit that out loud though. I couldn't and still live with myself.

"Looks like a white Nissan with a bearded man driving," Tom whispered.

"What are those marks on the side of the truck?" Benji asked.

"They look like bullet holes to me," Tom said.

"That's because they are," Joel confirmed. "There are also two armed men standing in the back with some kind of rifles."

"What does that mean?" Benji prodded.

"It means Xander was right to tell us to lay low," Joel admitted, sounding unhappy about having to give me credit for anything. "Could be a militia or a roaming band of thugs looking for trouble to get into. I say we wait for them to pass, then move on along down the highway until we get to town."

The truck was getting closer. Soon it would pass us and then, if it kept heading north, it would run into Sam—who by this point had probably sat down and gone into shock from his wound.

Zombie bite victims reported feeling disoriented after they're infected. This was according to early news reports from back before anyone knew it was going to be an epidemic. Their bodies shut down as a terrible fever overcomes them, just like people infected with HIV. It's the body's way of trying to fight off the virus. It doesn't work and it leaves the victim totally incapacitated. Sometimes, from what I've heard, they then experience organ failure. Within a few hours they lose the ability to think clearly; they can't communicate and then become agitated. At that point they aren't fully people anymore, but they aren't quite zombies yet either.

The first victims had no way of knowing what was happening to them. Poor Sam does. He'd know the whole way through what was happening to him. I couldn't begin to imagine that kind of fear.

Without thinking, I stood up and stared at the truck.

"What are you doing?" Joel demanded. "Get back down, you moron!"

Joel grabbed at my jeans, trying to yank me back down, but I pulled away from him and walked out into the middle of the road. The truck was barreling toward me. At first, I wasn't sure it was going to stop.

Great, I thought as the front bumper of the truck drew closer to my kneecaps. *I've survived the end of the world only to die by being run over.*

"What the hell!" I heard a man's voice yell.

The tires squealed as the truck came to a screeching halt less than ten feet from me. White smoke rose up and the smell of burning rubber filled the air. The two men in back had their faces covered. They were standing in the bed of the truck and pointed their weapons at me.

"Don't shoot!" I hollered. "We just need a ride."

The driver of the truck opened the door and stepped out.

"John?" One of the shooters cautioned him.

"It's all right," John said. "Just keep him covered for now."

He turned his attention to me. "Where did you come from?"

"Military base up north," I said, keeping my hands up. "We were overrun by a zombie horde."

"There is no such thing as a zombie horde," John replied matter-of-factly. "Zoms can't barely think for themselves. They're driven by hunger, like mindless insects. They are drawn to the living by sight and smell. *Period*. They don't communicate with other zombies and they don't work together."

"That's what we thought too," I said, trying not to tremble. I couldn't tell if it was the cold or the fear getting to me. "Until they knocked down the walls at Vandenberg and killed everyone we knew."

"Vandenberg's been taken out? Jesus."

"They were definitely working together," I added, feeling a little more confident. "Like they had some kind of hive mind."

"How'd you get down this way?" John asked, ignoring my suggestion.

"We walked," I replied.

"There are more of you?" John looked around nervously for an ambush. His guards did the same. "Come on out. Show yourselves."

Slowly Benji, Tom, and Joel stood up.

"Get your hands up where we can see them!" The guards swung around and trained their guns on the group in the bushes. Joel gave me an angry look.

"They're just little kids," one of the men shouted to the leader, who acted like he didn't hear him.

"Is that all of you?" John shouted.

"Yes it is," I said, shooting a threatening look at the rest of the group to keep their mouths shut about Sam.

"Get on out here," John ordered.

Cautiously the group walked over and joined me in front of the truck's headlights.

"Now," John said, seeming calmer, "where are you

headed?"

"Lompoc," I said. "Then farther down south toward the coast."

John laughed and shook his head.

"It's a good thing we found you," he said. "You'd never make it into the city without an armed escort."

"What do you mean?" Joel asked.

"Lompoc is a war zone now," John said, spitting on the ground.

"You mean zombies?" Benji asked sheepishly.

"Yeah," John said, "sure. We still got those. Plus there is the damn *Unity Gang* to worry about now."

"What is the Unity Gang?" Tom asked innocently.

"Hell on earth, son," John said causally. "It's a collection of bikers and rival gangs that got together after Z-Day to wreak havoc on the last of the living."

"You mean like a pack of outlaws?" Joel asked.

"Exactly," John responded. "Like a mega gang. They got a little bit of everything. Crips. Bloods. Latin Thugs. Hell's Angels. You name it. If the damned zombies don't get you, the Unity Gang will. All they live for is to rape, kill, and pillage. They do murder just for sport. That's why we can't never be too careful."

"That sounds terrible," Benji said with a visible shudder.

"You got that right," John agreed. "A lot of good citizens just barricaded themselves in after the zombies started eating people. Not the Unity Gang. They preyed on the weak, using the natural goodness of people and their basic human decency against them, tricking them into opening up their doors so they could bring helter skelter down on 'em."

This is the last thing we need, I thought. *More complications.*

I wondered if we would be able to talk John into giving us a car with some gas and getting us on our way.

"Most folks were too scared to do anything about it. They sat back and watched as these animals took advantage of their neighbors, praying it wouldn't be them next. It's enough to make a good man sick to his stomach."

"So you armed yourselves and took a stand against them?" Joel asked.

John smiled at him. He obviously liked the way Joel thought.

"You bet we did," John said. "We took back a bunch of neighborhoods from the dead and the damned, making a safe zone. We got food, water, electricity, indoor plumbing. It's almost like it used to be. We make sweeps outside the city looking for survivors and supplies when we're not on duty."

"You got clean beds?" Joel asked, sounding more and more comfortable with the situation despite the fact we still had guns trained on us. "We're exhausted and could use a good night's sleep."

"Sure." John shrugged. "We'll be glad to give you a ride and get you all set up, just as soon as you strip down and let us examine you for bite marks."

I swallowed hard, thinking about Sam. Right then and there I knew I'd done the right thing. Benji gave me a look that said he understood why I'd marched out into the middle of the road.

"Is that a problem, gentlemen?" John asked, noticing Benji and me.

"Not at all," Joel crowed, stripping down to his underwear like it was a hot summer day and he was about to plunge into a cool lake. He nodded to Tom who followed his lead. Benji and I did the same.

John signaled for one of the guys in the back of the truck. He came over with a flashlight held in his teeth so he could hold onto his weapon. It reminded me of something from the show *Cops*. He gave us a good onceover, then nodded to John.

"Well then," John said. "Looks like this lot is cleared for takeoff. Hop in the back and keep your heads down. Today's forecast calls for lead showers and a hail of bullets."

We dressed quickly and did as we were told. John got back in and turned the truck around, driving us back toward the city again. Deep down inside, I knew none of it mattered. Sam was dead no matter what I did. Giving him his last few human moments without added fear of being cut in half by an automatic weapon wasn't going to change his fate. Still a small part of me felt better, like I had done something good and made a difference—even though I hadn't, not really. I didn't know if it was the sound of the wind rushing by, drowning out everything but the hum of the engine, or just the fact that I was exhausted—but against all odds I slipped down in the bed of the truck and fell asleep.

CHAPTER SIX

I was in the darkness, surrounded by hissing demons. I could smell them, but not see them. I could feel the dread they inspired, an irrational fear that climbed up inside of me and grew like a weed until it overwhelmed me. I was afraid to move, afraid I'd give them a direction to lunge toward. But I was also afraid *not* to move, knowing that if I didn't do something to get away they would eventually find me.

Zombies don't sleep. They don't get tired. They just keep coming until they get you. You cannot reason with them. You can't plead with them. All you can do is run.

My legs felt like they were made out of lead. I could feel the sweat trickling down my back. I could hear my own shallow breathing, but it sounded like it was coming from somewhere else outside of me.

Something slithered through the darkness like a snake, only bigger and heavier. Every muscle in my body tensed up as I prepared for an attack of some kind. I felt a hand wrap itself around my right ankle, like an iron shackle, cold and hard. Electricity shot through me as a wave of panic crashed over me. Another hand wrapped around my calf, cold and unyielding, while the noise of a large creature dragging itself toward me intensified. The scraping across the ground sounded like mountains of sandpaper scratching inside my mind.

Searing pain shot through me and I screamed as the

zombie bit deep into the back of my leg. It was a crawler. I looked down to see tiny little zombie Sam staring up at me, blood pouring out of his mouth from the wound he'd just left in my leg. He was still in one piece but his legs didn't seem to be working. He hissed at me and stared with dead eyes, like a large snake.

Looking up, I saw zombies coming out of the dark mist on all sides. I was surrounded completely. There was no way out! I looked back down just in time to see Sam biting back into my leg. I screamed as loud as I could, filling my lungs with air several times in a row and yelling some more until I was hoarse. This was it for me. I was a goner now. They were going to tear me to shreds and there was nothing I could do about it!

I shot up, panting and sweating. I was in a soft bed under covers. There was a poster of Felicity James, the child celebrity turned reality star, staring down at me from above the bed. Before Z-Day I used to think about her all the time, but having the dead reanimate and try to kill you tends to change your priorities.

Where am I?

For a minute I couldn't remember how I'd gotten there. I pulled back the covers to examine my leg. It was fine. I noticed a scratchy tag had been scraping me in the same place I'd been bitten in my nightmare.

Am I dead? I thought. *Or better yet, maybe all this zombie stuff was just a bad dream. But this isn't my room. Where am I?*

I got up and looked out the window, surprised for a moment to realize I was dressed in pajamas. Pieces of the previous night were coming back to me: the walk, the guns, and getting in the back of the truck. I pulled the shades to reveal a suburban neighborhood. Bright sun beamed down on rows of identical homes with well-manicured lawns. Armed guards in khaki uniforms roamed the streets. They were the only indication that anything was off and not like it used to be before Z-Day.

Where's my sword? Panic shot through me. I didn't like

being unarmed. One thing I'd learned since the end of the world was that it was better to have a weapon and not need one than need one and not have it. Moto said that's an old cliché, but to be honest I didn't recall ever hearing it before things went bad. Maybe it's just universal wisdom. Who's to say what's old and what's new now that the world as we know it was over?

I scoured the room for my katana but came up short in my search. I did find my clothes at the foot of the bed. Someone had washed them, folded them, then set them in a neat pile for me. They were still warm to the touch. They smelled like fabric softener.

Maybe it was the same person who changed you into pajamas while you were sleeping, I thought. At least they hadn't changed my underwear. It was unnerving to think I had been so exhausted that I slept right through it. I didn't like being at the mercy of other people, much less being completely helpless in front of total strangers.

You need to pull it together. Remember your training.

Cautiously, I cracked open the door and looked out. I could hear people walking around downstairs, glasses clinking, women laughing. Then it hit me full in the face — the smell of someone cooking breakfast. It was like a dream come true. I opened the door and walked out: down the steps, past the living room and into the kitchen. A large, older woman in an apron was cooking scrambled eggs in a cast iron skillet. On the table was orange juice, milk, a pile of buttered toast, and a plate overflowing with bacon. I could feel myself salivating and my stomach gave a loud rumble in response. The woman turned to me and smiled.

"Good morning, sleepy head," she said in a chipper tone. "Glad to see you're up."

"Where am I?"

"You're in the safe zone in New Lompoc. You were out cold when the men got back last night. At first I was afraid of waking you up. By the time I got you changed and into bed I realized that wasn't going to be a problem."

So she was the one who put me in these pajamas, I thought. I was grateful it hadn't been one of the guys from the truck. There was a motherly quality about this woman that seemed to make it less embarrassing.

"I'd ask you how you slept but I already know," she continued. "Whole house could hear you snoring up until about twenty minutes ago."

God I hope I wasn't screaming in my sleep, I thought.

I didn't know why but I wanted this woman to like me. She had a kindness that hung over her like grace. She wiped her hands on her apron as she took the eggs off the stove.

"My name is Carol."

"I'm Xander," I said. She stuck out her hand and I shook it.

"Nice to meet you, Xander."

"How many people live here?"

"Usually not more than the three of us," she said, nodding her head toward the door where the two other women who had congregated to eavesdrop on us quickly scattered. One of them was around my age and cute as hell. She had soft brown eyes like melted caramel and long auburn hair tied back in a ponytail. She had lingered just long enough to make eye contact with me before vanishing into the house. "But on special occasions, when we rescue a group of kids off the highway, the number goes up a little bit."

I stood there staring at the food.

"You hungry?"

"Yes ma'am." I could barely control myself. The smell of the bacon was driving me mad. I hadn't had anything remotely as good as bacon since weeks before I saw my first zombie.

"Go ahead and dig on in," she said. "Eat as much as you like. Everyone else has already had their fill."

I sat down and began to tear into the bacon with both hands, shoveling it into my mouth. It was delicious. My fingers and tongue burned a little from the hot grease. Carol laughed.

"Slow down and chew your food now," she said softly. "You're going to choke to death."

Ignoring her, I shoved a full piece of toast into my mouth. I poured a glass of orange juice and downed it in a single gulp. The sugary sweetness hit me like a jolt. I could feel the life returning to me. Carol brought the cast iron skillet over and scooped a hearty serving of cheesy scrambled eggs onto my plate.

"Thank you," I managed in between bites.

"You are welcome," she said, smiling. "We're glad to have you here. We can use all the help we can get."

"Where are my friends?"

"The little one slept here last night."

"Benji?"

"That's the one." She nodded. "The twins stayed down the road."

"Where did Benji go?"

"John came for him this morning," Carol replied. "Benji wanted to check out the neighborhood and John said he'd take him around. I believe they're at his house now."

"Which one is John's house?"

"It's just down the block and around the corner," she explained. "Third house on the left. You can see for yourself when you're done getting cleaned up. I know John wants to talk to you. He was asking about you this morning before he took Benji on their walkabout."

Suddenly I didn't feel so hungry anymore. I didn't know why but the way she said it made me nervous, like a kid being told he has detention. There was something about John I didn't trust, but I couldn't put my finger on it. After all, he had saved us the night before. He'd given us safe passage into a dangerous town. He had given us a place to sleep, food, water . . . what was not to like about this guy? Still, I knew I had to trust my instincts. They'd kept me alive so far while a whole lot of people I knew had died. That had to be worth something.

"Where is my sword?"

"I honestly don't know," she said, turning away and cleaning a dish. "You will have to ask John."

I pushed my plate away defiantly.

"You finished eating so soon?" Carol turned back toward me.

I nodded in reply. They had no right to disarm me. My katana was a part of me. The thought of someone else touching it made me uncomfortable down to my core.

"Poor thing," she cooed, touching my face. "You just ate too fast, that's all. You probably haven't had food this rich in some time. The way you were shoveling it in, I'm surprised you didn't get sick."

There was no malice in her tone, only motherly concern.

"You're right," I lied. "It's been a while since I had any real food, much less bacon."

"That's all right. You go on up and take a nice hot shower," she said in a soft voice, taking the plate away from in front of me.

"You have *actual* hot water?"

I couldn't hide my surprise. I hadn't taken a hot shower since before I got to Vandenberg. The base only had group showers, like something out of physical education back in high school. We took turns with the girls. The girls always went first. Some days the water was lukewarm, but most days it was just a few degrees above ice cold.

"You take as long as you need." Carol smiled. "When you're all dressed and ready, come back down and I'll tell you how to get to John's."

I stood up and walked out of the room in a state of near shock. My feet carried me back upstairs. I went into the room and found my freshly washed clothes on top of my now made up bed. Without questioning it, I picked them up and marched off to the bathroom, locking myself inside and turning on the water. Sure enough, hot water flooded out, steaming up the room quickly. I undressed and got under the beaded stream. Within seconds I felt like I was melting away. The pure pleasure of that shower was so decadent I felt a pang of guilt shoot through me. I could still taste the bacon in my mouth. What was this place? Hotel California?

I didn't get out right away. After all I had been through, the least I could do was enjoy one moment of peace and happiness. I sat under the water and let it run over my body for a long time, clearing my mind of all thoughts.

When I came out of the bathroom, fully washed and in clean clothes, I could honestly say I felt like a changed man. For the first time in a long time, I had a belly full of good food. For the first time in a long time, I was clean. For the first time in a very long time, I felt fully human.

I put the pajamas back on the bed in a neat pile then bounded downstairs. Carol was just finishing up dishes in the kitchen.

"Thank you so much for the wonderful breakfast," I said politely, finally finding my manners again. I looked down at my hands, surprised not to find dirt beneath the nails.

"You are very welcome," she said pleasantly. "You ready to take a walk then?"

Carol gave me a long, thorough description of how to get to John's, then wrote down his address for me on a scrap of paper for good measure. I walked out the front door, feeling three sets of eyes on my back even though I'd only seen one. I was curious about that cute girl, but I didn't bother to turn and look back. There were far more pressing issues at hand.

Walking down the street felt surreal. Armed guards paced up and down the concrete with automatic rifles and dark sunglasses, ignoring me. It reminded me of pictures I had seen of Israel back when I was still in school.

I wouldn't want to get on their bad side, I thought, feeling the hair on the back of my neck involuntarily stand on end.

Other than that, things looked eerily normal—as in pre-Zombie normal. There wasn't a biter in sight. I should have felt relaxed but I didn't. A knot of muscles in my stomach contracted as I rounded the corner, passing a beautiful garden in someone's front yard, and headed down to John's.

I looked at the slip of paper in my hand, then back up at the house and laughed. There was no way in hell anyone could mistake this place for anything but John's place. Armed guards were posted in front of the residence as well as across the street. Two more guards stood watch at the door. I easily walked past the first set of guards, but was stopped by the guys blocking the front entrance.

"Name?" One of them barked at me.

You've got to be kidding, I thought. *Like anyone here doesn't know who I am by now?* Apparently John had a flare for the dramatic.

"Name?" he said again, growing more impatient, if that was possible.

"Xander Macnamara," I muttered through clenched teeth. Nothing happened for a minute, then both men stepped aside. "Hell of a way to greet people."

"John is waiting for you up in his office," the guard answered, ignoring my taunt. "Go straight on up."

I stepped into the house and the door shut behind me, making me feel more and more like a prisoner. The place wasn't all that different than the last house I had been in. The kitchen and living room were on the opposite side, but I had a feeling that when I got upstairs I would find two bedrooms and a bathroom, just like where I'd woken up. I heard what sounded like a video game going off in the other room. It all felt so familiar.

Cautiously, I approached the room and saw a big flat screen television nearly the size of the wall. On it, Mario and Yoshi were flying through a rainbow star.

"Awesome!" a small voice said from somewhere among the cushions. That could only be one person.

"Benji?" I walked around the sofa to find him sitting in a pile of comic books with the Wii controller in his hands and a half chewed piece of red licorice sticking out of his mouth. He hit pause the second he recognized me.

"Xander!" He jumped up and gave me a welcoming hug.

"What's going on?"

"You fell asleep last night in the truck," Benji said. "I guess the shock of it all just knocked you out."

"Yeah, I guess," I mumbled, rubbing the back of my neck.

"John brought us back here and dropped us off," he explained. "He came by this morning, but you were still sleeping. He said you needed your rest and not to bug you."

"A woman at the house told me that John has been taking you around, showing you stuff. What has he been saying?"

"You mean Carol?" Benji asked.

I nodded, impatient for his answer.

"Isn't she great?" he continued. "And who ever thought I'd get to have fresh squeezed orange juice again in my life? And bacon? Did you get to have some of the bacon or was it all gone by the time you got up?"

"I had the bacon," I assured him. "It was good. Now spill. What does John want?"

"Nothing." Benji shrugged. "So far as I can tell. He drove me around and told me about the boundaries and which parts of the city the Unity Gang has already captured. Most of it is over to the west of here. Oh, and he took me to an old comic book store and stood guard while I scoured for some new stuff. I got an original Spiderman in pristine condition! I know you have no idea what that means, but it is a big deal. Well it would be a big deal, if anything still mattered in the world, but it's still a big deal to me!"

I hadn't seen Benji talk this much since the base. I know it's petty, but a small part of me resented John for that as well.

"Where are the twins?"

"They slept on the other side of Ocean Boulevard," Benji said. "This street is for VIPs and stuff like that. John called it the Command Center. He says the twins were over in the soldiers housing."

"So you haven't actually seen them?" I asked. "He just told you?"

"Well, I watched as we dropped them off last night while you were sleeping," Benji said, a note of sarcasm infecting his words. "But I haven't seen them since then. No."

"What did John say about me?"

"He talked a lot about you," he said excitedly. "I think he really likes you. He asked all sorts of questions about you and your training and all about your brother."

"What did you tell him?"

"Not much. Truth is, I don't know much. All I know is the stuff about you looking out for me at the base. John said he thinks you are a natural born leader, a protector. That's what he called you."

"He did?" I didn't mean to sound so shocked. I just hadn't expected flattery. Was I becoming so jaded that I couldn't trust anyone anymore? This guy took us in and looked after us, but I was still looking for something wrong with him, some reason not to trust or like him. Maybe I was wrong.

Give him the benefit of the doubt, I thought, relaxing a little again. *If only for the hospitality he's shown you, the hot shower, and the delicious bacon.*

"It's just like you said it would be." Benji smiled. "They're taking back the city one block at a time. Once they get Lompoc turned around they plan on taking on other towns, cleaning them up too."

I was glad to see Benji happy again, even if I didn't know how long it was going to last this time.

"Cool," I said. "I'm gonna go talk to him. Be back down in a minute."

"Okay," Benji replied, turning back to his game without a care in the world. It was nice to see him finally getting to be a kid again. I could hear the sound of gold coins being snatched up as I hit the top of the stairs.

There was a hallway with an open door at the end. My instincts told me that John was in there, but I stopped at the first door and pulled it open anyway. I imagined that I'd find a bedroom just like the one I slept in the night before.

Sure enough, there was a bed in there. The rest was not at all what I expected.

Huge red and black flags hung from the ceiling with swastikas in the middle of them. I stood there in shock and looked around the room, seeing that it was stuffed from floor to ceiling with Nazi war memorabilia. There were SS soldiers' uniforms, weapons, even books. My eyes came to rest on the spine of one sticking out of the bookshelf — *Mein Kampf*.

Maybe this is why they hate the racially diverse Unity Gang so much, I thought. *John and his friends are white supremacists*!

The tiny little spark of suspicion that I had been harboring quickly blossomed into a fire of distrust. A flurry of wild thoughts ran through my mind as I tried to recall if I had seen a single person who wasn't white since we'd hooked up with John. None came to mind.

I knew there was a reason not to like this guy. He's a racist! That's why he called the war with the Unity Gang "Helter Skelter." It's a code phrase for a race war! He's like Charlie Manson or something. All those women are probably his sex slaves. I've got to get Benji and get out of here as fast as I can.

I knew I couldn't leave without my sword. I'd need a plan. We couldn't just bolt without attracting attention. This was bad! Cold chills ran down my spine as I felt a warm hand clasp me by the shoulder. I was totally screwed!

"So," John said in a deep, steady voice. "You've found our secret room."

CHAPTER SEVEN

I spun around to look directly into John's clear, cold, blue Irish eyes.

"Your secret room?" I sputtered. "You're into this stuff?" The words were out before I could take them back.

So much for playing it cool, I thought.

John laughed so hard his whole body shook.

"It's a joke," he said when he recovered. "Lighten up."

"So why is it here?".

"We didn't put it there," he roared. "I promise you that. These aren't our homes. We took over this whole block after Z-Day. We are still finding surprises."

"So why haven't you cleaned it out?" It seemed like an innocent enough question to me, but I could see I was starting to push his buttons.

Good to know I can, I thought. *That might come in handy later.*

"Believe it or not, we've got plenty to worry about right now," he spat, trying to hide his obvious frustration. "We'll get around to it when things slow down. I promise."

"Got it," I said, trying to act like a dumb kid as I turned and looked down at my sneakers.

"Come on then," he ordered. "My office is at the end of the hall. I wanna talk with you a spell."

We walked to the back of the hallway and into his office. After the Nazi war room, it was a bit disappointing how humdrum the place was. There was a map of the city with a bunch of stuff scribbled on it and crossed out. From the looks of things, it had been a hard month. John sat down behind the desk and motioned for me to take a chair as well. I sat and stared at him.

"So how do you like our fair city so far?" He grinned. "Not so shabby? Must be nice waking up without worrying that a zombie is gonna chew your head off."

"Where is my blade?" I didn't hesitate. I was prepared to go to war to get my katana back.

"It's safe," he casually countered.

"Why did you take it from me? You had no right."

"It's been decided that the citizens of New Lompoc shouldn't be armed," John said, casually trying to brush it off.

"Well I am not a citizen."

"No," he replied, leaning forward. "You are a guest."

I sat back and crossed my arms.

"As I was saying, only armed patrols are allowed to carry weapons."

"That's insane," I interrupted. "So you are telling me that if a wild pack of zombies were to march through town, the people wouldn't be allowed to defend themselves? Why? Are you really that threatened they might question your authority?"

"First of all," he managed through gritted teeth, the note of agitation no longer hidden in his usually honeyed voice, "there is no such thing as a zombie horde."

"Yeah? Then what ran us out of Vandenberg?"

"Second." He ignored my taunt. "The armed patrols of New Lompoc are more than equipped to handle the Unity Gang threat. Since we took over this territory we haven't had a single attack—zom or human related. The people are happy again. Life is finally returning to some sort of normalcy. You'd see that if you weren't looking for some way to tear us down."

"So it's simply share and share alike?"

"Pretty much," John said. "I get the feeling that you don't trust me much. I can't say given what I hear you've been through that I blame you entirely. What is it going to take to win you over?"

"You could start by giving me back my blade," I said without hesitation a second time.

John laughed.

"All things in due time," he replied, a knowing grin on his face. "For now, I was hoping you'd be interested in sticking around and helping out a bit. Word has it you are both a fierce warrior and a loyal friend."

I thought about Sam the minute he said it. God, I hope Benji didn't mention him.

"Actually, I have other plans, if you don't mind."

"You mean your brother in Hueneme?"

"That's right," I answered back curtly. "If you really want to help me out you'll hook me up with a car and send me and Benji on our way."

"You and Benji?"

"That's right."

"You're not interested in taking the twins with you then?"

"That's up to them. They were kind of a last minute addition, if you know what I mean."

"I do indeed." John winked. "I'm sorry to say that I can't let you leave right now."

"You can't or you won't?"

"It's not like that, Xander." He sighed. "Things are rarely as simple as they seem."

"Then explain it to me."

"Our little slice of paradise is pretty hot right now." He turned around and pointed to the map behind him. "The Unity Gang controls most of the west of what used to be Lompoc. We control most of the east. We control the northern entrance, to a degree. They still find ways to get around us. They control the southern exit, by and large."

"So we'll go around them," I suggested.

"It's not that easy," he continued. "There are no side roads that lead out. Just a wasteland of trails and hills. If the bikers don't get you, the cannibals might. And let's not forget that the Unity Gang isn't all that concerned with killing zombies. The hills just south of here are crawling with them. Some say the bikers are like old fashioned hillbillies. They set up shacks in the woods and keep zombies tied to the front porch as pets or guard dogs."

"I don't believe that," I admitted.

"It's true," John said in earnest. "Some even think they are good luck. Others fight them in pits or cages like wild animals, betting on who will win."

"Money doesn't mean anything now," I said. "What's the point of gambling?"

"They don't use money," John said. "Out in the badlands people trade sexual favors, food, booze, bikes, and just about anything else they can get their hands on. I've even heard stories of bikers gambling away their kids as slave labor to other gang members."

"But why?"

"Who knows. People with addictive personalities gotta find ways to keep feeding their disorder, end of the world or not. It's like a sickness."

"We can't stay here forever, John," I pointed out. "I know you want to convert me to your way of life, but I'm on a mission."

"Am I being that obvious?"

"Yeah, actually you are."

"Well," he said sheepishly, "can you blame me? You're very gifted for a young man your age. I hear you are good in a fight as well. That you stick up for your friends. That's brave. We could use good people like you. I'm fighting a war here. I'm trying to bring back a small piece of what we once had. You could be a big part of that. Then, when things calm down, when they are more under control, you can go on your way. What do you think?"

There was a twinkle in his eyes as he made his obviously

contrived confession. He had all the makings of a cult leader. It was clear now why he was in charge. He was charismatic. Other guys might be bigger or stronger or better fighters, but in the end he was clearly the brains of the operation as far as New Lompoc was concerned.

"I'm sorry," I replied. "This isn't my war. This isn't my town. I'm just passing through. I have to get to my brother. I can't afford to get caught up in your fight."

"I understand." He sounded disappointed.

"So you'll let us go then?"

"Of course. I'm not running a prison camp here."

"And my sword?"

"You can have it back when you go."

Something's not adding up here, I thought. *This just seems too easy all of a sudden.*

"Well then," I said, standing up. "It was a pleasure to meet you. Good luck with New Lompoc. Now if you will just give us a car and my katana we'll be on our way."

John smiled but didn't move. "I told you. You can't leave right now. The Unity Gang controls the southern corridor. For the time being, you're stuck with us."

Here we go, I thought.

"So I'm just supposed to stay here forever?"

"I'm working on a plan to take back the main highway," he told me. "I was hoping to get some help from you, maybe change your status from civilian guest to patrol?"

"How do I know you're not just making all this up to try to trick me into staying?"

"I am so glad you asked that," he replied, standing up. "I've been dying to show you around. Let's take a ride."

We walked back downstairs. I called out to Benji to come with us. John looked pensive for a minute, like he wasn't sure it was a good idea, but he didn't say anything.

"Why do you have a Nintendo Wii?"

"It's for first person shooters." John grinned. "You know, to train up new recruits? We can't afford to waste real ammunition rounds training in the field, so we do most of them here. Only Benji wasn't interested in that so he found the one game not suitable for training at all. He's been at it for hours now."

We both laughed. John opened the door and walked out. I followed after him, turning my head from the living room where Benji was saving his game play and crashing into a solid wall of muscle. Looking up, I saw a heavily tattooed man with rippling muscles in a torn Gold's Gym t-shirt. He had a gun belt on with two firearms showing and a large sword on his back. *My katana.*

"If it isn't Sleeping Beauty herself," he said, flashing a crooked smile down at me.

Anger flooded through me, robbing me of all reason as I lashed out at him.

"Give it back to me now!" I pounded both fists into his chest but he didn't budge an inch.

"Someone sure is grumpy first thing in the morning," the man spoke in a singsong voice. "After all the sleep you got I assumed you'd be in better spirits."

I stared at him in shock.

John stepped in to keep the peace. "This is Tank. You met him last night. He is my first in command. The other man in the truck was Bruiser." John motioned off to the side where an almost equally large man stood smiling at us behind dark sunglasses.

"Give me my sword," I said in a threatening voice to Tank.

He chuckled. "Nice to meet you too." He stuck out his hand and I slapped it away. My hand stung from the blow. It was like slapping a block of iron. He chuckled again, casting a glance around at the others who were shaking their heads in disbelief at my gall.

"I told you he had a lot of fire," John bragged.

"Chill now for a minute," Tank back peddled. "I'm just holding on to it until John says you can have it back. We share weapons here, like everything else. I saw this beauty sitting there and I knew it was important. I didn't want anyone else to get a hold of it and damage the blade. Last thing you need is some commando using it to chop wood or pop open locked doors. A masterpiece like this needs to be handled delicately, like a lady."

"I appreciate your concern," I hissed through gritted teeth. "Now hand it over."

"I've got an idea," Tank began. "Why don't we spar for it? You win, you get it back with no questions asked. If I win, I will keep holding on to it for a while. Deal?" He looked over to John to see if he would object, but he nodded his assent. I didn't know what Benji had told them but it must have been good. They were all eager to see what kinds of tricks I had up my sleeves.

"Fine by me," I agreed, stepping back and cracking my knuckles.

Tank looked surprised by my response.

I'm probably the first guy to ever challenge him head on, I thought. *If not the first, at least the smallest and youngest . . . and maybe the stupidest.*

I walked out onto the lawn and began to stretch. Tank took off his gun belt and set it gingerly on the ground before handing my sword to John to hold. He twisted his neck to the side and it gave a loud pop. I took up my first pose and let him walk toward me, like a moving brick wall made out of human muscle. For a split second I thought about what a terrifying zombie he would make.

"You want me to go easy on ya?" he asked, looking around to make sure everyone was watching as he popped his knuckles while mocking me.

The words were barely out of his mouth when my left heel connected with his jaw. When I saw his head turning, taking his focus off of me, I'd stepped forward with my right foot and planted it firmly in the grass. Then I twisted my body as I brought my left leg around as fast as I could, bending at the waist and pivoting to let the loose leg swing freely toward my target—his fat head. I'd seen plenty of big guys taken down by kicks like these in MMA matches, but I wasn't harboring any fantasies of a first round K.O. I didn't have the kind of power needed in my legs to pull off a stunt like that, especially against an opponent his size. As my foot came within striking range of his face, I tensed up and let the heel smack him good and hard to get his attention. It was, for lack of a better term, a smashing success.

I heard a loud crack as I followed through, spinning back into standing position, followed by a round of gasps from our onlookers. Tank's head twisted to the side but he didn't go down. He turned back toward me with an entirely different kind of smile. One I was certain his enemies knew only too well just before they died.

"Okay ya little bastard." He spat blood on the grass. "You wanna play like a big boy. Just don't cry when ya get hurt."

He advanced toward me, eager to land his first blow with those meaty paws. I tried to sweep his leg but it didn't budge. Instead, I was knocked off balance and he shoved me over onto the grass. He attempted to bring his weight down on my elbow first, maybe catch me in the head or the back of my shoulders, but I rolled out of the way and he landed on his ass. I didn't move fast enough though and he was able to pin me with his upper body and keep me from wriggling loose. I punched out feebly at him with my left hand, but he caught it in his mitt-sized palm and squeezed until shivers of raw pain shot down my arm. The more I pulled to free myself, the worse the agony was.

A plan formed in the back of my mind. If I could roll over in his direction, maybe I could flip my body around and knock him over with both feet.

Yeah, I thought. *And maybe you'll dislocate your shoulder in the process.*

But I wasn't ready to admit defeat. I wasn't leaving without my blade!

I started to twist toward him, but he must have sensed my plan. He moved so fast it blew my mind. I hadn't imagined a guy his size could be so agile! He spun around and locked my arm up, crushing my head into the grass with one of his gigantic legs at the same time. Leaning back, he held me in an arm bar. The pain was beyond anything I could describe. He was literally ripping my arm off! I thrashed in pure agony, screaming at the top of my lungs and beating the ground. All the air seemed to go out of my body and, for a moment, I thought I was going to pass out. Flashes of light began to pop behind my eyes.

"Say Uncle," Tank teased.

"No!" I managed. He leaned back again and the pain returned like a wave of sickness. "UNCLE!" I screamed at the top of my lungs while I slapped at the soft grass.

Instantly, he let up and jumped to his feet. Extending his hand, he offered to help me stand. My first instinct was to try to slap it away again, but I felt dizzy. I reached out to grab his palm, trying to keep the world from spinning.

"Whoa there," John cautioned, stepping forward to help. "Easy."

I closed my eyes and swallowed hard. Pain was still tingling through my arm and shoulder, but the humiliation was far worse than anything. Sure he was bigger than me, but that wasn't the point. Fighting isn't about size. It's about smarts. I'd seen small wiry monks easily defeat muscle bound madmen because they were smarter, faster, and most of all more controlled. I'd been none of those things.

If Moto could see me now he would be disappointed, I thought.

I opened my eyes and stood up. Tank rubbed his jaw with one hand and held me up with the other.

"Nice kick," he admitted, "even if it was kind of a cheap shot."

"Thanks," I countered. "Can I have my sword back now?"

"Sorry, but where I come from a deal is a deal," he said with a bloody smile. "Better luck next time."

Tank let me go and grabbed his guns from the ground, lacing on the belt again. John handed him my sword and he slipped it back over his shoulder.

"Well that was exciting," John said. "Now, if there aren't any further objections, let's go for that ride." He turned and walked over to the white truck from the night before.

Pride is your real enemy, I thought as I massaged my arm and shoulder.

What was done was done. I'd have to make the best of it. Being hostile to John and his buddies wasn't going to get me anywhere. For now I'd have to play along. I swallowed my pride and walked over to the truck, climbing in the back.

"That's the spirit," John said. "Hang on now, and keep low. We're heading into enemy territory."

He started the truck, the engine roaring to life, and began to back out. Benji got into a Jeep with Tank and Bruiser and followed us. I didn't have the strength or the will to argue anymore. I was glad to be in the back, away from John's prying stare. The cool breeze did wonders to help chill my embarrassment and dry the tears of shame that ran freely down my face in defeat.

CHAPTER EIGHT

Things were pretty much normal for the first part of the drive. We crossed over Ocean and went into another neighborhood that looked almost identical to the one we'd just left. Aside from the lack of traffic and the armed guards patrolling the streets on foot, it was just like any other day prior to the zombie apocalypse. Tank followed us, grinning at me as he drove.

Keep smiling you big idiot, I thought. *This ain't over yet. How's that jaw feel?*

We stopped in front of a random house and parked. Tank got out of the car and went to the door, knocking on it and yelling out in a booming voice. A minute later Joel and Tom came out dressed in camouflage from head to toe. They both seemed to be in good spirits. I was suddenly glad that Joel hadn't seen me lose to Tank. That seemed like more than I could handle at the moment.

"Hop up in the front," John hollered. I rolled out of the back and got into the front passenger side. Joel and Tom got into the back of the truck. Tank got back into his Jeep. "Believe it or not, you're going to want to buckle up. We're heading to the border of New Lompoc. Never know when things are going to get bumpy."

I sighed. Reaching back, I grabbed the safety buckle and dragged it across my chest, snapping it into place at my side. "Happy?"

I was still more than a little agitated about how things had turned out this morning and I didn't care if he knew it. After all, none of this would have happened if he hadn't taken my sword from me in the first place.

"You're a hard guy to win over," John said. "I thought for sure the bacon would do the trick. Oh well. Here we go."

John cranked the ignition. The truck roared to life. He screeched off. Obviously this wasn't how he saw things going either.

We pulled through a cul-de-sac and back onto Ocean, heading west. John had a long range walkie with him that kept going off with coded reports that made no sense to me. It was annoying to hear all the chatter.

"You got a radio station in New Lompoc yet?" I asked, reaching for the radio. He stopped me.

"We had one the first week. But it went down quickly. Drew in Unity Gang members like moths to a flame. They surrounded it and burned it to the ground." John looked upset.

"You lose a lot of good vinyl that day?" I said, trying to be funny. "Some *Three Dog Night* and *Saturday Night Fever? Abba?*"

"I lost my brother that day," he said, staring straight ahead. "They locked him in and burned the place to the ground. Aaron never had a chance."

"Sorry." I made eye contact with him for a brief second to let him know I truly was remorseful. I hadn't intended on stirring up bad memories. Seemed like nothing was going like I thought it would anymore.

"I appreciate that," John replied in a reverent tone, letting me off the hook. "Nothing to do about it now. I got a *Metallica* cassette in the tape deck, but now's not a great time to play it."

"Why not?"

"I gotta listen in for updates and reports," he explained, holding up his walkie. "A short conversation could mean the difference between life and death."

"Just sounds like gibberish to me," I protested.

We passed a bunch of old buildings that had been burned to the ground. From what was left of them, I could make out a Taco Bell and a Der Weinerschnitzel.

We must be getting close, I thought. *Man, I wish I could have some Taco Bell right now. I'd gladly fight off a hundred zombies for a Nacho Bellegrande and two Doritos Locos Tacos with a large Mountain Dew.*

"That's just because it's coded." He chuckled. "They got radios too so we have to keep changing the meaning of things. A couple of minutes ago a guy said 'blue bird on my shoulder' and another said 'cotton tail on the rabbit trail' — did you catch that?"

"Yeah." I shrugged. "Sounds like rhyming phrases from a kid's bedtime story."

"Far from it." John smiled. "The first means that we are en route to the gas station. The second means that patrolling units have confirmed we are on the move. We've been sighted coming up Ocean, most likely by snipers."

"You have snipers?" I asked with my jaw practically hanging open.

"Pretty cool, huh?"

I was actually pretty terrified. John and his group of military wannabe's were much more organized than I had expected. Sneaking away was going to be harder than I imagined. It was starting to look like I was going to be here a while.

"King is in the counting house," a voice squawked over the radio.

"Pocket full of rye," came the reply.

In the distance I could see the gas station. It was guarded like a fortress. Instead of feeling safe, it filled me with dread. We slowed to a snail's pace then pulled in through a line of armed guards who parted to let us pass. John drove through them like Moses parting the Red Sea and parked.

"Stick by my side," he suggested as he hopped out. I followed his lead, giving him a little room as one guy after another came up to him with questions. John had such a relaxed nature it was easy to forget he was in charge of this whole operation. Quickly I began to see that a whole lot of people counted on him for direction, for guidance, for support and encouragement.

"We're running low on lights," the first guy reported.

"Ask Jimmy," John replied. "He's in village four. Radio over to him."

"Thanks," the guy said and rushed off.

The next guy in line stepped up. "Janine told me to let you know they are having problems with the water purifier," the bald man groused.

"What kind of problems?"

"I don't know," He sighed loudly, scratching his patchy red beard. "She thinks something is wrong with the filter."

"Can you send Gilly over to look at patching it again?"

"I can, but I'm not sure a patch will fix it this time."

"We gotta try," John encouraged him. "If that fails we'll go to plan B."

"What's plan B?"

"I'm working on it." John smiled and the guy smiled back.

"Got it."

"Good man." He gave the guy a friendly slap on the back.

"We need more food rations," a short bald guy explained.

"Bruiser is bringing back some grub after our border run. How low are you?"

"Not critical," the guy admitted. "We're down to beef jerky and protein drinks. Another day and we're going to have guys scrounging in the streets for bags of chips and road kill."

"Let's hope it doesn't come to that." John laughed. "You're starting to look pretty thin as it is. Plus I'm not sure the birds can handle the competition. I've seen you tussle for meat. You're downright ornery when you need to be."

As the bald man walked away smiling and shaking his head, a short, wiry looking guy stepped up in his place, biting his fingertips in between words.

"Project Wild Turkey is still in play," he boasted, looking at me nervously.

John's face changed.

"Just a minute," he said, turning to me. "Can you give us a moment alone?"

I nodded. John put his arm around the small man and they walked away whispering to each other.

I turned to see the rest of the group hanging back near the gas station office. Benji had found an old arcade game and plugged it in. He was totally lost in playing *Galaga*. Bruiser watched from the side, excitedly cheering him on. I walked over to find the Parker twins sitting in the office playing with their newly issued hand guns.

"What's up?" I said, trying to sound casual.

"I heard you got whopped this morning," Joel goaded, picking a fight right out of the gate. "Brutal."

"I got in a few shots," I said defensively.

"Yeah," Joel shot back instantly. "I heard about your sucker punch. Man, you are lucky that Tank didn't tear you in half for such a low blow."

I could feel my face heating up as the anger flooded through me again.

"I see they gave you guys guns," I observed, recalling John's earlier remarks on the subject of arming civilians.

"Of course they did," Joel bragged. "John knows talent when he sees it."

"Made us go through some safety and shooting tests first," Tom piped up, trying to keep the peace. "Ammo is in short supply. They made a big deal out of explaining that we are supposed to exhaust all other means of fighting before we discharge our weapons."

"Does that mean you plan on staying here?"

"We are all staying here, genius," Joel chided, escalating the tension between us once again. "The road out of town is blocked by bikers and gang bangers. You'd better wise up and start playing nice if you have any brains at all. This is gonna be our new home for a while, and the way you're heading you're not making any new friends."

"I like it here," Tom offered. "I had hot oatmeal this morning with fresh fruit and a hot shower. It felt like things were almost normal for a minute. Did you get a hot meal?"

"They probably gave him cold cereal with water instead of milk," Joel taunted.

I decided not to mention the bacon and eggs. The last thing I needed was another fight. The truth was, I was relieved that the twins had bought John's propaganda hook, line and sinker. It meant I didn't have to take them with us when Benji and I snuck off. Suddenly a huge weight felt like it had been lifted off my shoulders.

Why would John go to such lengths to try to win me over? He hadn't put that much work into the others, so why feed me bacon and beg me to stay?

"They fed me." I shrugged. "That shower was something else."

"I just stood there for the longest time and let it wash over me," Tom confessed, his eyes sparkling with the happy memory.

"Yeah, me too. It was amazing."

Joel seemed a little perturbed that I'd stopped feeding into his taunts and insults. Whatever his agenda was, this wasn't it. It was like the guy couldn't stand to see me happy for even a second.

"I hear you earned a new nickname," he started in again. "Sleeping Beauty, is it?"

That's it, I thought. *I don't have to take this kind of abuse from him or anyone else.*

I balled up my fists and began to march blindly toward Joel, ready to finish the fight we'd started the night before, out on the bridge. I had every intention of smashing his brains in with my bare hands.

It took him a minute before Joel finally realized he'd gone

too far. I don't know if he thought the rest of John's crew was going to protect him or that I wouldn't respond to his jeers, but he looked truly caught off guard. His eyes dashed to his weapon on the desk then back to me, as if he was considering fending me off at gunpoint.

I hope he tries, I thought. *I'll have that thing out of his hands and shoved down his own throat before he knows what hit him!*

There was panic in Joel's eyes, but he forced himself past that. He puffed his chest and prepared for my first blow as I rounded the corner.

"What?" Joel shouted as I came within striking distance of him.

"We're going to settle this once and for all, Parker," I said in a calm, even voice. I thought I noticed a slight tremor move through him, but it could have been my mind playing tricks on me.

"Come at me, bro!"

"You ready or what?" I turned to see John standing in the door. Bruiser and Tank were behind him, smiling.

"Where are we going now?" I asked.

"To the border," John replied dryly. "You wanted to see the blockade for yourself, first hand. This is your chance." He turned and walked back toward the parking lot without waiting for an answer.

"This isn't over," I muttered under my breath to Joel.

"You can count on that," he replied, making a big show out of picking up his gun.

"Come on, girls," Tank yelled. "Pull on your dresses and let's get moving."

I waited for Tom and Joel to go first, then followed behind Benji, Bruiser, and Tank.

"Looks like you're equally popular with all the cool kids," Tank muttered to me. "You make quite an impression."

"I made quite an impression on your jaw, didn't I?" I said defiantly.

"You did," he said without malice. "It's still sore now

that you mention it. Hell of a kick."

"You planning on retaliating later as well?" I asked. "I'd like to know how many eyes I need in the back of my head to watch my back."

"Worry about the zoms, kid." He shrugged. "I got my eyes on something way more important."

"What's that?"

"The big picture."

John stopped at the Jeep and turned to address us.

"Listen up," he shouted. "We're going to save a little petrol by taking one vehicle."

"How are we all going to fit in there?" Joel asked.

John looked irritated at the interruption. I fought back a laugh as the rest of our group gave Joel the stink eye.

"Tank will ride up front with me," John explained. "Bruiser is going to ride the tailgate and keep lookout as spotter. The rest of you can cram into the backseat. Worst case scenario, if something goes down, the small one can sit on someone's lap."

Benji frowned at the suggestion. "I guess I don't mind," he said a bit selfishly.

"That's a relief," John retorted sarcastically. "Gentlemen, we are heading into what is for all intents and purposes a fully active war zone. We can be attacked at any moment without warning or just cause. I am only going to warn you one time to do exactly what I tell you to do. We got that?"

Everyone murmured their agreement.

"Keep your wits about you and you will make it out alive," John dramatically warned us. "Now get in."

Everyone climbed into the Jeep in the order he suggested, except me. I stopped John before he could get in the driver's side.

"I need a weapon," I begged. I was feeling really uncomfortable with the idea of heading into a combat zone unarmed.

"That's understandable," he agreed, reaching into his holster and handing me one of his firearms. I took it, letting the weight of it sink in. "Safety is on," he warned. "You know how to shoot one of these?"

"I do," I assured him. "I'm better with my sword though."

"Give it a rest, Xander!" John hit the roof. I thought flames were going to shoot out of his eyes. I froze up, not knowing what to say.

"The gun is fine," I backpedaled.

He gave me a fierce stare then softened. "Good. Let's roll."

Getting in last meant that I ended up in the middle of the backseat bench next to Tom. Benji sat between Joel and me to keep the peace. I was riding the hump. I could feel every bump in the road from the minute we passed the guards and bounced off the high curb. John took off down the road and immediately the loud roar of the wind blocked everything else out—but luckily I was in the unique position of being the only one able to hear and understand what John was saying. We were in our own little bubble, as the saying goes.

"Why is there so much security at the gas station?"

"Because of the fuel," John guffawed. "Obviously, they'd love to take this away from us. We've still got enough gas to keep things rolling another six months at this rate. We use it not only for the cars but for generators and heaters. It's not like there are any more refineries out there turning black sludge into liquid gold. This stuff is more valuable than diamonds."

"If they don't have gas, how do they keep their bikes running?"

"That's what we keep asking ourselves," he admitted. "Nothing gets past you."

There was that flattery again. I knew better than to fall for it, but it still felt good. John sure knew how to push people's buttons. Guy made it look effortless.

"Thanks," I said, trying not to blush.

"We think they have a stash of their own," he said. "After we regained control of our territory, first thing we did was go house to house and collect fuel. We pulled juice out of old lawnmowers, siphoned it from gas tanks, anywhere we found it. They must have done the same thing."

"And you're keeping it all at the gas station?" I asked.

"Now that wouldn't be very smart, would it?" He showed his devious smile once more. "Let's just say that we got it strategically spread out so that no one raid can rob us of it. Can you leave it at that?"

"Sure," I gulped. He never threatened me outright but it sure felt implied, just like the last time I asked for my sword back.

"All right then," he crooned. "Let's keep the chatter to a minimum now. We're approaching the border."

John shut off his radio and we rode in silence. I could hear screaming in the distance, and the roar of motorcycle engines. The barricade came into plain view. There was no mistaking it. A row of bullet ridden cars cut off one side of a major street from the other. The New Lompoc side was clean and covered with guards. The old Lompoc side was filled with trash, burning tires, and rowdy bikers hooting and hollering as they raced back and forth up and down the street. The sight of it made John's point on its own, but I was starting to suspect that had been the whole reason for dragging us out here.

We parked about a hundred feet from the border. John got out and signaled for us to follow without saying another word.

"Stay close together," Tank growled as we climbed over the sides of the Jeep. "And keep your mouth shut." He stared at me specifically before turning his back to me. My sword was only a few feet away from me and I needed it.

I ought to rip it off his back and give him a piece of my mind, I thought.

Instead, I followed the group to a staging area outlined with sand bags where a bunch of armed guards were hunkered down with walkie talkies watching the other side of the road. One of them turned around and saw John. He bolted up and ran to him with his hand out.

"No one told me you were coming," the man began, but John waved his concerns away with an easy gesture.

"Don't worry, Peter," he said. "This isn't a formal visit. Just taking some new friends on a little tour of our fine town is all."

Peter turned to us and waved.

"Welcome to New Lompoc," he crowed with an earnest smile. Those were his last words before the explosion knocked him off his feet.

CHAPTER NINE

It was like it was all happening in slow motion while Peter was waving and saying hello to us. Dreamlike, a bottle somersaulted head over end above him, the glass and fire catching reflections of the sun, sparkling and drawing our attention to it. It arced high over Peter like a satellite in orbit with no hope of ever returning to Earth. The next instant, it came racing back down, the weight of the fuel and the heavy glass bottle dragging it bottom first toward the top of Peter's head. For a brief moment it seemed like it would smash into his skull altogether. Our facial expressions went from disinterested to horror before his wondering eyes.

Poor guy doesn't have a clue what's about to hit him, I thought.

As the bottle hurtled toward him it spun less, the force of gravity correcting it until it was right side up with the thick bottom rushing down to kiss the asphalt. The flaming rag atop the sealed neck merrily danced like a wild-eyed, redheaded seductress, lost in the epiphany of the impending destruction it wantonly foretold.

Before any of us could call out to warn Peter, the Molotov cocktail smashed down next to him, narrowly missing the top of his head. There was a loud explosion as it burst, the flames greedily licking at the embarrassment of riches bestowed, a drooling puddle of pure fuel. Instantly Peter was knocked off his feet. Fiery hell shot up and engulfed his whole body as he screamed in pain.

In the distance, a man dressed all in blue stood laughing. At his feet were several more Molotov style cocktails waiting to be ignited by his Zippo lighter. Several men rushed to Peter, taking off their shirts and jackets and holding him down to put out the fire consuming him. Peter wailed in agony, panicking and having to be repetitively told to roll over and to not stand up.

Stop, drop, and roll, I thought. *This is why they used to try to teach us that in school.*

The sound of gunfire cracking off took us by surprise. I looked up to see Joel aiming at the man responsible for this tragedy and firing away.

"No!" John cried out. "Cease fire!"

Joel wasn't listening. His face was twisted up with hatred.

Something inside of him must have finally snapped!

"Put that gun down now! That is an order!"

"Come and get me, cracker!" The gang member loudly crowed at us, then turned and dashed toward a cluster of nearby buildings.

Instead of lowering his weapon and obeying orders, Joel charged forward. He cleared the barricade and began running after the culprit at a full sprint, determined not to let him get away.

"Stop him!" John ordered to Bruiser.

Bruiser nodded. He pulled out both his guns and rushed past the cars toward Joel.

Several men roughly patted Peter to make sure the fire was out. He moaned and shook in shock. Most of his hair and skin were burned away. There was a good chance that he wasn't going to make it, even if they did get him medical care. I could understand why Joel had been upset, but that didn't mean he should rush into unfamiliar territory and risk his life.

For all we know this is a trap, I thought.

No sooner were the words formed in my mind than the

yelling and shooting began. The man responsible for burning up Peter had turned the corner at a full dash with Joel in hot pursuit and Bruiser not far behind him. A second later, five Unity thugs had come running toward them, guns drawn, shooting wildly.

"Do something," Tom screamed.

"We can't," John protested. "If my men open fire they might hit your brother or Bruiser."

Joel just missed getting shot in the face by throwing himself at the ground. Bruiser wasn't so lucky. Being a big guy, he had a lot of momentum going as he ran full tilt to try to catch Joel. By the time Joel ducked down to avoid the muzzle being pointed at his face, it was too late for Bruiser. He didn't even know what hit him. The gun went off and the top of Bruiser's head came apart in a spray of blood, hair, and skin. He was dead instantly. Bruiser's full limp weight came crashing down on top of the gang member who killed him, pinning Joel's legs to the ground at the same time.

"Joel," Tom yelled in panic. "Get up and run!"

Joel frantically struggled to free himself, eventually pulling his legs out from under Bruiser's nearly headless corpse. Shots rang out from my right side as John's men took out two more Unity Gang thugs, causing the rest of the ambush squad to retreat back behind the building. All we needed was for Joel to get back over the line.

"Why aren't they shooting anymore?" I asked out loud, but no one answered me.

I looked at the buildings surrounding the intersection for signs of eyes in the windows but couldn't make out any.

"Hurry," Tom hollered.

Joel began to limp back toward us. The man who had thrown the explosive concoction brazenly walked out from behind his safe spot, pointing his gun at Joel.

"Behind you," John cried out, but it was too late.

Before Joel could turn and see what was happening, the man fired off two shots at him. The first pierced through his upper leg and came out the front of his jeans, covering them in blood. He faltered and began to pitch forward. He put his hands out to brace his fall, like a little kid. The second shot seemed to cut across Joel, entering somewhere in his back and coming out his chest. A tiny spray of blood came from between his lips as he fell flat to the ground.

Shots rang out from all sides as Joel fell out of the line of fire. The gang member jerked as the volley of bullets pierced him as if a live wire of electricity was running through him. He fell over, twitched briefly, then went still.

Tom wailed in disbelief at the horror unfolding before him. Tank and another patrol member held him back. John rubbed his brow and shook his head in disgust. Joel's head moved as he started to get up, but he fell back to the ground. Then he began to slowly crawl toward us.

"Let go of me!" Tom shouted. "We've got to go help him!"

"It's not safe," John howled.

At that moment, almost as if to back up his warning, a pack of four zombies came wandering out from down the street. The air rumbled as the sound of motorcycle engines roaring to life besieged our senses. We heard loud yelling and hooting as the bikers fled the scene.

"Where did *they* come from?" Benji asked in surprise.

"Unity Gang probably brought them with them," John yelled over the crackle of gunfire that ensued. "They keep 'em as pets and fight them. I told you it was bad." John turned and stared at me.

It was too much to take in at once. Things had gone from bad to plain psychotic. Joel was still inching forward, pulling himself along. He wasn't going to make it. What started out as four or five zombies was now easily up to thirty. John glanced around. They were coming out of buildings in packs. The gunfire wasn't doing much to slow them down. Their bodies seemed to absorb the rounds. Only a direct shot to the head would stop them from advancing.

"Get back in the Jeep!" John yelled. "We're leaving now!"

"No!" Tom cried out in protest. "We have to save Joel!

We have to save my brother!"

"It's too late for that," John hollered back. "Now get in or get left behind."

Benji scrambled up into the Jeep. He curled up in a ball in the backseat, keeping his head down and covering his ears. The sound of gunfire was all around us, like a chorus of exploding high grade fireworks. I followed him in, taking the passenger seat. John started the Jeep and put it in reverse. Tank dragged Tom, desperately kicking and screaming, to the car.

"Get in or I'll knock you out," Tank warned him.

Tom tried to pull himself free but Tank grabbed him by the arm and yanked him around, delivering a hard punch to the stomach that knocked the wind out of him. Tom doubled over and Tank wasted no time throwing him in the back of the Jeep. Tank was only part way in the vehicle when John took off, slamming the pedal to the floor and leaving a trail of rubber behind.

Tom lay next to Benji, crying mournfully. Tank didn't say anything. I opened my mouth to speak, but John cut me off.

"Not a single word," he growled, his voice low like a coiled snake ready to strike.

I shut my mouth. We rode in silence until we got back to the first neighborhood. John pulled up in front of his house and shut the engine off.

"Everyone inside the house now," he demanded. There was no longer any pretense of friendliness about him. We climbed out of the car and stood staring at John, waiting for further instructions. He looked like he was about to explode.

Now we're seeing the real John, I thought. *A coward who leaves fallen men behind.*

My look must have said all of that and more because John suddenly turned on me.

"I've had just about enough of you for one day," he said. "Tank, see to it that these brats are secured until I decide what to do with them."

"My pleasure," Tank replied.

"Lock them in the secret room and put a guard on them," John barked. "I've got some business to take care of and I don't want them causing any more trouble or even accidentally getting anyone else killed."

Before Tank could reply John floored it, taking off down the street.

"Well, ladies," Tank began with a slimy grin. "You heard the man. Let's go."

He marched us upstairs to the room covered with Nazi memorabilia. I hadn't bothered to tell Benji and Tom about the decor. Their surprise was as genuine and deep as mine when I first saw it.

"You like it?" Tank asked. "I decorated it myself."

"You did this?" Benji asked in surprise.

"Yep," he proudly responded. "I'm a bit of a collector, or at least I was before Z-Day. John's house burned down during the riots so I offered him mine to set up headquarters in. There is some reading material you can flip through while you wait to see what John plans to do with you."

"You can't keep us locked in here like prisoners," I feebly objected.

"That's where you are wrong," Tank corrected me. "We can and we will. Consider yourselves lucky. If it were up to me I'd just take you out back and shoot you for what happened back there."

And if it were up to me I'd chop off both your hands and leave you to the zoms, I thought.

"My brother is still out there," Tom cried out suddenly. "We have to go back for him."

"I hate to be the one to tell you this kid, but by now your brother is either dead or craving some serious brains. It's his own damn fault too. I never seen anything like that before. It was like he had a death wish." Tank spit out a string of curse words that made Benji blush.

Tom's jaw clenched and I could see he was plotting how to repay Tank for his insult.

"That's his twin brother," I said. "Show some

sensitivity."

"I thought you two hated each other," Tank replied.

"We didn't hate each other," I fumed. "We disagreed. Besides that's no reason to leave him to zombies. How would you feel if someone did that to one of your family members, then laughed about it?" An evil look came over Tank's face, like a dark cloud throwing a moody shadow across his eyes and forehead.

"I've known Bruiser almost my whole life," he said in an even, steady voice. "He was better than a brother to me. He's saved my life countless times. Now because of your idiot brother's actions, he's dead."

"Sorry," I offered as guilt flooded over me.

"Save your apologies for John," Tank roared, his tone hard as nails. "I don't give a crap what you children think. Just remember this, you ever talk that way to me again and I will twist your head off like a dinner chicken. Now sit down and shut the hell up."

Tank shoved us deeper into the room and slammed the doors. He locked them from the outside.

Of course, I thought, picking myself up from the ground and testing the handle. *The secret room locks from the outside. That's why John wanted to keep us here.* Tank wouldn't want people just wandering in and discovering his Nazi obsession. Before Z-day he kept it under lock and key. After the world came apart, and he was helping to run a white paramilitary splinter group that was fighting off mostly minority gang members, it wouldn't matter if people knew he was a bigot.

"It's locked from the outside," I explained without them asking.

"What do we do now?" Tom wondered, pacing back and forth and chewing on his fingernails.

"Nothing we can do. We wait and try to come up with a plan."

"We have to help Joel," Tom reiterated. "We have to go back for him."

"I agree," I said. I looked over at Benji and he nodded. "First chance we get we have to make a break for it. We'll grab Joel on the way out of town and never look back."

"How are we going to get out of Lompoc when the Unity Gang controls the highway out?" Tom asked. "You saw what they're like. They're animals who killed my brother for no reason at all. It's not like we can just explain that we're not part of their war and they'll let us pass through."

"I don't know," I admitted. "But we will find a way."

I sat down with my back to the doors and closed my eyes to think. Things were not going according to plan at all. Somehow I knew they were going to get worse before they got better. I felt guilty about Joel's death, even though it wasn't my fault. Yeah I didn't like the guy. He kept challenging me. He kept picking fights for no reason. He was a pain in the butt from the minute he saved us at Vandenberg. That didn't mean I wanted him dead, did it? No. It didn't.

I was exhausted from the events of the day and my mind was starting to play tricks on me. I was going to leave Joel and Tom behind. That's the truth. I was going to grab Benji and sneak out of town the first chance I got. Now I was going to have to risk my life again to try to help Tom. But how? Nothing came to mind but more problems when I asked myself that question.

Without even realizing it, I drifted off to sleep again.

CHAPTER TEN

The sound of the door unlocking woke me from a deep, dreamless sleep. I scrambled to my feet and hurried over to the bed where Benji had passed out. Tom sat in the corner staring at the wall, as catatonic as Cameron in *Ferris Bueller's Day Off*. It had grown dark outside. I quickly scanned the room for signs of a clock. All I saw were Nazi symbols and swastikas.

Abruptly, the door swung open and Tank stood there looking as intimidating as ever. "Rise and shine, kiddies," he sang out condescendingly. "It's dinner time."

The cute girl I had seen earlier in the day stepped out from behind him with a tray full of soup bowls. She walked into the room and set one down in front of each of us. The contents looked like piping hot beef stew with a square of yellow corn bread on top. When she set the bowl down in front of me, she stared deeply into my eyes for a long time. Up close she was even more beautiful than I had imagined. I was speechless. Then without a word she turned and marched quickly out of the room.

Another woman I didn't recognize came from behind her and gave us all large glasses of water. I gulped half my glass down at once. I hadn't realized how thirsty I was.

"Easy there runt," Tank scolded. "You're only getting one bathroom break, so take it slow, amigo."

"Where's John?" I demanded. "I want to talk to him."

"And people in hell want ice water," he said in a mocking voice. "In case you hadn't noticed, John's a pretty busy guy. He'll get to you when he has time, princess. Now eat your chow and shut your yap."

Tank slammed the door shut and locked it again.

"You think it's safe to eat?" Benji delicately turned over his portion with a large spoon, like it might explode at any second.

"I guess so," I said, taking a cautious first bite. It tasted good, really good. "Tastes fine to me."

"What if he poisoned it?"

"I think if John wanted to kill us he would just take us out and shoot us," I mused.

"Yeah," Benji agreed. "Or let Tank twist our heads off like chickens."

I turned and looked at him in shock. He laughed. I tried to fight it back, but soon I was laughing too.

Things have just gotten ridiculous so fast, I thought. I looked over to see that Tom wasn't eating. He'd turned himself more toward the wall and was muttering under his breath. He was taking what happened to Joel pretty hard. It made me stop giggling.

"That's not funny," I said, spooning in a few bites. "Eat up. We're gonna need our strength."

We chowed down in silence for a while. When I reached the bottom of the bowl I found something unexpected. At first I thought it was a seasoning leaf. I dug at it with my spoon to unearth it from the soil-colored sludge of the stew and saw that it was a piece of plastic. I pulled it out to reveal someone had stuck a tiny plastic bag at the bottom of my bowl, but that wasn't all. There was paper inside.

A note, I thought. *Someone snuck a note to me. But who? And why?*

I unwrapped the plastic and removed the paper from it, being extra cautious not to get it wet. I unfolded the tiny square of paper until it was the size of my palm. There were tiny words etched into its surface in perfect little letters.

The guard change happens at midnight. The spare key is hidden in the spine of Mein Kampf. Check the map in John's office. The road south is not guarded by Unity Gang. You've been lied to. Eat the evidence when you are done. Good luck!

I leaped up and grabbed the book off the shelf.

"What's going on?" Benji asked.

"I'm not sure," I replied honestly, flipping the pages down and pulling at the spine. The glue gave a gentle sigh and came loose. A shiny silver key slid out and plopped onto the bed. I picked it up and shoved it in my pocket.

"What's that?" Benji probed.

"I will tell you later," I promised, crumpling up the note and jamming it into my mouth. I chewed it up as best as I could and swallowed it whole. I could feel the sharp edges tickling as it slid down my throat.

A moment later the door opened again.

Just in time, I thought. *Any longer and I would have been caught.*

The cute girl came back in and cleared the dishes away. I tried to make eye contact with her, to let her know I had gotten her message, but she wouldn't look at me. She was in and out of the room in under a minute. Tank sauntered in after she left, looking annoyed to be stuck babysitting a bunch of kids instead of being out there chasing down gang members.

"All right," he grumbled, sounding grumpier than ever. "Time for bathroom breaks. Who has to go?" Benji stood up and walked toward the door.

"Good," Tank said. "Now let me remind you that if you try to escape you will be killed without hesitation. No warning shots. You got that?"

Benji turned white. His young legs began to tremble a little. He was unable to answer, so he nodded his reply.

"Fantastic," Tank chortled, pulling him out of the room. He shut and locked the door again.

I turned to Tom. "I know you can hear me in there," I whispered gently to him.

He didn't budge. He hadn't touched his food either. His eyes were moving back and forth a lot and he kept blinking, but that was about the only sign that he was still in there.

"We're getting out of here tonight. First thing we do is steal a car. Then we go looking for Joel. You don't have to do anything. Just be ready to go when the time comes and don't slow us down. You got that?"

Tom closed his eyes and shook his head. "Got it," his small voice croaked.

It made me sad to see him this upset. He was always the fun one, the peacemaker, the guy telling us all that everything was going to be okay. Losing his twin brother to the chaos out there had turned him into a hollow shell. I knew I didn't have to explain to him that there was a good chance we wouldn't be seeing Joel again, that his brother was dead and gone—or worse, transformed into a monster.

The lock clicked several times and the door swung open once more. Tank shoved Benji back in.

"Next," he said.

I stood up. "I'm next."

"You know the drill." He frowned. "You make a break for it or try to be a hero and I will rip your arms off for real this time. Is that clear?"

"I understand."

"Then let's go."

Tank led me out and locked the door. He slid the key back into his pocket.

That's not going to be a problem anymore, I thought.

We walked down the hall, passing John's empty office. My eyes lingered on the big map on the wall. Tank shoved me on before I could get a good glimpse of it.

"Keep going," he said roughly.

There will be time later tonight, I reminded myself.

I walked into the bathroom and shut the door behind me, locking it even though I knew Tank could easily knock the door down if he wanted to get to me. I turned the water on and did my business. While I was in there alone, I went over my plan. At midnight I would strike, unlocking the doors to the secret room from our side and pulling them open. Hopefully, there would be no guard there, but if there was the element of surprise would work in our favor. I'd cover his head with a pillow case and choke him out. Then we'd all have to sneak out, find car keys, steal a car, sneak out of the neighborhood undetected, and slip back to the heart of a war zone to look for a missing person—all before high tailing it out of town with bikers chasing us.

This is insane, I thought. *There are too many things to plan, too much left to chance. It's never going to work.*

I beat back the pessimism with an internal pep talk: *It has to work. I have no other choice. Whatever happens, we'll make it work. We will fight until we are free and on our way. Sure the odds are against us, but it's been that way since Z-day and we've survived. We will adapt to whatever surprises come our way.*

Adapt and survive. That was what Moto always said.

A loud banging at the door brought me back to reality.

"Hurry up in there," Tank yelled. "I ain't got all night."

I flushed, pulled up my pants, washed my hands, and unlocked the door again.

Tank practically yanked me out of the room and shoved me down the hall.

"When are we going to see John?"

"Tomorrow," he responded. "He said he'll sit down with you first thing after church."

"*Church?*" I gave him an odd look. Somehow I couldn't picture them as God fearing Bible thumpers.

"That's right, little sinner," he said. "What? Did you think we were a bunch of Godless heathens like them biker trash?"

"Doesn't the Bible say to turn the other cheek?" I asked.

"It says a lot of things," Tank scolded, growing annoyed at having his faith challenged. "I'm not up to a theology lesson from a snot nosed punk kid like you right now. So shut it."

"Sorry," I offered, turning my stare to the ground to give

him the impression I truly was.

"You know," he pondered, unlocking the door. "We were all hoping things would turn out different with you."

Before I could answer, he shoved me into the room. I collided with Benji and we both fell on the bed. The door clicked again and I knew it was now locked shut. I tiptoed over and put my ear to the keyhole, listening for the sound of footsteps. Benji tried to speak but I waved him silent with my hand. It sounded like heavy footsteps pacing back and forth in the hallway.

I pointed over to the corner where Tom was still sitting staring off into space. Benji and I huddled around him to whisper.

"What's the plan?" Benji asked.

"The guards get changed at midnight," I said.

"How will we know what time it is?"

Tom pulled back his jacket to reveal a kid's wristwatch. The time was eight-thirty.

"That takes care of that." I laughed. "Thanks Tom."

He blinked in reply.

"So how are we going to escape?"

"I am still working on that." I chuckled.

"What does that mean?"

"It means there are a lot of things involved in this escape," I said, annoyed. "There is a whole lot that can and probably will go wrong. We need to be honest with ourselves about that right from the start if we are going to make this work. We need to stay flexible and never let go of our goal."

"Freedom," Benji whispered.

"Joel," Tom mumbled.

"All the above," I added.

For the next few hours I kept my mind busy, turning the plan over and over in my head, mostly to keep myself from falling asleep again. I dreamed up one possibility after another and then imagined what I would have to do to overcome the obstacles they presented. I thought about

Tank's words, how they had hoped I would go along with their plan from the start and join them. It would have been a whole lot easier to escape if I had gone along with their plans for me. I wished I would have thought that through a little more, instead of just blurting out whatever came to mind. It was too late now for regrets.

When it got close to midnight, Tom tapped me on the shoulder and pointed to the door. I knelt down again and put my ear to the keyhole once more. I could hear loud snoring. At points, it even shook the door slightly. A dull, male sounding voice resonated on the other side. There was some commotion that sounded like someone standing up. The door moved. For a moment I was afraid they were going to open it and check on us.

I glanced back to see Tom and Benji ready to pounce. I waved them back with my hand. It was too late to pretend we were sleeping. A few tedious moments passed and then I heard the men talking outside.

"It's a ridiculous assignment," the voice said. "They are just kids. How much trouble could they be?"

"It's not up to you to make that call," the other voice said. "John wants us to keep an eye on them. That's what we're going to do."

"I thought he said the kid with the sword was joining our movement?" There was heavy sarcasm in his voice. "Thought he was supposed to be officer material. Guess that didn't work out."

"Stop asking questions or I will have you court-martialed," the voice threatened.

"Take it easy."

"I've been stuck watching a door all day," the man said. "I'm hungry and I'm tired. See you in the morning."

I heard one of them walk away. It sounded like the other slumped down into almost the same position the first had, with his back against the door. This part was going to be easy. I would simply unlock the door, pull it open fast, and choke the guard out. With a little luck he'd have a set of car keys on him. That meant all we had to do was check the map and get my sword on the way out. No way was I leaving without it!

I turned and made the thumbs up to Benji, who took one of the pillowcases off the bed and held it ready to bag the guard's head. Tom grabbed a bronze bust of Hitler off the shelf. If the guy made too much noise we were going to knock him out. I only hoped Tom wouldn't hit him too hard.

The closer it got to midnight, the more Tom seemed to come back to life. There was a growing fire in him, fueled by revenge. These people were misguided, no doubt about it. It was wrong to hold us against our will, wrong to treat us like kids, but I didn't think they deserved to die for it.

The guys got real close to me. I put the key up to the lock, threading it into the key hole and slowly pushed it all the way in. Making as little noise as I could, I turned it until the door clicked. We all froze in fear. I put my ear to the door but didn't hear anything. If the guard was sleeping up against it, the click could easily have woken him.

At least I know Tom will clobber him if he tries to come through before I get it open, I thought.

Just when I figured I couldn't take any more, I heard a low snore coming from the other side of the door. I nodded one more time to the guys, then stood up and yanked it open. The guard, a small, middle aged man with a bald spot on the back of his head, fell over into the room without making a sound. Benji threw the pillowcase over his head and Tom hit him hard twice on his crown. He went limp almost immediately.

"Well that was easier than I expected," I whispered.

I turned out the guys pockets. He had a small square of chocolate and a deck of playing cards. There were no keys. This was going to be harder than I had imagined.

"Stick close to me," I ordered, slipping out the door and picking up the man's dropped gun.

The house was dead quiet as I walked down the hall to John's office. I stopped and listened for signs of life, but there were none. It was almost as if we were the only ones left. The thought gave me chills but I didn't know why.

"Okay," I said. "Keep your eyes open. If anyone comes near or if that guy gets up, don't hesitate to raise the alarm. It's going to take all of us to get out of here in one piece, and we are not leaving anyone behind this time."

I went into the office and partially shut the door. Using only the light coming in the window from the cracks in the blinds, I traced a line with my finger across the map from where we were to the barricade. I checked for routes from there that led down toward the highway. There was one that ran along an old cemetery and came to what looked like a dead end. We had been lied to by John for sure. The only way out of town was right through the far side of New Lompoc, miles from where the war was happening. There was no way for me to know that this morning when I had first seen the map, but now that I had been to the fight it couldn't be more obvious.

"She was telling the truth," I mumbled in disbelief. Before I could turn to tell the others the good news, I felt two sets of big arms loop around either side of my neck and pull me off the ground. The air came out of me in a rush as they tightened like two angry, tattooed boa constrictors. My feet kicked uselessly at the ground below. I heard my gun drop to the floor.

"Well, look who came out for a midnight stroll," the man's voice said.

Tank was going to strangle me to death. It had been a trap and I had walked right into it.

CHAPTER ELEVEN

"My daughter cannot tell a lie," Tank crooned, his voice coming out of the darkness. "She just has too big of a heart. Poor thing. I blame myself for naming her Tammy. People don't realize it's short for Tammany, which of course is Irish for honesty."

If I could have drawn in a breath I might have told him I was Irish too. I was not above playing the race card, especially since I knew the guy was a white supremacist. It was no use. My head was swimming. His arms felt like they were made out of metal. I scratched at them but he didn't give an inch. It was as if he couldn't even feel it.

"It's only one of her weaknesses, unfortunately," he said causally while I kicked and fought for air.

Had he been in the room the whole time waiting for us? She'd set us up? Of course she did. Why would she help us? It didn't make any sense. He told her to trick us so he would have an excuse to get rid of me. John was still hoping to turn us to his side, and Tank was worried I might challenge him in the months to come. With me out of the way, things could go back to normal. First I had to fight off Joel and now Tank! The biggest difference being that Joel only wanted to kick my butt. I had no doubt that Tank was trying to kill me.

"The other is her beauty," Tank mused absentmindedly, as if he strangled sixteen-year-olds to death every day for sport. "She gets that from her mother, may she rest in peace.

Don't feel too bad. You're not the first to fall for her act. The note-in-the-soup trick works every time. You eat the evidence and no one can blame me. I'm just doing my job, keeping you from escaping. Later on I will tell John you confessed to being a Unity Gang spy and that it was no accident you were on the road waiting for us. John's a great man but he suffers from paranoia, especially since his brother burned to death."

My vision was going completely black. Tiny little pops of light appeared and vanished. I renewed my struggle. *Where are my friends? Why aren't they helping me?*

"Usually I don't take this much pleasure in killing a non-zombie," Tank confessed, "but ever since you sucker kicked me in the jaw, I've been looking forward to the moment when I would finally get to watch the light go out of your eyes."

At the rate he's going it won't be much longer now.

I went limp and let him hold me up.

Let him tire himself out, I thought. *I'm going to need all the brain power I have left if I am going to get out of this. Think! Think! Think!*

Moto had taught me how to slip out of attacks from behind, but in every instance they involved having my feet on the ground. I never imagined I would be up against a giant. My mind raced, trying to think of weapons I might have on me. My pockets were empty. I could try to head-butt him unexpectedly, but there was no guarantee that would work. More than likely it would just upset him more and he'd snap my neck like a twig.

Tank was still talking, but his words were starting to sound farther away. They had a dull echo and I couldn't tell if they were coming from inside my head or not. My fingers instinctually found his hands and gripped them. They felt like knotty branches from a tree.

His fingers, I thought. *That's it!*

The short training sessions Moto and I had done on Chin Na came flooding back to me all at once. By applying a small amount of force on his joints, I could produce a huge amount of pain, forcing him to release me. Just twisting his hand the wrong way would be enough to completely bring him under my control if I did it right.

I took both my hands and wrapped them around the index and middle fingers on his right hand. Using all the strength I had left, I bent them back hard and fast. A loud roar erupted out of Tank and he dropped me. Air flooded back into me but I didn't let go of his fingers. Tank reached back to slap me away, but I bent his fingers back even more and he yelped in pain, falling to his knees. Tears flooded his eyes, washing out the shock and anger. He rapidly panted in pain, unable to speak. I twisted his hand extra hard until I felt the bones snap and Tank screamed at the top of his lungs, unleashing a torrent of obscenities in the aftermath. With my free hand, I knuckle punched his windpipe and he went silent as he choked for air. My strength was coming back to me now. I was angry and flooded with adrenaline.

Tom and Benji came rushing into the room, but stopped and stared when they saw Tank on the ground holding his throat. I quickly maneuvered behind Tank and put him in a sleeper hold, using my forearm to choke him out. Despite his size, he gave me almost no resistance. Eventually, he fell to the carpet floor like a heavy sack of flour and remained there, motionless.

"Did you kill him?" Benji asked in shock.

"I don't think so," I said, my voice raspy from being choked out so long.

"He's just unconscious," Tom informed us, placing his fingers on Tank's neck and checking for a pulse.

I picked up the gun and handed it to Tom. "Cover him," I managed to croak out through my swollen throat, "while I go through his pockets. If he moves at all, go ahead and shoot him."

""What happened?" Benji inquired as I fished out Tank's car keys.

"It was a trap. The girl who was helping us is actually his

daughter. They planned on killing us all and telling John we were spies for the other side."

"That's crazy," Tom said. He seemed to be finding his grip on reality again now that it looked like we were going to escape.

"It gets worse," I went on. "The road out of town is actually on the New Lompoc side. Which means John was trying to trick us into staying and fighting in his war. We never needed to go to the border in the first place."

"So what happens now?" Tom stared at me.

"I guess we head south and leave town," Benji suggested. "And pray they don't have a trap waiting for us there too?"

"No," I said, shaking my head. "We promised Tom we'd find Joel. I know we didn't exactly get along like best friends but we can't leave without finding out what happened to him."

"Thanks," Tom said. "You're a good man."

"How are we going to get out of the house without raising an alarm?" Benji asked.

"We march right out the front door," I said darkly, retrieving my sword from Tank along with another pistol. I checked the blade to make sure it was still in pristine condition. The small sliver of light coming in the window danced across the steel. "God help anyone who tries to get in our way."

"We'd better hurry before one of them comes around," Tom prodded.

We rushed down the hallway, taking the steps two at a time. When we got to the front door, Tom stopped and waited for my response. I drew my blade and nodded. He held his pistol tight with one hand and yanked opened the door with the other, but there was no one outside.

The Jeep was parked by the curb. Suddenly, a loud yell rang out upstairs and lights flashed on in the kitchen.

"Let's go," I cried out, rushing outside.

Benji and Tom were right behind me. We climbed over the side of the Jeep and I hopped in the driver's seat. I had the keys in the ignition and the engine running in just a heartbeat.

Tom and Benji pointed their guns at the front door. The short man we'd ambushed at the secret room came running out with his gun drawn. Benji and Tom both let off several shots that seemed to explode over his head, forcing him to run back into the house for cover.

I peeled out, racing up the street and turning onto Ocean toward the direction of the border. I wasn't exactly clear on how we had gotten where we were. The last thing I wanted to do was go by the gas station and ask for directions. They'd be after us now in no time. The plan was getting more screwed up by the second.

"Turn left up here," Tom advised, pointing at an intersection with a strip mall. "I'm pretty sure John took us this way on our personal tour the first morning before you arrived."

"You got it," I replied, glad to have a distraction.

We drove past armed patrols, but they didn't even turn their heads as we went by. No one had sounded the alarm yet.

Tank was obviously going rogue, I thought as I rubbed my sore throat. I could still feel his arm crushing my windpipe.

"Turn right up here," Tom directed. We rounded the corner and I could see the barricade in the distance coming up fast.

"What are we going to tell them?" Benji asked.

"We'll think of something," I lied.

One of the armed guards held his hand up as we approached and I slowed to meet him.

"Let me do the talking," I insisted. Tom and Benji nodded. I stopped to meet the guard.

"What are you doing out here this time of night?" He didn't seem upset or alarmed by our presence, just curious.

"Tank sent us out," I said calmly. "Said we'd have a better chance of looking for his brother Joel at night since zoms slow down after dark."

"I wish that were true," the man replied. "I'm Harvey. Park over there." He pointed to a line of vehicles. Benji shook his head no but I pulled over and parked anyway.

"What are we doing?"

"We're finding Joel and getting the hell out of here," I whispered. "Just do what I do."

"We're going to get caught," Benji said.

"No," Tom said in his normal, relaxed voice. "Everything is going to be fine."

"No one would suspect in a million years that we would come back here," I suggested. "They probably think we made it out of town already. Tank's going to have a lot to explain to John."

We got out of the car and walked over to Harvey.

"How's Peter?" I asked.

"He's had better days," Harvey admitted wearily. "I didn't see it but I hear it was like he was consumed by a giant fireball. Most of the skin was burned off his body. He's still alive but he's in serious shock."

"Jesus," Tom gasped.

"We got some medical supplies and they are doing what they can for him," Harvey said. "Bunch of animals those Unity Gang creeps are. It's bad enough we have to fight off the zombies. The last thing we need is to fight with each other."

"Amen to that, brother," I agreed, slapping him on the back and walking toward the line of cars. "What happened?"

"You should know," Harvey said raising an eyebrow in surprise. "I heard you were here but John rushed you away to keep you all safe."

Yeah, I thought. *That's one version of what happened.*

"I meant after the attack," I corrected myself, not skipping a beat or contradicting his story. "When the zombies swarmed."

"I got called in about an hour later," Harvey explained. "The official report is that they pushed back the zombies and held the line, but just barely." He turned to Tom. "After the fighting was done, they looked for your brother but didn't find him. There was no body. Either the Unity Gang came back for him or the zombies turned him. Sorry kid."

"Let's hope it's the first then," Tom groaned.

"I hear you," Harvey replied. "Zombie ate my wife right in front of me. Nothing I could do but watch her scream in unfathomable pain as they ripped her arms and stomach apart with their bare teeth. We were leaving town, heading south, when some jerk in a truck broadsided us and left us for dead. I was pinned in. She got out to look for help. I couldn't do a thing."

"That's terrible," I offered.

"It gets worse," he cautioned us before plunging further into his twisted tale of woe. "Hours went by and eventually the zombies were drawn to a new kill zone by the smell of fresh meat. They left me there. I got to see my dead wife reanimate before my eyes. Can you imagine?"

"No," Tom practically shouted, shaking his head from side to side.

"Later, when John's men found and freed me, I hunted her down," he said. "I was the one who killed her."

"I'm so sorry," I sympathized.

"Don't be," Harvey explained. "It brought me a lot of comfort to be the one who did it, to know that she is at peace now and not walking the earth looking for people to eat. I would want her to do the same for me if our roles had been reversed."

"I never thought about it like that," I admitted. It sounded horrible no matter how you looked at it.

"I hear people tell stories all the time about how they lost one of their friends or family members under similar circumstances," he continued. "The story goes that they couldn't bring themselves to kill their loved ones, so they got eaten instead. I am proud to say I didn't hesitate when I saw my Suzie. I put her out of her misery with a single shot to the head. I did the Lord's work here on Earth during his last days. I know she is smiling down on me, that I will see her again at the right hand of Christ when he returns to rule over this world."

"I appreciate your kind words" Tom told Harvey, "but I am going to find my brother. I can feel it."

"I wish you luck," Harvey sincerely replied.

"There he is," Benji shouted, pointing to the middle of the road past the barricade. Sure enough, Joel was limping slowly across the intersection. His clothes were torn and his skin looked ashy and gray. There were bite marks visible up and down his arms. He had been turned. He was already gone.

Tom didn't hesitate. He turned and jogged toward Joel, calling out to him.

"Son, don't!" Harvey yelled. Armed guards trained their weapons on them but Harvey called for them to stand down.

"What is he doing?" Benji asked.

"I don't know," I said, "but it doesn't look good."

The walkie talkie on Harvey's hip began to chirp and I heard Tank's voice coming over it. We were out of time. Soon it would be too late to make a run for it and get out of town. We'd be stuck here forever as John's slaves or worse—target practice for Tank's goon squad.

"Get back to the Jeep," I ordered Benji.

"What about Tom?"

"I don't think he's coming with us," I said, turning and walking back as fast as I could without drawing attention to myself.

Harvey held up his walkie talkie to his mouth. He looked confused by what he had just heard.

"Say that again?"

"Those kids are Unity Gang spies," Tank screeched. "They've already killed two guards and stolen top secret intel from John's house. Don't let them get away."

I didn't wait to hear Harvey's response. I fired up the Jeep and started to pull away. Looking in my rearview mirror, I saw Harvey pull his gun out and point it in our direction. Behind him Tom screamed as Joel began to bite his neck. Gunfire rang out as the armed patrol shot them both dead. Harvey turned to see what had happened, but Benji and I took off.

"Well," Benji said, "at least you kept your word. Even if it was totally crazy for you to do that."

I drove along a series of side streets, down by where the map showed the cemetery, hoping to avoid getting caught or running into that dead end. I kept an eye out for any off road opportunities we might come across to slip out of town. Having a Jeep meant we could easily make our own path, but the last thing we needed was to get stuck out in the middle of Unity Gang territory or surrounded by zombies in a muddy field without even a tree to climb up.

After fifteen minutes I found a small dirt road behind some track houses that looked like it ran along the highway as a fire route. We drove along, passing a cluster of wild cows, and eventually came up onto the highway itself. There was not another car in sight. I drove around a corner feeling elated that we'd managed to sneak out of town, until I saw the row of cars blocking the highway ahead. In the center was John's truck. He was standing in front of it with his arms folded. The expression on his face was pure rage. Next to him was Tank with his right hand bandaged. I stopped the car in the middle of the road.

"What do we do?" Benji said in a panicked voice.

I looked in the mirror and saw a row of lights heading our way, blocking our escape. They had chosen this point in the highway for good reason. There were hills on either side of us that prevented our escape even in a Jeep. We were in the lowest point of the road. The only way out was forward.

"I don't know," I conceded.

"Can we ram them?"

"I don't think so. More than likely they'll blow holes through the Jeep if we try and we'll bleed to death."

"What are we gonna do?"

"Our only hope is to try to reason with them," I

concluded at last. "Maybe we can convince John of our innocence, tell him Tank was trying to kill us."

Benji looked white with fear. He was trembling all over. I had a horrible sinking feeling in the pit of my stomach like I had just swallowed poison. Slowly, I pulled the Jeep up.

"That's far enough," John yelled through cupped hands. "Shut off the engine and throw out the keys."

I did what he told me to do.

"Step out of the vehicle with your hands up."

Benji and I exited the Jeep and stood there. I still had the handgun tucked into the front of my jeans and my katana on my back.

"Throw down your weapons," he insisted.

"No," I shouted back.

"Excuse me?" John looked genuinely puzzled.

"Tank tried to strangle me to death earlier," I yelled. "He told me he was going to kill me like he'd killed the last visitors you had, then tell you we were spies."

"Sounds like something a spy would say," Tank retorted.

"We didn't kill anyone," I explained. "We trusted you and now two of our friends are dead."

"Put down your weapons or we will be forced to shoot," John demanded again.

"Then shoot," I hollered back. "All we want is to be on our way. If you are not going to let us go, then you're going to have to kill us. We are not going to surrender and have Tank finish us off later when you're not looking."

"You heard him," Tank roared. "They are traitors. Shoot them!"

"Hold your fire," John said turning to Tank.

"Oh come on!" Tank screamed. "You saw what they did to my hand! They came here with one purpose and one purpose only, to get information to take back to the Unity Gang."

"Then why didn't they cross over when they got to the border?" John asked. "If they are working for Unity, why would they take the road that leads away from the biker hideout?"

"You're not serious, are you?" Tank puffed out his chest. "They're just trying to mess with your head. For all we know, this is an ambush and Unity Gang riders will be all over us any minute now. Think about it!"

I unsheathed my sword and held it out in front of me.

"Lower your weapons," John said in a calm voice. "I need to have a word with you before you go. I promise you will leave here unharmed."

Tank seethed with anger. He turned and punched his huge fist into the side of John's truck, denting the door.

Cautiously, I inched forward. I kept my blade out but I left it at my side. Benji got behind me. Armed guards pointed their guns at us. If they were going to kill us, it wouldn't take much.

"I hope you know what you're doing," Benji said.

"Me too, kid," I replied.

John walked out and met me between the cars.

"This is a real mess," he said. "You gotta understand how this looks from my side."

"It looks like the neo Nazi you put in charge as your first command tried to murder me and my friends, from where I'm standing."

"Tank's a good guy," he insisted. "You don't know what we've been through. He's got trust issues. That's all."

"And now thanks to him, so do I," I fired back. "Look, this doesn't have to be complicated. Tell your men to stand down and let us go. You'll never have to see us again. End of story."

"I wish it were that simple," he said, scratching his head.

"It is that simple," I flatly pointed out.

"Maybe if you left the kid," John said. "As a sign of good faith. That might work."

Benji grabbed the back of my shirt and buried his head.

"What's the matter?" John asked, looking down at him. "I thought you liked it here? You can have all the video games and comic books your little heart desires."

"No way," I said. "It's not gonna happen. Benji is my responsibility and I am not leaving him behind."

"There now," John said with admiration in his eyes, pointing at me and smiling. "Can you see why I need your help? You are the perfect balance of warrior and philosopher, loyal to the bitter end. No wonder Tank is intimidated by you. You stick around and I will make you my second in command. Tank will have to answer to you!"

I looked over at Tank. A murderous rage was visible in his face. As tempting as it might be to take John up on his offer, I knew that it was just a matter of time before that man finished me off.

"That is a tempting offer," I lied.

"Isn't it?" John flashed us that sly grin, as if to say he knew he'd already won when he hadn't. "I'll tell you what . . ."

He cocked his head to the side like he was listening for something. Then I heard it too. A low growling, like a herd of wild animals shuffling toward us off in the distance. Only it wasn't livestock we were hearing. The unmistakable smell came downwind toward us. John and I both realized it at the same time.

"Zombies," he said right before one of his men let out a high pitched scream that tore our attention away.

CHAPTER TWELVE

The next thing I knew, there was wild gunfire going off in every direction. A zombie horde, just like the one that had taken over Vandenberg, had come up from the south and taken John's lynch mob completely by surprise. The men were so focused on our discussion they hadn't seen the monsters sneaking up on them. Several unlucky souls were torn apart before they could even get a shot off.

John wasted no time. He ran as fast as he could past us toward the Jeep. He climbed in the driver's side and started the engine. I thought he might use the open topped vehicle to try to save some of his loyal subjects, but instead he quickly turned around and took off back toward New Lompoc. I watched the red of his taillights disappear in the darkness in stunned silence.

The coward just ditched his own men!

I turned back to see Tank had a zombie by the throat and was holding him off the ground. The undead monster snapped and lunged at his face but couldn't reach him.

"What do we do?" Benji pleaded.

Once again, I didn't know the answer. The cars behind us were backing away, following John's pitiable example of retreat. In no time, the zombies would be past the line of vehicles and heading toward us.

We need to take one of those cars, I thought. Plain and simple. *We can't go back to town now. There is no other way.*

"This isn't going to be pretty," I warned him. "Do you trust me?"

"You don't sound like you're planning something truly crazy when you ask that or anything," Benji sarcastically replied.

"I am," I promised. "Let's just hope it's crazy enough to work."

I took my gun out and held it in my left hand. I held my sword up in my right. Benji, who didn't have a weapon, got behind me again, using me as a human shield.

I took off at a solid run toward Tank. When I got close enough I aimed the gun at the zombie's head he was holding. Tank's eyes grew wide. I think for a minute he thought I was going to shoot him. He turned as if he was going to throw the snapping zombie at me, but before he could I shot the creature right between the eyes. Thick, gooey, black decaying blood and dark brain matter splashed across Tank's face. He dropped the writhing corpse and it went still. I sprinted past Tank while he screamed hateful curses at me, wiping the mess from his eyes.

A long haired teenage zombie in a Slayer shirt moved up along the side of John's truck. With one downward motion I cut him in half with my sword. His mouth and arms kept reaching up for me. The dead thing was so determined to feast on my flesh that it didn't even notice it had been sliced in half! Before the top half could topple over, I snapped my blade back and severed the spine from the head. It fell over in three pieces at my feet.

"Nice one," Benji said encouragingly.

I grabbed the door handle to John's truck and yanked it open.

"Get in fast!"

Benji scrambled past me and up into the passenger side. By the time I shut and locked the doors, he was buckling himself in. I turned over the ignition and, without hesitation, the engine purred to life. Benji smiled at me.

You gotta love Ford trucks, I thought.

I looked up to see Tank staring at us with fire coming out of his eyes.

Geez, I thought. *You'd think the guy would be happy we just saved his life.*

I glanced in the rearview mirror. There were about a hundred feet of zombies behind us. Once again, we were between a rock and a hard place.

"Hang on," I warned. "This is gonna be one rough ride."

Tank reached down with his good left hand and brought up a handgun. He pointed it at us just as I threw the truck in reverse and plowed down a row of zombies. The gun went off and Benji and I automatically ducked down. The bullet went into the truck's grill, hitting something metallic but not stopping us. Another shot went off and punched through the top of the windshield, spraying us with a fine mist of glass shards.

"Stay down!"

Behind us, the loud sound of clanging rang out again and again as we mowed down one zombie after another. We were surrounded on all sides now by the walking dead. They beat their slimy hands against the truck, pressing their bodies against the doors. I could still hear the gun going off, but the shots weren't reaching us now. They were hitting the dead and being absorbed. The zombies didn't even seem to notice.

Well, I thought. *At least we have one less problem now.*

"We're stuck on something," Benji shouted.

I knew without looking he was right. We'd run down over a dozen of the creatures at least. The rags that were once their clothes were coming off of the zombies and getting twisted up in our axle, preventing us from backing up farther and escaping.

"Hold on," I said, shifting into drive. "I'm going to try to dislodge him."

Loud thumping on the back window of the truck scared both of us. We hadn't expected them to get into the vehicle. Usually zombies can't climb.

I must have accidentally popped some of them into the truck bed when I floored it, I thought as I drove back through the zombies, freeing the one trapped under our wheels.

"Look out!" Benji shouted, pointing out the front window.

Tank was standing just outside the edge of the zombie horde pointing his gun directly at us. I was going too fast to stop. It was too late to duck. He was going to shoot me and I was going to run him down. I saw the look of fear in his eyes as we came down on him. He pulled the trigger again and again, but nothing happened.

He's out of bullets! He used them all up when he was trying to kill us earlier.

The front of the truck slammed into Tank, knocking him over. It sounded like the grill cracked. Steam poured up from the headlights.

"Aw man," I groaned. "He is gonna be pissed if he lives through this."

"Serves him right," said Benji.

"Let's try this again," I said, putting it in reverse and backing up again. This time we had more of a path. We cleared the zombie horde with almost no resistance. The last thing I saw was them climbing over each other to get at Tank.

"They got him," Benji said.

"Looks like it," I agreed, turning the truck around to face south on the highway. "Better him than us."

We drove off and, as we picked up speed, I could hear the damage we had done. It sounded like metal was grating on metal. Every couple of minutes the whole truck would shake with a violent tremor and give off a high pitched squeal. Still it ran. I intended on taking it as far as the thing would carry us. No way we were going on foot after that last zombie horde.

"That doesn't sound good," Benji said. "Are we going to be able to make it all the way to Hueneme in this?"

"We'll be okay," I assured him, despite thinking pretty

much the same thing. "We'll see how far this thing can take us, then swap it for another ride when one becomes available. Just try to relax. The worst is over for now."

"The sound is driving me nuts," he complained. "Makes me think the whole truck is gonna come apart at any minute."

I remembered John telling me he kept a Metallica tape in the cassette player of the old truck.

"Let's see what John left us for tunes," I said, turning on the switch.

Heavy metal music poured out loud and clear. Lightning fast guitar picks and pounding drums filled up the cabin and blocked out most of the grating sounds. *And Justice for All*, one of my favorite albums. Benji and I lost ourselves in the music for over an hour without either of us talking. I beat out the rhythms on the steering wheel and he sang all the lyrics he could remember. It was probably the most fun I'd had since we left the base.

I was afraid to take the truck up over 45 mph. Every time I got it going that fast, the whole chassis would shake violently and Benji would unconsciously dig his nails into the paneling on his side. I knew at this rate we wouldn't get anywhere near the base until the next afternoon, but I didn't mind. I was so happy to be away from New Lompoc in one piece that I couldn't complain.

We saw a couple of drifter zombies in various states of decay along the way. One of them looked more like a skeleton than a human. Its skin hung off it like loose sheets in the wind. It was missing part of its left arm, and its face was sunken in and decayed so badly, with just wisps of what must have been hair left on its rotted skull, that it was nearly impossible to tell if it had been a man or a woman when it was alive. It wandered into the middle of the road like a lost ghost looking for the way back to heaven or hell. It was so close to true death that it didn't even take notice of us as we came barreling down on it from the higher grade. I took my foot off the gas and let us drift by, getting a closer look as I swerved around it. As we rolled past I noticed it didn't have any eyes.

We passed plenty of other cars as well, but not one of them looked suitable to drive. Even though the pickup was on its last legs and barely limping along, I wasn't going to chance swapping it for another car that might strand us out in this no man's land.

Most of the cars were smashed up in some way or completely burned out. They looked like they had gotten into accidents with thin air. I wondered to myself if the drivers had hit other cars on the road in their panic and abandoned the vehicles or if a zombie horde like the one we encountered had overrun them as they sat in traffic.

When Z-day came, everyone had tried to flee at once. People up north thought if they could just get down south they would be safe. People down south tried to flee up north to get away from the zombie outbreak. Everybody thought they could run to some other place, some magical land that hadn't been affected yet. They thought they could wait it out. They were wrong.

When we got to Vandenberg, we learned that the outbreak had happened all over California at almost the same time. No one knew how it had started but there were rumors. One story said that it came from China, from a sick traveler who brought it with him when he landed at either LAX or SF. They say he attacked a stewardess on the airplane who then took it with her to several places around the world on an international flight.

That's the "patient zero" theory any way.

Most people believe that it spread first among the homeless population in California. So many transients flock here to escape bad winter weather and they are virtually unprotected out on the streets, forgotten and abandoned. The city of Los Angeles had a 'no questions asked' bus-out program to ship homeless people from skid row to the Las Vegas Strip on a one way ticket. It wasn't really legal but it wasn't quite illegal either. With the economy taking a crash, there were too many needy people who actually wanted help and not enough shelters. No one on the City council thought they would be shipping the zombie virus to a tourist destination. It hit Vegas after it hit California, then spread like wildfire all over the Midwest and eventually the East Coast.

It's funny, I thought. *In every major movie the end of the world always starts in New York City. But in reality it all began on the West Coast, in California. Seems kinda ironic.*

People don't talk about it much, but the truth is the virus went haywire south of the border even before it hit Vegas. Migrant workers carried it with them back to their homes in Mexico. Once it got in, it was impossible to stop. It spread down to Mexico City almost overnight, then out to the rest of Latin America and the Caribbean. People in Florida could see the black smoke out over the sea from fires burning in the lost island of Cuba long before Vegas was lost.

One of the last acts of Congress was to place travel restrictions on Europe, stopping foreigners from coming in and banning visits to or from Mexico, along with a halt on all imported products. The fact that they thought this would stop it, after years of poor border enforcement, only underscored just how screwed up our political system was in the end. By then it was too late. It spread up into Texas, New Mexico, and Arizona in less than a month. After that, well, we just don't know what happened. No one does. The whole world went offline.

The tape ran out with the final licks of *Dyer's Eve,* the frenetic, unrelenting drum track chasing the lightning fast thrash guitar to the end like a galloping horse. I reached up and shut off the radio before the cassette could flip again.

"You don't like Metallica?" Benji turned to me surprised.

"Who doesn't love *Metallica*?" I answered. "I just thought we could use a break is all. We've played it straight through now twice."

"I used to play them nonstop before *Ever Rest* came out." Benji said it like a confession. "I forgot how good they are, how much I love them."

"You a big fan of Jax?" I asked.

"The biggest," he said.

"So did you buy the album the minute it came out on iTunes, or just download it from the Pirate Bay?"

"When that first album came out, I was like six," Benji said. "I was barely getting over *The Wiggles,* you know? I got into metal a little over a year ago. Listened to everything I could get my hands on. A lot of it on Youtube at first. I didn't want to pay for stuff I didn't like."

"Piracy never occurred to you?" I said. "You know, test drive it and if you like it buy it later?"

"I didn't trust it," he said. "You never know what you're really getting when you download a torrent. One time my friend Craig accidentally got some real nasty stuff."

"You mean like a virus?"

"He got one of those," Benji said. "Eventually. Wiped out his whole hard drive. I'm talking about illegal stuff, the kind of stuff that would get you sent away before Z-day."

"Ah," I said, not wanting to push.

"Really gross stuff with kids."

"Got it," I said, trying hard to change the subject. Even after everything I'd seen, the thought of coming across some horrible image from the dark side of the deep web just made me super uncomfortable. There were plenty of sick people in the world before Z-Day. They just weren't as easy to spot is all.

"He wasn't even looking for it," Benji said. "That's the worst part. It was hidden in a download labeled as music. After I heard that, I lost all interest in downloading."

"So what kinds of bands did you get into?"

"At first it was like *Van Halen* and *Motley Crue*. I dabbled in *Alice in Chains* for a bit."

"They are good," I agreed. "You gotta be in the right mood. Like *Soundgarden* or *Rage Against the Machine*."

"I tried harder and harder music, like *Pantera* and *Slayer* and *Helloween*," Benji said. "I used to think they were the greatest bands in the history of music."

"Yeah? What happened?"

"All that went out the window when I heard *Ever Rest*," he said. "Jax did things with a guitar I didn't know were possible. It was like hearing Jimi Hendrix for the first time or Randy Rhoads. Amazing. I stopped listening to anything else."

"A real fan, huh?" I said. "I remember that feeling."

"Did you feel like that when you first heard Jackson?" Benji pried.

"Well no," I confessed. Benji looked disappointed. "Don't get me wrong, I love his music. He's like Slash in a lot of ways, but more moody and complex."

"Exactly," Benji said. "So who made you feel that way?"

"Rob Zombie," I blurted out. Benji gave me a confused look. "You never forget your first love. My brother tells me his was *Foreigner*. Says he fell in love when he heard the song *Jukebox Hero* on 45."

"What's a 45?"

"I don't know," I said. "Some kind of recording they used to use to listen to music, I think."

"What's the story with your brother anyway?"

"What do you mean?"

"I don't know." He shrugged. "You talk about him all the time but I still don't know a thing about him."

"Where do I start? I don't want to bore you to death with it all."

"It's not like we have a whole lot else going on right now."

"Except being in the middle of a zombie apocalypse fleeing for our lives?"

"After the last few days, I could use some boring conversation," Benji admitted. "I'm starting to feel like I will never see normal again."

"I understand. Well I told you he is a corporal in the marines, or at least he was before Z-day. Now that all the armed forces are working together, I don't really know how ranks work anymore."

"Yeah you told me that," Benji said, suddenly taking a big interest in my family life. "Is that his real name? Moto?"

"No." I laughed. "It's kind of a joke, but it isn't at the same time. They used to have those commercials for Motorola cell phones on television all the time, you know . . . the one where the guy's voice goes all high pitched? He says 'Hello Moto!'"

"I remember," he said. "Did he have that phone or something? Why did that stick?"

"You don't understand," I told him. "His real last name is Ishimoto."

"I thought your last name was Macnamara?"

"It is," I said. "My dad was stationed in Japan when he was in the marines. He was married to his first wife, Jane. I never met her."

"Isn't that weird?" Benji asked. "Thinking that someone else could have been your mom? I never really got that."

"Stay focused," I interjected. "This story gets a little complicated and I don't like telling it all that much so I really don't want to have to repeat it."

"Sorry," Benji said.

"It's fine," I went on. "Now where was I?"

"Jane?"

"Right," I said, picking up my train of thought where I had left off. I hadn't told the story in a while so I was trying to remember the best way to tell it without confusing him.

"So I guess Jane got tired of waiting for my dad to come back from Japan. She sent him a letter saying she wanted a divorce and that she had found another guy—like some traveling businessman, I swear I'm not kidding, to run off with."

"Wow," he said. "Harsh."

"They were high school sweethearts, the way my dad tells it," I continued. "He was devastated. He started drinking more than he should have and running around bars in Tokyo. That's where he met Aiko, Moto's mom. I never understood if she was a singer at the bar he went to or if it was just karaoke."

"So what happened?"

"I guess they started running around together. Dad said she really helped him turn things around when he was in a bad place. I asked why he didn't stay in touch with her after he was transferred to Germany. All he told me was that she was busy with her singing career."

Benji was completely absorbed in my family history.

"I wish I would have asked him more questions," I said. "It's too late now. There are so many things I would have liked to know. When you're a kid they tell you what they want you to believe and you never think to pick apart the answers, not until later when you're older. By then it's old news."

Benji nodded.

"My dad met my mom when he got out of the service. She was a car service girl on roller skates at one of those retro hamburger stands. He said he used to go there all the time. He'd brag about the amazing onion rings and how thick they were, but now I think he just went there to check out the girls in short skirts."

"I don't get it," Benji said.

"Don't worry," I said. "You will soon enough. He said it was love at first sight. They were married in under a year. He spent a good chunk of his military money on a house and a new car. He used to joke he spent more time in the car cruising than he did at home before he met my mom. She hung up the skates when I came along."

"Where is your mom?"

"She passed long before Z-day," I said bitterly. "Cancer."

"I'm sorry," Benji sympathized. "I didn't know."

"It's not your fault. It's not anybody's fault really, except maybe God. Funny thing is, my dad got all religious after that. Then one day out of the blue there was a knock on the door and there was Moto. He'd tracked my dad down and come to confront him for leaving his mom."

"I thought you said he was transferred?"

"That's not what Aiko told him," I explained. "She was ashamed of getting into trouble, especially by an American. In her culture there are strong prohibitions against being with foreigners, so she tried to say Moto's father was this older Japanese guy who owned a factory a couple of towns over. The only problem was that Moto was clearly part white. The other kids teased him mercilessly, growing up. He says they called him a half-breed and a mongrel. He says he used to get beaten up every day walking home from school. Still his mom wouldn't tell him the truth."

"That's terrible," Benji said.

"That's what I said," I agreed. "Moto says it made him stronger though. He says he finally confronted his mother one day and she told him the truth—except the way she told it, my dad had taken advantage of her and left her in trouble. Moto was mad. He wanted to track down his father and challenge him to a fight. He wanted to restore his mother's honor."

"Did they fight?"

"No." I laughed. "Once my dad explained everything to him there was no reason to scrap. Moto believed him right away. The truth has a certain ring to it. I guess his mother had lied to him about a lot of things to him growing up. My dad told him he could stay with us if he liked. He was like fifteen years old at the time and didn't speak much English. We got him a tutor and he did really well. He always was a fast learner. We adopted him on his sixteenth birthday and made it official."

"Were you happy to have a big brother?"

"I was a little weirded out at first," I confessed. "My friends kept giving me a hard time about him. He was kinda odd the first year, but I guess that was just a cultural issue."

"What turned things around?"

"He saved me from getting beaten up one day after school."

"Like the way you saved me back on the base?"

"Pretty much," I said, nodding my head. "He didn't have any friends in his own grade so he used to follow me around. He said he was practicing his ninja stealth skills."

"Cool." Benji smiled.

"I didn't think so at the time," I admitted. "Then I got jumped by these older kids from middle school one day. He came out of nowhere. It was like he literally appeared out of thin air. One minute I was getting pummeled and the next he was there, fists moving so fast I couldn't keep track of them. After that we got along much better."

"So you started training with him?"

"Believe it or not, I didn't," I confessed. "It wasn't until later when I got older that I realized what a valuable resource he was. I guess part of being a kid is taking things for granted."

"Did everyone call him Moto or is that your nickname for him?"

"Oh yeah," I said. "I almost forgot the point of this story. So his name was Yasho Ishimoto when he came to live with us. My dad had it legally changed to Patrick Macnamara when we adopted him, but by then I had gotten used to calling him Moto. He liked the nickname. He said it allowed him to keep a part of his identity. He was proud to take his father's last name, but he didn't want to lose who he was in doing it. My dad was so happy to have him as a son. We hadn't been doing too well since my mom died. Moto changed all that. Suddenly my dad was like a new man, not just to Moto but to me as well."

"Why?" Benji asked.

"I think he saw a lot of my mom in me," I said. "He never said it, but that's my guess. He loved her so much that just looking at me hurt him. When Moto came, it gave us a chance to be a family again. Instead of focusing on what he lost in life, on Jane or Aiko or my mom, he could put all his energies into us. Suddenly we were going camping and hunting and to big sporting events. Moto gave him an excuse to do all that stuff, you know — to show him how

Americans lived, but I think my dad loved getting a second chance."

"That's an amazing story," Benji said. "And you've been close to your brother ever since?"

"Yep," I said. "I trust him with my life. He's about the only person left I can say that about."

"I hope you can say that about me one day then," Benji said with a smile.

"I'm sure that day will come, little man," I assured him.

"Can we pull over? I need to go to the bathroom."

"One or two?" I asked.

"One," he said tentatively. "I think . . ."

"I know what you mean," I said. "We've been in the car a long time. I'll tell you what. The sign said we are almost to the 101 split. We can pull over when we get to the coast and go on the beach."

"I'm not going to make it that far," he warned me.

"Why didn't you say something before then?" I tried to hide my annoyance but I was too tired.

"It just kinda crept up on me," he said defensively.

"Fine," I said. "We'll take this next exit. But you better keep your eyes peeled. If you so much as think you see a zombie, we're flipping around and you're holding all the way to Ventura."

He nodded, holding his pants and squirming. I pulled the battered truck down the off ramp and toward a side road that ran parallel with the highway. In the distance, the first rays of sunlight were starting to come up.

CHAPTER THIRTEEN

We drove down a small street that dead ended at a private school. It had a huge field and a large parking lot full of cars.

"What is this place?" Benji asked in surprise.

"Looks like one of those fancy schools for kids whose parents are extremely rich," I blandly commented.

"Why are there so many cars?"

"I don't know. It's a bad sign though."

"It is?" Benji turned to me in surprise.

"Cars mean people," I explained. "So where did they go?"

"Maybe they're hiding in the school," he suggested. "Like a commune. Maybe they've stockpiled their resources and are surviving until help comes."

"Maybe," I said. "And maybe they're all zombies now. Maybe the whole place is crawling with hungry, undead monsters just waiting for us to walk through those doors so they can snack on us."

Benji swallowed hard. "Do you think so?"

"I don't know. We have to be careful." I turned the truck around and pointed it back toward the way we'd come. If things did go bad, I was planning on driving back up the off ramp rather than looking for the freeway entrance.

I put it in park, set the brake, rolled the window down, and got out. Benji followed me. I could feel pins and needles shooting through the lower half of my body. We'd been traveling for so long I hadn't noticed that my legs had fallen asleep. I grimaced as I forced myself to walk them back to normal.

"Are you just going to leave it running?" Benji asked.

"It's not like anyone is going to steal it," I said, immediately regretting my choice of words. Now if someone came running out of the bushes and took off in the truck, I would feel like a total moron.

I shook the feeling off. More than likely if we saw someone they'd already be dead. Stealing the truck would be the last thing on their agenda, right after eating us alive and picking their teeth with our tasty bones.

"Besides," I continued, "I'm not so sure it will start up again if we kill the engine."

"It's barely hanging on," Benji agreed.

"Right. So this way if something happens we can run back and jump in the truck and take off right away. Worst case scenario is you lock yourself in and take off without me."

The large American flag above us whipped freely in the wind, drawing our attention.

"I'm scared," Benji said.

"I'm here," I said, drawing out my blade. "Let's just get this over with as quickly as we can."

We walked slowly up to the front of the school and opened the doors. The hallways were empty upon first inspection. Part of me wanted to walk around the school, do a full sweep of the grounds, but the urgency to go to the bathroom overwhelmed me. Inside the hallway were doors clearly marked *Men* and *Women*. I walked cautiously to the end of the hall. Peering around the corner, I found both sides empty.

"Do you see anything?" Benji whispered. He was nearly dancing around now and holding his pants at the crotch.

"Looks clear," I said. I pushed open the bathroom door and checked under the stalls. The place was deserted.

"Hurry," Benji said, now literally hopping back and forth.

"Okay. Do your business but don't waste any time. I'll keep watch outside the door. If you hear me yell, you pull up your pants and get out of there. Got it?"

"Got it," Benji said, pushing past me and running into the stall. I shut the door to give him some privacy. The hallways were eerily quiet. I understood that we were basically in the middle of nowhere but it didn't make sense to see all those cars just sitting out front.

Maybe there was a football game or something, I thought. *Maybe they parked their cars and took a bus to a sporting event.*

Looking back toward the way we came in, I noticed a huge cross hanging above the door.

It's a Christian school, I thought. *Maybe they were all raptured.*

A loud flush quickly pulled me back to reality. I heard the water go on in the bathroom as Benji washed his hands. I propped the door open.

"Everything okay in there?"

"Better than ever," Benji said.

I took my turn while Benji waited outside. It was nice to have a moment's privacy even if I was too paranoid to really enjoy it. I cleaned up and walked back out.

"I'm hungry," Benji said when I came out.

"Well that didn't take long," I countered.

"Can we search the school for food?"

"Feels kind of like we're pushing our luck."

"Puh-leese?"

"Okay," I said. "But at the first sign of trouble we're high tailing it back to the truck and getting out of here. Agreed?"

"Yeah," Benji agreed.

"If I so much as see a dead body, I am out of here."

We set off into the school at a snail's pace. It was just too much to believe there was no one there. We searched all the classrooms, but all I found was a flask of whiskey in one of the teacher's desk drawers.

We ended up in the teacher's lounge. I opened the fridge but knew the minute the door swung open there was nothing edible in there anymore. It smelled horrible, like a pile of rotting tuna fish sandwiches.

"What about the cafeteria?" Benji asked as I gagged and shut the door. "Or maybe some of the vending machines?"

"Good idea," I agreed.

We popped a couple of the machines on our way and grabbed handfuls of junk food. Both times I waited to see if the sound of breaking glass would attract anyone, but there was nothing. So far as I could tell, we truly were all alone.

The cafeteria had a bunch of frozen food that had gone bad. There were tins of dried pasta and sauce but we'd have to cook them and I wasn't comfortable sitting in one place that long, even if we could get a fire going.

"What about these?" Benji pointed to two large tins that read FRUIT COCKTAIL on the side.

"They're better than nothing," I said.

We rummaged around and found a can opener then peeled the top off one. I grabbed a ladle and Benji used a wooden spoon. We sat down and ate the sugary concoction of peaches, pears, and cherries without conversation. When we were both too full to take another bite, I stood up and turned on the water. It was cold but clean. I rinsed my face and gulped down several refreshing handfuls. Benji followed my lead. I could feel the life returning to me.

"Did you ever think you'd be so happy to eat canned fruit?" Benji asked. We both laughed.

Then I heard something and I froze in place. Benji saw the look on my face and turned his body toward the door. I motioned for him to stay still. We sat there for a while, not making a sound.

"What is it?" he whispered.

"I don't know," I said. "It sounds like a radio picking up static."

I took out my sword and held it in front of me as I walked toward the sound. Behind the kitchen was a small hallway leading to the gymnasium. The doors were closed. There was a smell in the air that reminded me of an old campfire that had burned out. I held my hand out to signal Benji to stop. He froze dead in his tracks. Leaning over, I peeked into the gym through a window in the closed doors. I lowered my sword when I saw the bodies spread out on the floor.

"What is it?" Benji asked.

"I found the people," I said cheerlessly. I tried the door but it was locked. "Stand back."

Benji stood against the wall and I kicked the doors several times to try to get them open. They held fast together despite my best efforts. Loud booming sounds echoed down the hallway with each kick.

If there are any zombies here, they'll know right where to find us now, I thought.

I gave the door one last kick with everything I had in me. It popped open and the stench of the dead bodies hit me full in the face. I fell over and threw up sticky peaches in syrupy nectar. Benji helped me back to my feet.

"The smell doesn't bother you?"

"I'm used to it," Benji said. "I mean, as much as anyone can ever get used to it. What happened here?"

We walked into the room, stepping over the bodies of whole families—parents and kids alike. Their faces were purple and swollen and their eyes bulged horribly out of their heads.

I found the radio and shut it off. In the middle of the room were the remains of a large fire and several empty bags of charcoal. I knew what had killed these people.

"Carbon monoxide poisoning," I reasoned.

"What?" Benji asked. "How did that happen?"

"They tried to light a fire in here," I noted. "I don't know if they were planning on cooking or just trying to stay warm. With no ventilation, it didn't take long to kill them."

"How is that possible? This place is huge!"

"It doesn't take much," I said. "We used to do a lot of

camping. One time this old couple next to us in the campground put their barbeque away under their trailer, thinking the coals were extinguished. They went to bed with their windows closed because it was cold. The coals reignited in the middle of the night. The fumes came up through the floor boards and killed them in their sleep. They looked just like this when the paramedics showed up to take them away the next day."

"How'd they know to look for them?"

"Ranger found them," I said. "Came around to collect the campground fees and when they didn't answer he got nervous. I guess he could smell something funny. Smelled just like this."

"Is it safe to be in here?" Benji looked around nervously.

"Yeah," I said. "It is now. They look like they've been dead for a while. That's why there are so many cars in the parking lot. They probably came here to wait out Z-Day together thinking there would be safety in numbers. They were listening to the radio for updates. More than likely they just got ready for bed and went to sleep but never woke up."

I glanced around until I found a well dressed man. I bent down and rummaged through his pockets, pulling out a set of car keys with an alarm.

"What are you doing?"

"Getting us a new ride," I said. "Thanks, buddy."

We headed back outside toward the parking lot. There was still no sign of life anywhere, but I was less worried now. If zombies had been here they'd already discovered there was no food for them. It wasn't likely they'd be drawn back by the smell of two random teenagers over the scent of two hundred plus rotting corpses. I held the keys up in the air and pressed the alarm over and over. Finally a dirty black Cadillac Escalade chirped.

"Let's hope the battery still has some juice left in it," I said as we hurried over to it in excitement. I hopped in to the plush leather interior and shoved the key into the ignition. Instantly, it came to life. I felt like fighting back tears as the air conditioning hit my face on full. Benji climbed around in the backseat.

"Look at this," he said, holding up cans of energy drinks.

Turning around I saw that there were cases of water, energy drinks, and diet soda.

"Nice going," I said. Benji smiled. "You leave anything in the truck?"

"Just that *Metallica* tape," Benji said.

"This thing has a six disc CD player in it," I said. "It's not going to do us any good."

We drove back out the way we came and got back on the highway. There were no signs of life along the way and I was grateful. Despite being knocked-out tired, it felt good to be in a luxury vehicle instead of that broken down truck. Benji grabbed us both a couple of sugar free Red Bull's and we knocked them back as fast as we could. I tried turning on the stereo, but it just kept telling me the GPS couldn't find the satellite so I shut it off. I was definitely going to miss that *Metallica* tape.

In less than ten minutes we turned onto the 101 Freeway and made our way down to the sparkling ocean. I noticed we only had a half a tank of gas. That bothered me. The Escalade was a real gas guzzler. There was no way we were going to make it to Hueneme without stopping to refuel. I wasn't sure I would make it much longer without sleep, Red Bull or no Red Bull.

"So what's the plan?" Benji asked.

"I'm thinking we should try to stop in Santa Barbara. Look for gas and food."

"Jackson is from Santa Barbara," he said.

"Oh yeah?" I thought he was just making conversation.

"He's got a mansion on the beach," Benji said. "I saw it in People magazine. It's in an exclusive gated community. The whole neighborhood is probably deserted."

It's not a half bad idea, I thought. Rich areas would have loads of supplies and weapons. *Who knows? Maybe we can even clean up and take turns sleeping.*

"Do you think you can remember how to get there?" I asked as Benji's eyes went wide with excitement.

"Sure I can," he said. "This is gonna be awesome!"

Benji could barely contain himself the rest of the way. We made good time passing through Gaviota and Isla Vista without incident, and saw only a few stalled and empty cars. In Buellton I was tempted to stop for gas but saw zombies milling about in the weeds near the side of the road and knew it was too risky. Benji saw them too but he didn't say anything. We were both beyond exhausted.

They look just like migrant workers from the fields, I thought. *Only I know no one works the land anymore.* For a minute it made me think of how good things used to be. We never really appreciated it until it was all gone. We were always looking for something better, the new thing to get into. Now I'd give anything to just have things go back to the way they used to be—even for one day!

The canyons winding down to Santa Barbara were idyllic and empty. We pulled into town and Benji guided me off the freeway and up a hill to an area with a cliff that overlooked the ocean. We made a couple of loops through the abandoned area looking for the entrance to the neighborhood where Benji's idol lived. It was like the world had never ended. We were just two exhausted kids looking for a rock star's mansion so we could get an autograph. Eventually, we found the gates that led to his small plot of heaven.

"This is it," Benji said confidently.

"Are you sure?" I asked.

"No doubt about it," he replied.

The electricity was out on the call box. We had to leave the Escalade behind and go on foot, climbing over the fence. It made me uneasy to be on foot out in the open. You never knew when you were going to be cornered by a small horde of flesh eaters.

A lot of these homes are only used in the summer, I told myself. *Rich people buy them for the real estate investment and then they sit here unused all year long. What a waste.*

Benji led us down a curving side street to a house with a large metal gate with the Ever Rest band logo on the front. This was Jackson's mansion. No mistaking it. I laced my fingers together and helped Benji over the wall by letting him step into my hands and boosting him up and over. Slinging my katana on my back, I scaled the bricks on the side of the gate and swung myself up. The front door was locked and I sure didn't feel like trying to bash it in.

We walked around the side and into the backyard. There was an infinity pool that appeared to run off into the ocean. Benji sat down on some of the patio furniture and began taking his shoes off. He had blisters covering both sides of his feet, but nothing too serious.

"You wanna check the house before we relax?"

"I'm really tired," Benji said. "I think the Red Bull is wearing off."

"That and the adrenaline," I said.

"I just want to dip my feet in the pool." He sounded defeated. "Catch my breath for a second."

"That sounds like a great plan," I said, yanking off my boots and peeling off my socks. I rolled up my jeans until they were well past my knees, then waded onto the top step of the pool. The temperature was already rising outside and the cool of the water felt decadent against my feet and calves. Benji hurriedly rolled up his pants and joined me, letting out a satisfied sigh as his feet went under.

"That's amazing," he said, breathing out the words like a long, relaxed sigh.

"Yeah," I said, staring across at the ocean. "And the view doesn't hurt either."

"Can you imagine living like this?"

"Lifestyles of the rich and famous," I chirped in my best British accent, trying to sound like Robin Leach.

"I'm not saying he didn't earn it," Benji added quickly, wanting to preserve the image he had of his favorite musician. "It's just epic. I wonder how many famous people he's had in this pool?"

Benji's words trailed off. We sat in silence for a long time, splashing water with our feet, thinking about the perfect life that Jackson Everrest had once lived and knowing in our hearts that this was only a tiny part of it.

"It's getting hot," I said, standing up again.

Benji didn't budge. He stared defiantly at me as if to say he had no intention of leaving.

I unbuckled my belt and took my pants off. I folded them in a ball and set them off on the grass, along with my sword and my shirt. Without further warning I jumped into the pool in just my boxers, making a loud splash. At first there was the shock of being fully submerged in cool water, but it quickly changed to bliss.

"I can't believe you did that!" Benji stood up and was yelling at me. My impromptu cannonball had sprayed him good. He had water dripping from his hair and all down his shirt.

"You're free to get me back," I said. "Unless you're too chicken?"

Benji peeled off his clothes down to his boxers as fast as he could then jumped in, narrowly missing me with his feet. We got into a loud, splashing contest for about five minutes that ended with us both laughing hysterically. It was great having him around. In a lot of ways he had become like my kid brother.

"Truce," I said.

"No way," Benji replied with another hand splash aimed at my face. "I win!"

"Okay," I said. "Don't be a spaz. You win."

The chlorine was burning my eyes. I closed and wiped them, trying to restore my vision.

"Xander?" Benji's voice sounded strange but I couldn't see him. That last shower of water had gotten me good.

"Hold on a minute, Benji," I said. "I think I got something in my eyes."

I swam under the surface of the pool and opened my

eyes. I loved the way it felt to be fully submerged in the water—like I was floating. When I came up, I saw Benji standing in the shallow end with his hair dripping water all over himself and his hands thrust high in the air. Just past him on the patio was a very familiar looking teenage girl pointing a shotgun straight at him.

"Who are you people and what do you want?" she said, turning from Benji to me.

I held my hands up and smiled. I couldn't help it. The girl threatening to kill us if we didn't give an answer that she liked was none other than Felicity Jane.

CHAPTER FOURTEEN

"What are you smiling about?" she fumed, turning on me.

"Nothing," I said. "I just wasn't expecting . . ."

"What?" she said fiercely, fear in her voice. "A girl with a shotgun?"

"A celebrity. I mean a reality television star. Guess we're all on our own version of reality TV now."

"If you're trying to convince me not to shoot you," she said, cocking her head to the side, "you are doing a really bad job."

"I'm Xander. And this is Benji."

"Are you stalking me? Is that why you're here?"

"A little full of yourself," I scoffed, "aren't you? We didn't even know you'd be here so how could we be stalking you?"

"Then why are you here?" She waved the gun around, aiming first at me and then at Benji.

"Could you put that thing down?" I was starting to get ticked off. "Please, before you hurt someone."

"Not until you explain what you're doing here."

"Okay," I said. "No need to go psycho on us."

"Start talking," she threatened, turning the gun fully at me.

"We're heading south to Hueneme. Our place got overrun by a zombie horde. We've had a really crazy couple of days on the road. We just need a place to relax and recharge."

"So why did you come here?"

"Benji is a big fan of Ever Rest," I explained. "He remembered the location from a magazine article he read. We thought this area would be less populated, meaning fewer zombies to fight off. Most of these rich people don't even live in these mansions full time anyway."

"We never thought anyone would actually still be here," Benji added.

Felicity lowered the shotgun at last. A puzzled look came over her face. "Hueneme?" She scratched her head. "I don't get it."

"His brother is a big shot in the armed forces," Benji said. "He's stationed there."

"We had some trouble coming down," I said. "We're exhausted. If we could just sleep for a while, maybe rummage for some supplies, we'll be on our way."

She stared at us for a minute, thinking.

"We'll have to ask Jax, but I'm pretty sure he won't mind. He has more than enough rooms, even for uninvited guests." She practically hissed the last part of the sentence.

"Jackson is here?" Benji's mouth hung open in surprise.

"Yeah, but he's sick. I wouldn't get your hopes up that he'll perform a personal concert for you." Sarcasm dripped from every word as she spoke.

At least she's not pointing a shotgun at us anymore, I thought.

"You said he's sick. Be honest. Is he infected?" I asked.

She turned her full rage on me. "No he isn't," she practically screamed. "He's just sick. Okay?"

"Okay," I said, holding my hands up for fear she might shoot me. "Chill out. We're your guests. Be cool."

"Then act like guests instead of intruders. You can start by getting dressed."

"Um," I said, looking a little lost.

"What is it now?"

"We didn't really bring towels to this pool party."

"You were just planning on drying out in the sun?"

"Actually, we were so happy to see a clean pool we didn't really think much at all," Benji said, jumping in and saving me.

Instantly Felicity softened. Benji has that affect on people. Yet again, I was really glad he was with me.

"I'll get you some," she offered. But then she turned and glared at me like I was an enemy. "Wait here."

She walked back into the mansion leaving us alone.

"Dude," Benji said. "I can't believe it's actually *her!*"

"I know," I confided. "I can't believe how mean she is in real life. This was not what I was expecting at all."

"What is it with you two?"

"What do you mean?"

"It's like on one level you're both fighting and saying rude things to each other," Benji began, "and then on another level something else is going on."

"I don't know what the hell you're talking about," I said. "I think the sleep deprivation is getting to you. Quiet, here she comes."

Felicity came back with large, ultra fluffy towels that smelled like roses. It was like we had died and gone to heaven. Benji and I quickly toweled off and redressed, ditching our boxers and going commando while they dried out in the sun. When we were back in our jeans, Felicity led us into the house. There was a large kitchen with huge windows that looked out onto the ocean and pool. To the side of that was a huge living room with several big flat screen television sets and a couple of super comfy looking couches. There were pictures of lightning striking the ocean hanging all over the walls. They looked like the ones people used to sell prints of at the mall, only fancier because they were real. In the middle of the room were several guitars and an amp, right next to a video game console.

"Follow me," Felicity said, leading us down a long hallway deeper into the house. Platinum albums with sales numbers in glass cases lined the walls, along with pictures of Jackson with famous people like former President Bill Clinton and Bono. We passed a couple of guest rooms with the doors barely cracked. There was also a small, normal looking office and a studio space.

"That's his private studio, but believe it or not he usually writes in the living room."

Felicity Jane is playing tour guide for us as she takes us to meet Jackson Everrest, I mused. *Maybe we died back in New Lompoc. It would make more sense. I'm sitting in the truck with a bullet from Tank's gun in my head, bleeding to death right now while ravenous zombies tear me apart and Benji screams bloody murder. There is no way I am actually here!*

"How many people are staying with you?" Benji asked, snapping me out of my twisted fantasy.

"It's just Jax and me right now," Felicity said.

"Are you dating?" Benji looked up at her innocently and she smiled. I was glad he asked. I was just as curious about that as he was, but after the way she took everything I said wrong I didn't plan on asking her myself.

"No." She laughed. "Jax is a close friend, like a brother."

"Does he know he's in the friend zone?" I asked, trying to be funny. I regretted saying it even before she turned her head and gave me an evil glare—a glare that felt like she had physically punched me in the guts.

"Jax can date anyone he wants," she said. "Our relationship is special because we've never tried to be anything more than friends. Just because I'm an emancipated minor doesn't change the fact that I am sixteen and he is twenty-four. Why am I explaining all this to you?" She threw her hands up in disgust. "I don't owe you anything."

"I'm sorry," I confessed. "I didn't mean anything by it. I am really tired and I was just trying to be funny. I'm an idiot. Please forgive me."

She fought back tears. I had hit a real nerve but I couldn't see why. I really needed to learn to keep my trap shut.

Felicity Jane was one of the few celebrities I'd had a crush on and now that I was finally meeting her in person, I couldn't seem to stop putting my foot in my mouth.

"I didn't mean to snap at you," she said. "I shouldn't take my stress out on you. You gotta understand that you are the first living people I've talked to other than Jackson since Z-Day happened."

"You don't need to apologize to us," I said, cautiously reaching out and putting my hand on her shoulder to comfort her. "We came barging in unannounced and I have been kind of a jerk. I promise I will mind my manners from here on out. No more excuses."

She laughed as tears streaked down her face.

"You have been kind of a jerk," she said, wiping her face. "Thanks for that."

Benji looked back and forth from her to me like a confused dog. To be honest, I didn't really know what was going on either. I just stood there awkwardly with my hand on her shoulder for too long. I stepped back to give her some space and she took a deep breath.

"I've gotta check on him first," Felicity said. "Hang back and wait for me to call you in. Okay?"

"Got it," I answered.

Felicity opened the large doors at the end of the hallway. Inside, it was dark and cool. I could make out a huge bed but not much else. The sound of the ocean was mixed with some kind of chanting coming from somewhere inside the room. She left the door cracked slightly as she went in. It seemed strange just standing there, but I was determined not to do anything else to set her off.

Eventually she came back, stepping out and shutting the door behind her. Benji looked crushed.

"He says you can stay as long as you like. There are guest rooms you can sleep in. Most of them have clothes in them. You're welcome to help yourself to whatever you need, including food and water from the kitchen."

"Do you have hot running water?"

"No," she said. "We still get cold water from the faucet and it's clean, for now. The toilets still flush, but there is no way to know how long that will last. It's not like someone is working at the sewage plant anymore. I think we're just lucky that most of this neighborhood is abandoned, like you said."

"What about drinking water?"

"Jackson has a huge supply," she explained. "We moved it to the kitchen after things quieted down."

"From where?" I asked.

"From the panic room," she pointed out. "We were in there for over a week. Once the electricity went out, we decided to get out. They say you can't get stuck in there but your mind starts to play tricks on you in small spaces like that."

"You must be running pretty low on supplies."

"Not really," she said. "Jackson was raised Mormon."

"I knew that," Benji said, proud of himself.

"I don't get it," I said. "What does that mean?"

"It means he kept a stockpile of food and water hidden in the house," she said. "Mormons believe in being prepared for the end of the world. They will probably play a role in rebuilding the country if the military ever gets things under control. Jackson left the church when he was fifteen but old habits die hard, as they say."

I was growing more tired by the second. Now that I knew we could actually relax and rest, it was like my body was rebelling against me.

"What do you do about lighting? What I mean is, do you use candles?" I yawned. I didn't feel like waking up in pitch black in an unfamiliar place, even if it was a mansion.

"Sometimes," she said. "If it's overcast. The stars provide a lot of light, believe it or not. We have a backup generator that's capable of providing plenty of electricity, but Jackson doesn't like to use it at night. He's worried that light will bring looters or zombies."

"That's actually really smart," I said.

"You look exhausted."

"I am."

"Go ahead and crash out," Felicity suggested. "We can talk more when you get up."

I was happy to have an excuse to go lie down. I was almost feeling dizzy.

"Thanks," I said. "I'll take this room." I cracked open the door to see that it was beach-themed with soft shades of blue.

"You gonna crash with your brother?" Felicity asked Benji.

"He's not my real brother," Benji said.

Thanks kid, I thought. *Throw me under the bus to the hot celebrity chick.*

"Okay then," she said with a smirk. "How about your own room?"

"Thanks again," I said, making eye contact with Felicity. She held it for a second too long then pulled away.

"It's not a problem," she countered. "I'll get him set up. Go to sleep."

"Promise me you'll wake me up right away if anything happens," I said fiercely.

"I will," she replied casually. "Don't worry. Like I said, you're the first people to set foot on the property since the zombie outbreak—living or dead. We're safe here."

Even though I had no way of verifying her words, they made me feel better. I shut and locked the door.

I checked the closets and under the bed, making sure they were all clear. I checked the bedroom window. It was high. If someone wanted to get in that way they'd have to break it and climb in at chest height. I'd have plenty of time to defend myself.

I locked the window carefully then set my sword by the side of the bed. After what happened in New Lompoc, I wanted it within easy reaching distance. We really were lucky to get out of that place in one piece.

Far luckier than the twins, I dismally remembered.

I sat on the bed and looked around the room. It was quiet. Almost too quiet. I was overly tired and anxious and excited by everything that had happened. The last thing I remembered thinking was that I didn't know if I'd be able to fall asleep. I woke up briefly some time later, on top of the bed in my clothes, fingers touching my katana. I took my shirt off, rolled over, and fell back asleep. If I dreamed at all, I don't remember it.

I woke up a few hours later, feeling calm and refreshed. It was still dead quiet outside. I put my shirt back on, grabbed my blade, and opened the door. The sun hadn't quite gone down yet but the light coming down the hallway had that golden quality to it that suggested we weren't far from night. I could hear the sound of music and voices mixed with laughing. I walked out, rubbing my eyes.

"Hey, sleepy head," Felicity greeted me. She seemed in a much better mood. Light danced in her sea green eyes as she stared at me.

Maybe she got some sleep too, I thought as she asked me how I slept.

"Like the dead," I said.

"That's either the best joke in the world or the worst pun," said a guy's voice to my left. I turned to see Jackson Everrest standing and holding a toy guitar in his hands, smiling amicably. He didn't look sick at all. Benji was next to him, smiling. It took me a second to realize they were playing Guitar Hero, one of my favorite video games of all time. Jackson was actually a character in one of the latest versions. If you got to the highest level you had to battle him to complete the stage.

"Thanks for letting us crash here," I said, trying to play it cool.

"Well it's not like I had a choice, did I?" For a moment I thought he might be mad that we had let ourselves in after all. "We the living have to stick together now. No more 'mine and yours.' We have to work together if we're going to survive."

I let out a huge sigh of relief at the words. *He really is cool*, I thought. *Imagine that.*

"You actually play Guitar Hero?" I asked, changing the subject.

"I love this game," Jackson said. "Have you ever played it?"

"I have," I said, laconically.

"Are you any good?"

"I've cleared the game once before," I said, trying to sound modest. You don't just brag about your fake guitar skills to one of the world's most legendary guitar soloists of all time. "I assume you shred at it."

"Believe it or not I'm just mediocre at the game," Jackson said. "I've talked to other musicians who have the same problem. Playing buttons is totally different than playing strings. I do okay though. Benji here has been giving me a run for my money. Wanna give it a go?"

No way, I thought. *One of Rolling Stone's top ten guitarists of all time just challenged me to a game of Guitar Hero in his living room. I can't believe this is happening!*

"Sure." I shrugged, trying to keep my cool even though my heart was racing in my chest harder than if a hundred zombies were chasing me. "I'll give it a shot."

Benji gave me his fake guitar controller and I slid the strap over my neck. They'd already unlocked most of the levels so we selected intermediate play and I started playing some *Slipknot*. Benji's character had been the girl with the pigtails in the pink skirt. I didn't bother to change it, odd as it was. Jackson had selected himself.

Fitting enough, I thought as I made short work of the song, racking up extra points with the glowing blue notes and the whammy bar.

Jackson had a little more trouble than I expected. He missed a bunch of notes in a row. Then again he had been sick, according to Felicity.

When we polished off *Slipknot*, we played some *Metallica* and then *Black Sabbath*. At that point I could see that it wasn't just feeling under the weather that was holding Jackson back. He had serious timing issues hitting the buttons. What was going on?

I can't believe I'm beating Jackson at Guitar Hero, I thought. *This just doesn't seem possible.* I tried not to focus on it too much for fear it would distract me. I could see him getting frustrated that he wasn't doing better at the game. He tried to hide it, like when he missed a note he'd turn and play it off like he was distracted, or start telling us a story from when he was on tour.

"Ozzy's tour manager worked with us on the Australian leg of our last world tour," he said, when he missed a bunch of notes in a row on *Paranoid*. "Great guy. Real solid."

We reached the battle stage of the rock legends version. That meant we had to play against the computer's choice for us to advance to the last level of the game and win. The guitarists included Dave Navarro, Joe Satriani, Jimmy Hendrix, Slash, Carlos Santana, Jimmy Page, Jack White, and last but not least, Jackson Everrest. I was randomly matched up against Hendrix. Luckily I had played against Hendrix before. I matched him note for note on *Purple Haze* for the first part of the song and did a decent job keeping up the rest of the way through. It was enough to advance, but just barely.

"Not bad," Jackson complimented me. "If they ever figure out how to turn these things into real instruments you'll have a smashing future."

"Thanks," I said, setting the plastic guitar down and taking a seat on the couch next to Benji.

I hadn't noticed while I was playing, but Felicity had moved closer and was watching us both intently. I turned to look directly at her and she looked away toward Jackson, trying to pretend she hadn't been looking. Her nacre skin seemed so soft and white, like light from the moon was glowing off her. Her hair fell in bright red vibrant curls against her neck, standing out in shocking contrast. I got the feeling she could sense I was staring at her so I looked away quickly, trying to pretend I was yawning.

The computer began to shuffle through the remaining guitarists, looking for a match for Jackson. All the characters whooshed past at once until one was left — Jackson Everrest.

"This is like a nightmare," the real Jax said. "Like an evil computer version of myself come to life to torment me. Wish me luck."

"Good luck!" Benji practically shouted.

Even though it was one of his biggest hits, *My Soul to Take*, Jackson seemed to have trouble with it from the start. He needed to switch fingers to hit the lower keys and his timing was really off. He quickly grew frustrated as his artificial avatar blazed through the notes effortlessly while he kept getting loud reverb clangs from hitting the plastic keys too late. He cursed and spat on his own floor. No one said anything. During the long guitar solo he stopped and took the controller off altogether, giving up. I looked over at Benji who could barely hold in his surprise.

"It's a stupid game anyway," Jackson vented in frustration. "I don't know why I keep messing with it."

The screen flashed the words YOU LOSE as the avatar Jackson flicked his pick at us and threw up a devil finger salute.

"Jackson," Felicity said calmly, "it's okay. It's just a game."

"I know," he said, reaching over and flicking on his guitar amp. He picked up a black Les Paul from the stands near the console and plugged it in. He put his foot on the amp and rested the bottom of the guitar on the top of his thigh. "Can a game teach you this?"

Jackson ripped into a guitar solo filled with racing notes and mind melting progressions. Benji's jaw literally fell wide open. I'm pretty sure mine did too. It was far beyond anything we could possibly have imagined. Jackson looked up at us and laughed out loud.

"You really are fans?" A satisfied smile spread across his face before we could nod in reply.

Was Jackson really begging for our attention by putting on a private show for us in his living room? I didn't have to ask because before we could answer him he began laying into the instrument again, giving it all he had. The sounds coming out of it were unreal and we were transported into his world. His hands moved so fast, they almost seemed to blur. He was like a guitar god! He finished and Benji and I wildly began to applaud him. The look on his face said it all. His ego was just getting a taste of what it really wanted.

"You want more?"

Benji practically leaped to his feet in response. I turned to look at Felicity. She looked slightly annoyed that Jackson was acting up for attention. I shot her a look that was somewhere between 'I told you so' and 'what can you do?' She let out a heavy sigh, like the whole weight of the world was on her shoulders. This wasn't just her being upset that Jax was showing off. This was something deeper, something not visible on the surface.

"That was amazing," I said, standing up.

Jackson stopped playing mid-song and turned to me. Benji just stared with his mouth hanging open like a prize bass. A quick glance down told me that Felicity had to stifle back a laugh with the back of her hand. I had just been shown what Jax could really do.

"I hope you don't mind me interrupting, but I wanted to rinse off and get cleaned up before dark. The sun is almost all the way down and I heard you're not partial to indoor lighting. A wise decision, I might add, but one that leaves me pressed for time."

"Of course," Jackson said, setting his guitar down. Benji shot me an angry look for interrupting our personal once-in-a-lifetime concert. "The guest bathroom is three doors down the hallway on the right. There should still be towels in there. I haven't had any company since the maid was last here, other than the lovely Felicity Jane."

"Awesome," I said, walking past him and down the hallway.

I turned on the water and was splashing my face when there was a knock on the door. I opened it to find Felicity.

"Here," she said, handing me a thick, brown candle and a book of matches. "Just in case it gets too dark to see."

"Thanks," I said. She stood there a minute, like she had something else to say. She bit her lip. I was sure she was going to share a secret with me. I waited, but after she still didn't say anything, I started getting annoyed.

"What?"

"Nothing," she muttered. She turned and walked away. I shut and locked the door.

"Geez," I griped out loud to myself. "What's her problem?"

I lit the candle and shook out the match. The smell of sulfur filled the small room, making my eyes water. I blew my nose on some tissue then went to throw it away and stopped dead in my tracks. Sitting in the wastebasket was a bunch of hypodermic needles.

I leaned in to get a closer look. There were wads of cotton with what looked like dried blood on them. The realization hit me all at once—Jackson was a *drug addict!* That's why he was sick. He was trying to get off heroin. Was that why Felicity was here?

I decided not to mention it to Benji. The last thing he needed to worry about was his idol being a junkie. I'd only seen stuff like this on television, but I'd heard that dope fiends were capable of anything when they were going through withdrawal.

It might not be safe to stay here long, I thought. *Let's just hope he has enough stuff to keep him high as a kite until tomorrow. We'll have to leave soon for sure.*

CHAPTER FIFTEEN

I ran a cool bath and used a hand towel to sponge away the chlorine from the pool. It wasn't nearly as good as the hot shower I'd taken in New Lompoc, but it wasn't as bad as I thought it might be either. For the moment we seemed to be safe. I knew that it could change at any minute, but I pushed the thought out of my mind. The recent madness and chaos and insanity taught me that it was more important than ever to hold on to the good times. You never knew how long they were going to last.

When I got back out to the kitchen, everyone was sitting around the kitchen table eating by candle light. They'd covered the windows with black sheets to cut down on the amount of light they put off.

That may be the only reason they haven't been attacked up here yet, I thought.

Benji had opened up a can of Chef Boyardee beef ravioli and was eating right out of it with a fork. He looked more content than I had ever seen him. Jackson was picking at a bag of freeze dried ice cream, the kind we were told astronauts ate when we were little kids. I knew now why Jax wouldn't be eating. The drugs were all he cared about. That's how he stayed so skinny. Felicity had what looked like a plate of steaming beef fajitas with rice and beans.

"I thought you said you didn't have gas or electricity." I said. "How did you cook that meal?"

Felicity looked up at me and smiled.

"It's from the food rations kit," she explained. "Cooks in the bag, ready in under five minutes."

"You're kidding?" I said. "That's amazing. It looks like real food."

"Survival in style," she said. "Plus all I have to do is throw out the bag when I'm done."

"Too bad it tastes like low end fast food," Jackson said, still picking at the chalky pink block in front of him. The fire he'd had in him earlier was steadily going out. Now he looked pale and sickly. He'd used up all his energy trying to impress us.

"Really?" I said, a grumble rolling through my stomach as if on cue. "I'd kill for some Carl's Jr right about now." Felicity made a face I couldn't decipher.

"Felicity, would you please be so kind as to make our guest one of our finest meals-in-a-bag, my love?"

"I can make it," I said. "You enjoy your food. I'm sure I can figure it out."

Jackson dismissed me casually with a wave of his hand. I found the bags of ready-to-eat meals on the counter. They had every kind of meal I could imagine, from sweet and sour pork to beef stroganoff to lasagna. I grabbed a bag that read *Jamaican Chicken* and flipped it over to read the directions. It said to pour water into the top portion, seal, then pull a cord on the side and it cooked right in the bag. I took some bottled Voss off the counter and got it to work.

"There is still some soda in the fridge," Felicity said.

"Thanks," I said, opening the door and pulling out a two liter of Coke. Nothing in the fridge was cold.

I guess the video game console is more important than the food, I thought sarcastically. *Why do they even bother to keep this stuff in the fridge if they aren't going to keep it cool?*

I grabbed my meal bag. It was now piping hot, so I pulled the top open and steam poured out along with the smell of delicious chicken.

"Grab it from the bottom," she suggested.

It was cooler down there. I took the whole bag and my cola to the table and sat down next to Jax. I was so hungry that I dug right into my meal, not caring if I burned my tongue. The last thing we'd had to eat was the fruit cocktail back at the high school and I'd thrown up half of that.

"How is it?" Jackson asked.

"Surprisingly good for food from a bag," I said in between bites. I was suddenly overcome with hunger. "You're not going to eat?"

"Naw," he said, flicking his freeze dried ice cream away from him. "I played in Jamaica once. Big benefit in Trenchtown. Home of Bob Marley and the Wailers."

"Did you get to meet Bob Marley?" Benji asked. Felicity giggled. Jackson smiled and turned to him.

"I wish," he said good-naturedly. "Bob Marley died before I was born."

"Oh," said Benji, looking embarrassed.

"You know what?" Jackson continued. "You can still feel his spirit when you walk through the streets there. He stood for love and peace and unity through music and that message is still alive today. So in a way, you can say he lives on and I did meet him there."

Benji blushed. He had bags under his eyes. He looked almost as exhausted as Jackson.

"How long did you sleep this afternoon?" I asked.

"He didn't," Felicity said. "He followed me around asking questions about my career as a child actress, and whether or not I had a twin sister for when I shot *Double Trouble in Acapulco* like he read on some fan site. He's got quite an active imagination."

"How do you know if you don't ask?" Benji looked worn out. He was getting fussy at being teased. His battery was going down. It had been a long day by any standards.

"After that, Jackson was up and feeling better," Felicity said.

"That's when he challenged me to a guitar battle," Jackson said. He was starting to look green around the gills.

If I hadn't seen his trash in the bathroom I might have asked to inspect him for bite marks. "He's got the heart of a rock star."

Let's just hope he never inherits any other rock star organs, I thought.

"He's been up for almost two days now." I gave him a worried look. "I think it's time to get some rest. We wanna get back out on the road tomorrow."

I expected Benji to put up a fight at the suggestion of going to bed but instead he looked relieved, as if he had been waiting for someone to order him around.

"You can use the bedroom next to the one Xander slept in," Felicity said. "That way you will be close to each other."

"Does it have a bathroom in it?" I asked.

"Yours does," she said. "Why?"

"I think I broke the one in here," I said, turning to Benji. "Don't go in there."

"Good night," he said, standing up. He couldn't get out of there fast enough.

"I think I'm going to call it a night as well," Jackson said.

"You feeling okay?" Felicity asked with a note of fresh concern in her voice.

"Better than okay," he said with a sad smile. "I'd say this is the best I've felt in years and I have you all to thank for it."

"Thank you so much for letting us stay here," I said, trying to show my appreciation. "It was very kind of you."

"It's not a problem. In a lot of ways I was waiting for you. Now I can finally relax knowing that she will be taken care of if anything happens to me."

"You're really sick then?"

"Nothing is going to happen to you, Jax," Felicity said fiercely. "You are going to be fine."

"In more ways than I can explain," he said to me, ignoring her. He put his hand on my shoulder and stared into my eyes. "Take whatever you want. I mean it. I have more than I will ever need. I have been very blessed in this life. I never understood that before. I wasted so much time on so many useless things in this forgettable world. I wish I could do it all over again."

"You've brought a lot of happiness to people all over the world with your music," I said, and I meant it. "Kids like Benji. You have a wonderful gift."

"They never tell you that it comes with a curse," he said cryptically. "It was nice to meet you." He walked over and kissed Felicity on the head. A single tear escaped from her eye and rolled down her cheek, just like the way Demi Moore soundlessly cried in movies.

"Sweet dreams, angel," he said. "See you in the morning."

He turned and walked out of the room, back down the long dark hallway full of awards and honors, disappearing out of sight.

"I guess that just leaves you and me," I said. "You feeling tired?" She shook her head no. She seemed to lose all interest in her fajitas. "Me neither. Must have been the nap. What do you want to do now?"

"You don't have to do that," she said in a voice just above a whisper.

"Do what?"

"Act like everything is okay. I know the bathroom isn't broken. You figured out what's wrong with Jax. Admit it."

"I guess I did," I said. "The trash can was full of used needles and bloody cotton balls. It doesn't take a genius to put two and two together with that kind of evidence. You want to talk about it?"

"It's not his fault," she said. "Drugs are a big part of the music industry."

"You mean like they are in Hollywood?" I didn't know if I was stepping over the line. I hoped I didn't sound condescending.

"Exactly. So now you know why I am here. I came here to try to help him get clean, before the zombies took over the whole world."

"Why didn't he just go to rehab?"

"He did," she said, letting out a big sigh. "We met in rehab, actually. In Malibu."

"I don't remember you going to rehab," I said. "What were you addicted to, if you don't mind me asking?"

"It's fine. I was taking prescription pills. A lot of them. It started out as a way to get through long days on the set, but before I knew it I was taking something every hour just to get by. I had several doctors giving me almost anything I asked for. I'm lucky I didn't end up like Michael Jackson."

"Isn't that the kind of thing the tabloids would have a field day with? Under-age actress checking into Betty Ford?"

"My agent worked hard to keep it out of the news," Felicity said. "She told everyone that I was suffering from exhaustion. We canceled the Disney movie I was supposed to be shooting in Fiji. She threatened to sue anyone who let it out. They wanted me to go on *Celebrity Rehab with Dr. Drew*. My mom wouldn't have it. She said I needed to be away from the cameras, that they were part of my disease. She was right. I checked into the in-patient rehab program and stayed there without television or computer or any contact with the outside world for thirty days."

"That doesn't seem so long," I said.

"It felt like an eternity," she confessed.

"Were all the people there celebrities like you?"

"No. That's what made it so hard. Most of them were just rich kids with drug problems caused by boredom and privilege. There were a few housewives, a CEO who snapped under the pressure and started shooting junk, and a horror author strung out on speedballs."

"Anyone I would know?"

"Probably." She shrugged. "I know it doesn't really matter now but I don't feel comfortable naming him."

"Yeah," I said. "Sorry. Force of habit. Go on."

"Jackson was the only other famous person there," she said. "The others didn't treat us all that well, to be honest. They were pretty nasty. Detoxing off drugs can really bring out the worst in you."

"What would they do?"

"They'd throw stuff in my face when we were holding outside sessions," she explained. "Stuff they'd read in a magazine about my father dating girls my age, or about my little sister's death. They'd talk about my mother and call me names, or quote lines from movies I'd been in. It got really bad. At one point I honestly wanted to kill myself."

"That's awful," I said.

"It really was," she agreed. "Jackson was the only person who treated me well. We'd sit up all night talking, just like this sometimes. He even threatened to hurt a guy who made sexual advances toward me. He was like my guardian angel."

"Let me guess," I said. "His drug of choice is heroin."

She nodded. "He was doing one of those huge concert tours across America. This was before he was famous. Seven big name bands touring together. A different city every night. He was filling in for another guy who had overdosed and almost died. You'd think the band would have learned its lesson. Instead, the bassist introduced Jax to the needle just so he'd have another buddy to party with on the road. By the time he got home he was totally strung out."

"So he checked into rehab?"

"Eventually," she said. "He was court ordered into it after an incident down on Skid Row where he almost died trying to shake down a dealer for more dope. The guy stabbed him and left him in the gutter. Missed his kidney by about a half an inch or he would have been a goner."

"Wow," I said. "I never knew."

"It's not a story he usually tells. He claims he lay there almost bleeding to death for a long time. He doesn't remember much except waking up in an ambulance, handcuffed to a gurney. He swears he saw my face floating above him, but I think he just says that to make me laugh. He's a performer at heart. He's always on, you know?"

"You got clean. So why couldn't he?"

"I had a great support system," she said. "People talk all

this trash about my mom pushing me into Hollywood, but she's been really great. They forget that she was a single mom with no help from my dad, trying to give me and my sister a good life. I begged her to try out for commercials when I was a kid. She didn't push me in any way. If it were up to her, I would have stayed in school like a normal kid."

"The tabloids really make it seem the other way," I agreed.

"After I got out of rehab, no one would hire me," she said. "They said I was an insurance risk, like I was going to eat a bottle of Tylenol in my trailer and overdose. There were some dark times when it looked like my career was over. I mean, one day I was starring in a movie with Johnny Depp and the next I was washed up."

"I thought you said no one knew you went to rehab?"

"The media might not have known," she said with a twisted grin, "but the studios have better people working for them. These aren't TMZ rejects. We're talking former police detectives and private investigators. They knew even before I checked in. When you're spending hundreds of millions of dollars on a movie, you don't want any risks."

"Is that how you ended up on reality television?"

"Pretty much," she admitted. "My agent had several offers from unscripted shows and low budget horror movies. *Star Dancing* was the only one on prime time on a major network. It was supposed to be my comeback vehicle, but we all know how that turned out."

I nodded. It was just when the zombie outbreak was taking off in California. Most people still thought it was only something that affected homeless people and the perpetually poor. *Star Dancing* was being filmed in Hollywood. Seven couples were matched up. Sports heroes from basketball and football were paired with famous writers and celebrity chefs and political pundits and movie starlets. An all-star panel of celebrity judges weighed in every week. These included a famous choreographer who had worked with Janet Jackson, as well as the stereotypical nasty celebrity with the English accent who never liked anyone.

Ewan Crowley had earned his success working with the Royal Ballet. He was both feared and loved by American audiences for his vicious attacks on the shows performers, as well as his cunning word play. It was almost impossible to earn a compliment from him. As the season wore on, his behavior grew increasingly erratic, driving ratings through the roof in the process. One week he brought a linebacker to tears with his razor sharp tirade. The next week, he scolded a national news anchor for her choice in wardrobe. Rumor was the studio executives were constantly receiving complaints about him and threats of lawsuits. He was single-handedly responsible for their ratings spike and he knew it.

So when in the final month of the contest he walked on stage during the middle of Felicity Jane's tango performance with her partner, famous opera singer Mario Antonio Puccetti, everyone thought he was just pulling another of his stunts. That was until he severely bit Mario in the neck on live television. The video went viral overnight. Millions of people saw it, people who would never watch a show like that in the first place. A month later Z-Day was announced and shortly thereafter the internet went down.

"So you stayed in touch with Jackson after you got out?" I said, trying to change the subject. Her eyes had glossed over with the dark memory of her televised catastrophe.

"I did," she said. "Like I told you, he was a big brother to me. He was living in Studio City, working on his own album. That's all he did those days—just record tracks and go to meetings. I was nearby, just over the hill, so we'd go to meetings together. He got signed from those early recordings and went on to make his album."

One of the most celebrated albums of all time, I remembered. In under a year, Ever Rest's first album was bigger than *Appetite for Destruction.* Growing up, there wasn't a kid on my block that didn't know the lyrics to every song. We even memorized the music video and tried to recreate it at home while listening to him.

"The song *Calamity Jane* is actually about me," she said with some embarrassment.

"Wow," I replied. I was kinda at a loss for words. It was hard to imagine being part of something so massive. "So how did he end up back on drugs then? I mean, it sounds like he was doing so well without them."

"He's an addict." She sighed. "Like I said, it's a big part of the rock and roll lifestyle. There are only so many times you can turn down drugs before that little voice in the back of your head tells you that you can get away with partying just a little bit. That's all it takes; just once and you are hooked again."

"That's crazy," I said. I couldn't relate like she could. I didn't really understand what drove people to put poison in their bodies that would kill them. Maybe it was because I had this great family life with my dad and Moto. Maybe Jackson didn't have that kind of constant reassurance. It just seemed nuts to throw away all the good fortune and talent he was given on getting wasted.

"I think he did it because he was lonely," she said wistfully. "Out on the road all the time, no support system, no one to really love you. It takes its toll for sure. When he got back, he called me and confessed everything. He said he had a stash up here and that he was trying to wean himself off."

"Why didn't he just go back to rehab?" I asked. "It worked once. Wouldn't it work again?"

"He thought he could do it on his own," she said. "He was embarrassed. He had a real hard time admitting it to me. A lot of guilt and shame goes along with being an addict. It's hard to understand if you've never had this kind of problem. People just think, well why doesn't he stop using? It's not that simple. His body is so used to the chemicals he's been putting into his system that if he were to just go cold turkey, there's a good chance he would die."

"I didn't know that," I said. "I've always wondered."

"Most people don't realize," she said. "Plus it's painful.

His body wants more and more and he is giving it less. That's why he's so sick. He was supposed to be stepping down, but then Z-Day happened and it's not like he can just go to his dealer. He's been using more than he's supposed to be using, hiding it from me, and now he's almost out."

"I didn't mean to pry," I said, feeling bad now that she had to explain all this to me.

"No," she said. "You didn't pry. I offered. It feels good to be able to talk about this with someone. I am glad you are here."

"Me too."

"You wanna take a walk outside?"

"Is that really safe?"

"It has been," she said. "Usually I just stay on the patio and look out at the ocean. It's really pretty with the light from the moon hitting the water as the waves roll in."

"Let's do it," I said, standing up.

We walked outside and sat on the patio. The moon was almost all the way full. It was huge and white, putting off a soft light illuminating everything below. Looking out over the ocean I saw what looked like a man jogging along the water's edge. There didn't appear to be anyone chasing him.

"What's that?" I said, pointing at him.

"I've seen him down there before," Felicity said. "Just jogging along like nothing ever happened."

"Maybe that's his way of trying to get back a piece of his old life."

"I think you're right."

Without saying a word, she reached over and took me by the hand. We sat in silence, watching the man disappear from sight in the distance. Being with her felt easy, like being totally at home. I could see why Jackson would want her with him while he battled to get sober.

"I'm tired now," she said after a while, standing up and stretching like a cat. "Time to go to sleep."

I got up and we walked back inside, locking the door behind us.

"Thanks for listening."

"No problem." I shrugged.

She leaned over and kissed me on the cheek. "I'll see you in the morning," she said, walking down the hall.

I stood rooted in place for a moment, distracted by her unexpected display of affection. Slowly, I forced myself to head back down to my guest room. I locked the door and sat on the bed, daydreaming about possibilities until sleep finally took me under.

CHAPTER SIXTEEN

I remember having bad dreams all night, but couldn't remember what they were about for the most part. Maybe it was the "Jamaican" chicken trying to fight its way back out. Maybe it was the feeling of dread that had come over me shortly after I locked myself in for the night. I tossed and turned for a while, trying to fight off a string of nasty thoughts with little success. I thought about my brother dying, about the bodies piled up at the school we visited, about Joel and Tom. No matter how hard I tried, I could not seem to calm my mind. Eventually the dark emptiness of sleep pulled me under all the way.

I had a series of overlapping, graphic dreams early in the morning before waking up. They slipped one into the next — like watching several short movies on fast forward as I fought to wake up. The last thing I remembered before getting up was running on the beach with Felicity. We were serenely holding hands while zombies in the distance surfed on huge metal pieces of a jumbo jet they'd pulled apart and taken right out of the sky, mid-flight. That part was kinda like a cool music video.

Benji was in the dream too, dressed just like a tiny version of Jackson. I was worried about him so I chased him up the beach and back into the house. He locked himself in the guest bathroom, trying to hide. I knocked down the door in time to catch him shooting heroin in his arm.

"Don't worry about it," he told me. "It's just a little death to even me out."

I looked down to where he had put the needle in and saw that the skin around the mark was dying and turning gray. Soon it began to spread up his arm and across his body until he had the same complexion as the walking dead. His eyes turned solid black and he let out a roar as he transformed all the way into a zombie. The last image I remembered was him lunging at me while I stood rooted to the ground in total shock.

I woke with a start, sweating in spite of the room being cool. The sun was up, and it had to be late. I couldn't believe I'd actually slept in after tossing and turning all night long.

Almost immediately my dreams faded away, leaving me grasping to remember what they were. I shook my head to wake up and went out toward the living room. Benji was sitting on the sofa looking completely catatonic. It reminded me of Tom after Joel got shot.

Man, I thought. *That seems like years ago instead of just days. Time is moving way too fast.*

"What's up?" I asked.

He didn't answer me.

I heard the toilet flush and Felicity came out of the bathroom. Her eyes were red raw from crying and she still had streaks of makeup on her face. She threw herself into my arms and hugged me, sobbing so hard that her whole body shook.

"What is going on?" I asked. "Who died?"

Benji turned and glared at me. Felicity pulled away. She looked really hurt for a second, then it faded.

"Jackson killed himself last night," she said at last.

Cold shock ran through me at the news. How could I have said something so stupid and insensitive? I was always saying or doing the wrong thing around her! *I am such an idiot*, I thought.

"What?" I finally asked. "I'm so sorry. Oh my God. How, I mean, why did he do it?"

She waved a piece of paper in her right hand at me. I realized it was a suicide note.

This wasn't how things were supposed to go today, I thought. *I was just hoping to get up, grub down on a portable meal of hot space age blueberry pancakes, and hit the road. This definitely complicates things.* It might have sounded cold but the last thing I was looking for at that point was another complication. After what happened in New Lompoc, all I wanted to do was just get to Moto's base and settle in. The sooner I could put this madness behind me and forget about it, the better.

"He left a note," she said.

"What does it say?" I asked, feeling lame.

"It says that he knew he wasn't going to make it anyway and that he just wanted to go out with one last high on his own terms," she said. "It says that he's a coward for not trying harder and not saying goodbye but that he's thrilled he got to spend one last night with his real fans doing what he loved, playing music. It's beautiful and totally screwed up and I hate him so much right now for doing this, but I miss him too much to be angry."

She burst into tears again and this time I held her close to me. I glanced over at Benji, who seemed to be just as affected by this tragedy as Felicity was. He looked up at me with the sadness of a lost child.

"It's going to be okay," I said to both of them. "I know this is hard but the worst is over. You'll see."

"Are you still planning on leaving today?" Her words were muffled as she spoke into my shoulder.

"I was, before I heard about Jackson. I just woke up so it all feels like part of my dream right now."

"I want to go with you."

"Of course," I agreed. "That's a great idea."

"What are you going to do with Jax?" Benji looked up at us with his big puppy dog eyes swollen from tears he was fighting back. I had been wondering the same thing. Was he propped up in bed? Did he smell already? Was she sure he was even dead?

"I found him in bed," she said as if she was reading my thoughts. "He was naked. His body was blue. He felt ice cold. His eyes were open. There was no sign of life in him at all. It just didn't seem real, you know?"

"How long ago was this?"

"About an hour. I was going to put him in the bathtub. I don't know why. I'm not thinking clearly right now. I just feel so crazy inside."

"We could bury him in the yard," I offered sympathetically.

"I thought about that," she said, "but now I think we should just leave him where he is. After all, this is his house. He was happy here. He died happy, with friends and fans who loved him."

"I understand," I said softly. I wasn't trying to be more insensitive than I already had been, but I was glad we weren't going to spend a lot of time digging up a grave for him. I wanted to get moving as soon as we could. Plus it seemed crazy to bury him given the condition the world was currently in. There were dead bodies in various states of decay pretty much everywhere you went, some just lying there stinking and others walking around and trying to kill you. Leaving a guy dead in his own bed like he was peacefully sleeping didn't seem so heartless when you thought about it in those terms.

"Besides," she said, walking to the patio door and sliding it open. "I'm not sure how much time we have left here."

"What do you mean?" I asked.

"See for yourself."

I walked over to join her and what I saw blew my mind. There on the beach was a huge tanker ship with some kind of foreign writing on the side that looked Russian. Up on top of the ship I could make out twenty or thirty former humans in various states of decay ambling around. One of them fell over the side while I was watching and splashed into the ocean. Looking down, I could see a handful of zombies making their way out of the water and roaming listlessly on the sand in search of food. If the jogger went for his morning run today, he was going to be in for a big surprise!

"When did that thing get here?" I asked in near panic. I had been intending on doing some Tai Chi in the backyard and stretching before we left in the impossible hope of bringing my life back to some sense of normalcy and routine. *That's out for sure now*, I thought.

"I don't know," she said, a little too casually for what the situation called for. "It was just there when I got up this morning. I didn't see any zombies until an hour ago, and those were still on the top deck. Must be only a matter of time until they find their way up into the neighborhood."

Why is she being so casual? It's not like those are fire ants coming to spoil a picnic, I thought. *These are undead demons from the depths of hell, devoid of all mercy, coming to rip us to shreds in a horrible, violent death!*

"We need to get out of here," I said. "We left the Escalade at the entrance to the community near the gates. It has some gas left. We'll figure the rest out as we go."

"That's not necessary," she replied. "Jackson has a fully fueled Lexus SUV hybrid in the garage. It gets like a million miles to the gallon. He loaded it with water and two extra cans of gas after we came out of the panic room. There is even a first aid kit under the passenger seat."

"Wow," I said. "I'm surprised he planned an escape route. The way he acted last night was like he never planned on leaving this place, no matter what."

"It wasn't for him," she explained. "It was for me. He said he wanted to make sure when the time came I could just grab food and leave. He really was the most thoughtful man I knew."

"Benji," I said. He turned and stared up at me again, ungluing his eyes from the floor. "Why don't you grab some plastic bags and help Felicity pack up all these portable meals? We don't want to leave anything behind that might be helpful on our trip. Got it?"

"Yeah," he said, wiping tears off his face and standing up.

"What are you going to do?" Felicity asked.

"I'm going to grab my sword and check out the Lexus. Make sure it's fired up and ready to roll with no surprises. I want to be out on the road in the next ten minutes. Who knows how long we have?"

"Okay," she said, sounding aloof as she turned and sauntered into the kitchen. I shook off her attitude, chalking it up to grief over Jackson's suicide.

I jogged back to the guest room and fetched my sword, then made a pit stop at the bathroom before heading off to the garage. I splashed some cold water on my face to wake myself up. There was a bottle of pills on the counter with the lid off. I picked it up and read the label. Soma. I wasn't sure what they did but I was certain they were responsible for Felicity's condition.

Cut her some slack man, I thought. *It's been a very traumatic morning for her by any standards.*

I decided not to bring up her apparent relapse, but that didn't mean I wanted her doped out. We might literally be running for our lives at any moment, fighting these undead monsters. The last thing I needed was a spoiled celebrity with a pill habit slowing us down because she was high and thought they looked pretty. I stuffed the rest of the bottle in my pocket and headed out to the garage.

The Lexus was fully gassed and stocked as promised, and the keys were in the ignition. I fired it up and the engine purred to life. This was a true luxury vehicle, and my heart practically sang with joy. With this car and the supplies we were bringing, there was no reason we couldn't get to Hueneme and safety at last. I didn't mean to get my hopes up. If the last few days had proved anything it was that things could turn out horribly different than you expected, with little or no warning at all. Still it didn't hurt to be optimistic, did it?

"Wow," Benji said, setting down a shiny black trash bag

full of ready-to-eat gourmet meals. "It even has television screens in the back of the headrests. I wonder what's in the DVD player?"

"Jackson's last tour footage," Felicity said as she popped open the back and set another shiny black bag inside. "The car was a gift from his record label. They thought he'd like seeing himself. They really didn't know much about him."

"So he never drove it?"

"Oh he did," she said, "but mostly to the store and back to get supplies. He used the CD player, but he didn't have long road trips to take with small children. That's what the players in the back of the seats are really for. Can you imagine Jackson taking friends on long distance trips and making them watch him play a concert in Prague? He was way too humble to do something so egotistical."

Yeah, I thought, *but he's still the same guy who played his video version in Guitar Hero and, when he lost, threw an impromptu concert in his living room to prove his expertise. Not really what I'd call humble.*

I knew I shouldn't be so hard on Jax. I had only met him once, but it didn't take much to see the guy was plagued by the types of demons that traditionally torment all creative types. His inability to conquer them cost him his life at a young age. If we didn't get moving, we'd be tortured soon by worse.

"Hop in," I said, sliding into the driver's side and positioning my katana between my right leg and the center console for easy access.

Benji didn't hesitate to climb into the back. The idea of watching a free rock concert in a comfy leather luxury vehicle while drinking a Coke didn't strike him as all that bad. However Felicity seemed to be taking a bit longer to get her act together.

It's probably the drugs, I thought, tapping my pocket. *Here we go.*

"I was going to grab something," she said.

"We really need to get moving," I told her.

She hesitated for a minute then gave up. "Shouldn't you open the garage door? We don't want to get carbon monoxide poisoning in here."

Benji's head shot up at the suggestion.

"It's far too ventilated in here for that," I said, thinking back on the pile of dead people in the gym from the day before. "Besides we're only going to be in here a minute. The last thing I want to do is risk opening the door and having an unexpected guest come barging in."

"The gate didn't stop you," she teased.

"Get in," I repeated. "And put on your seat belt."

Felicity finally complied. Once she was in and buckled up, I locked the car doors and hit the garage door opener.

The barrier rolled up, blasting us full on in the face with bright sunlight. Luckily there were no signs of zombies, probably owing to the high walls and iron gate. I pulled out of the garage and rolled down the driveway.

"How do I open the gate?" I asked Felicity.

"Just pull up and it will open automatically."

"Even without electricity?"

"It's wired to the backup generator," she informed us, "in case of earthquakes."

I pulled up and the gate slowly swung open. We drove out onto the asphalt and a loud thump hit the right side of the car. Benji screamed at the top of his lungs. I turned to see a wet, rotting corpse in a sailor's uniform pounding his fists on the side of the Lexus.

"What are you waiting for?" Felicity yelled, finally shaken from her pill-induced state of relaxation. "Drive!"

I pulled down the street to the main gates. They were already open. The Escalade was where we had left it, but the doors were torn off now and one of the tires was missing. Whoever hit it had left it up on the spare tire jack.

"Glad we didn't try to make a run for the Escalade," I said.

"Me too," Benji chimed in.

I looked over and noticed Felicity was violently shaking.

Poor thing, I thought. *She probably hasn't seen a lot of zombies, being locked away in that prison palace with Jackson this whole time. She doesn't know how common it is to see these creatures, or what worse horrors await. She's in for a huge surprise!*

We pulled down the Mesa and back toward the highway. Along the way, Felicity gasped as we passed carcasses of people and animals left out for the flies and scavengers. The air was hot outside but we had a nearly unlimited supply of AC thanks to the Lexus, so she didn't have to smell the scent of rotting death that had settled over most of the world. Surprisingly, we only saw a few zombies on our way to the freeway onramp and they were all a long distance off.

I drove around a stalled car abandoned in the middle of the freeway and took off south toward Ventura. We were driving past Santa Claus lane in Carpenteria when she spoke again.

"I want to go to Ojai," she said.

"It's a little out of the way," I responded. "For now we need to stick to the plan and just drive straight through to the military base."

"I want to go to Ojai."

"It's beautiful out there," I said, trying not to sound condescending, "but now's not the time."

"You don't understand," she argued. "My mom lives there. I haven't seen her since the zombie outbreak."

"Maybe you can talk some of the soldiers into taking you on a trip out there," I said.

"They are going to lock us up like prisoners. I don't want to stay there. Who knows how long we have left? We could die at any moment out here. If I am going to die I'd rather be at home with my mom."

"It's not a great idea."

"Isn't it? Listening to you talk about your brother all the time made me miss my family. Why should you be the only one who gets to do what he wants? Why are your plans more important than mine?"

I rolled my eyes. She was just trying to guilt trip me into doing what she wanted, and I knew it. Sure she missed her mom, but it just wasn't safe to go wandering off into the countryside.

"What the hell is that?" I asked.

"Don't change the subject," she said. "Don't be passive aggressive."

"No. There is something going on up ahead."

We'd reached the point in the road where the freeway veered off along a narrow strip between the ocean, a set of railroad tracks, and high cliffs. It was the final stretch between Santa Barbara and Ventura. Usually cars flew up the five lane road on both sides as fast as they could. Instead, we saw a line of cars stretching the wrong way across the road three deep, effectively creating another road block. Surly looking guys with beards on motorcycles rode up and down the freeway on either side.

"Unity Gang," I mumbled.

"What?" Felicity asked. "Who the hell is the Unity Gang?"

"It's a coalition of bikers and gang bangers from all over the state working together to rob, rape, murder, and extort survivors. This is bad."

"What are we going to do?" Benji asked, looking terrified again.

"I don't know."

"Turn around," Felicity shouted.

"I can't."

"Then stop the car and just back up," she yelled.

"You don't understand,. They can easily run us down with those bikes. I don't think it's a good idea to agitate them."

"So we're just going to surrender to them and let them have their way with us?"

I realized that Felicity had a lot more to lose than we did because she was a girl. While we might escape with just being target practice, there was no way they would let her go. She looked like she was on the verge of a nervous breakdown. Obviously the pills had worn off.

"We're going to play it cool," I said, trying to be calm. "When the time comes we will fight, but not until I give you the signal. We'll bust through those cars, even if we have to push them all out of the way and haul ass to Ventura. We're not leaving anyone behind. I promise."

I put my hand on her arm and looked her in the eyes.

"Do you trust me?" I asked.

Her lip trembled but she nodded.

"What's the signal?" Benji asked.

"Me pulling out my sword. Don't make a move until I do. If I have to get out of this car, I'm leaving a trail of bodies for zom food in my path."

Two motorcycles loudly roared next to us as they pulled up alongside the Lexus to escort us into position. I pulled toward the front of the blockade and let the car idle as I put it in park. The good news was that the hybrid was so quiet it might have sounded like I turned off the ignition, especially with all the ruckus from the bikes.

A greasy looking biker in a leather vest with long black hair walked over to us and tapped on my window. I rolled it down. His name was sewn on his cut. RABBIT. *That's an odd name for a tough biker,* I thought.

"Where are you coming from?" he asked.

I could feel Benji's eyes burning a hole through the back of my head from his seat. We couldn't tell him that we were in New Lompoc. For all we knew, John might be looking for us. I wouldn't put it past him to put a bounty on our heads for what happened to Tank.

"Are you retarded?" he asked when I didn't answer.

"Sorry. We are coming from Santa Barbara, up on the Mesa."

"How long you been there?"

Why did he want to know? And how was any of this his business? I could feel Felicity starting to squirm in her seat.

"Since the outbreak started," I said.

"So why did you leave?"

Who does this guy think he is? Mister twenty questions?

"A tanker washed up full of zombies," I said. "They came ashore and started taking over the neighborhood. I thought we might be safer in Malibu."

"You're not gonna have much luck down there," Rabbit said, sounding more like an overly helpful gas station attendant than a thug. "Whole place is overrun with the walking dead."

"We still gotta try."

"Suit yourself," he snapped.

The words left me feeling kind of relieved. It sounded like they planned on letting us pass. Then I noticed that Rabbit hadn't taken his hand off the car. He leaned in and looked around past me.

"Whatcha carrying," he asked, looking back over to Felicity and winking, "aside from this pretty girl?"

Felicity pulled her skirt down and put her legs together. *Man*, I thought, *it must be scary as hell sometimes to be a girl.*

"Just some food rations and water," I lied. If they found out about the gas they'd want it for sure. For a biker, fuel was maybe even more important than air. It was how they maintained control over the area. Without it they were just a scary tribe of guys on foot.

"We're going to need to take a look," he said.

"We're kind of in a hurry," I explained. "And we don't have much to spare."

Rabbit chuckled.

"You don't get it do you, sport?" He spat on the ground. "I'm not asking."

"We're not looking for any trouble," I said, holding my hands up. For a moment I considered flooring it and trying to fight our way out right then and there while we still had the element of surprise on our side.

"Well I guess this is our lucky day then, isn't it?" He scoffed at us. I could feel Felicity trying to make herself smaller in her seat.

"Now this is what's going to happen," Rabbit said. "You're going to step out of the vehicle and we are going to search it for things we might find useful to our cause."

"So basically you're just going to steal all our stuff."

"We've claimed this road," he said, undisturbed by my outburst. "The toll for driving on it is generally half of whatever you are carrying, depending on how valuable we determine your cargo to be. We're not monsters like them Unity Gang. We're Sons of the New Dawn. We use what we take to fight them off, keep them from taking over all of Southern California. You might not think it's noble, but then again who cares what the hell you think?"

I began to fidget with the blade. I saw Felicity cast me a wary glance. The last thing she wanted was a fight, but I was fairly certain that, noble or not, it was going to come down to that. There was no way I was letting a gang of deluded bikers steal all our stuff and kidnap Felicity.

"Now get out of the car," he said coldly, adding with a smile, "pretty damn please."

"No," I said casually, wrapping my hand around the base of my blade. I figured I could yank the door open and knock him over, then hop out and begin carving up anyone who got in my way. It wasn't the best plan I had ever come up with, but I was starting to get really angry. I'd been through too much to let them take my chance of getting back to my brother away from me. I was sick and tired of other people derailing my plans with their nonsense.

"Excuse me?" he said, looking genuinely shocked. "I don't think I heard you correctly, little man."

"You heard me," I said in a low growl.

He shook his head in disbelief and laughed.

"All right then, you little idiot," he said, reaching in and grabbing me by the shirt. "We're going to have to do this the hard way."

I smiled at him. My right hand was crossed over my lap with my fingers on the door handle. My left hand was now wrapped around my blade.

"What are you smiling about?"

I didn't answer. *I'm smiling,* I thought, *because in just a few moments the same fingers that are pulling on my shirt are going to be laying on the hot asphalt permanently detached from your body, you punk biker scum.*

Just as I was getting ready to make my big move, a booming voice came from behind Rabbit.

"Rabbit! What's taking so long?"

His expression changed and he let go of my shirt, backing out of the window. He turned and I could see his buddy, a much larger version of himself with the name SCAR stitched on his jacket.

"Nothing," Rabbit said. "They are just getting out of the car now."

Scar walked over to the window and looked in. His expression changed dramatically when he saw Felicity.

"Holy Jesus," he said, sounding almost like a convert. "Do you know who that is? That's Felicity Jane!"

Rabbit looked confused. Felicity came back to life. The guy was obviously a fan.

"Who the hell is Felicity Jane?" Rabbit asked.

"Only one of the hottest and most talented actresses of her generation," Scar said.

Felicity blushed and pulled down the visor on her side to check her makeup. I rolled my eyes.

This isn't happening, I thought. *A second ago we were ready to battle for our lives with hardened biker scum and now we're being accosted by a die-hard fan. Unbelievable!*

Scar leaned in the window to get closer.

"You probably don't remember me," he said, the heat of his breath practically in my face. "I met you at Comic Con last year. I stood in line for over an hour to get a picture with you."

"You were at Comic Con?" I asked, laughing dismissively. "What for?"

Scar turned and gave me a nasty glare.

"You see what I've been dealing with?" Rabbit protested.

"I was in *Starfire Galaxy*," she said. "I played the child queen of the warrior Amazonians."

"Ursa," Benji said from the backseat. "They made that poster from the movie stills of her in the fur bikini. It sold like a million copies."

I suddenly remembered the poster on the ceiling in New Lompoc.

"What are you doing here?" Scar asked.

"My friends and I are heading to see my mom in Ojai," she said. "I haven't seen her since the outbreak and I am worried about her. We were taking her and my stepfather food and water. He's diabetic so I am really concerned, you know?"

"Right," Rabbit scoffed. "A minute ago they said they were going to Malibu."

"I'm sorry," Scar said in a soft voice. "We gotta take half your supplies. It's our policy."

"You can't make an exception for me?" She leaned over and gave him those sad eyes.

"I wish I could, but the rest of the guys wouldn't understand," he said. "I promise you we won't take the car though. We will need some of the gas, but that's it. You really have no idea how huge a fan I am."

"If you're really a fan then you won't rob me," she pouted, turning on all her charm. "I need this stuff for my mom. Please?"

"I can't do it," he said, sounding really torn.

"I do remember you. You were so sweet after waiting all that time. You brought me a teddy bear and I gave you a signed DVD for being so nice."

"That's right," he said, sounding shocked and pleased. "Do you still have the teddy?"

"I named him Rasputin. He's at my mom's house."

"That's amazing," he said. "Rasputin . . . I like that."

"I have an idea," I said. Scar and Rabbit glared at me for interrupting but I pressed on. "We have a spare can of gas in the back next to the water. That's got to be pretty valuable right? Why don't you take that and let us get on our way?"

Scar stopped to think it over, running his dirty fingers through his salt and pepper beard in the process.

"Yeah," he said. "That might work. Go ahead and pop the hatch."

I did, and he walked back and took both gas cans instead of the single one I offered. I was glad that we were driving a hybrid. There was no telling when or how we'd be getting gas again. The last thing I needed was to run out ten miles from the base and have to fight my way across an urban jungle filled with zombies and bad guys.

"You know you're lucky," Rabbit said with a nasty grin. "Usually when someone mouths off we just take the whole car and make them walk to Ventura on foot."

I didn't say anything for fear of upsetting him further.

"You're very kind," Felicity said. "I hope our contribution helps your cause."

"I remember you now." He laughed. "You're that broad from *Star Dancers* whose partner got chomped on live air. Yeah. I saw that on the internet. Funny as hell."

Felicity blanched and went silent. She sat back down and pulled on a pair of sunglasses, looking ill.

Scar slapped the side of the Lexus with his big, meaty hand.

"You are clear to go," he said. "Good luck Miss Felicity Jane. Say hello to your mother for me."

CHAPTER SEVENTEEN

The bikers moved the cars blocking our path and waved us through. We drove along the deserted highway in silence for a while.

"That was close," I said.

"Yeah," Benji said. "I thought for sure you were going to freak out and get us all killed."

"Thanks for the vote of confidence, bro," I said, flabbergasted.

"Just saying." He shrugged.

"You're awfully quiet," I turned to Felicity. "It's okay now. We made it out, thanks to you."

"Yeah thanks," Benji said. "I guess being a celebrity still has its advantages."

"You okay?" I asked. "You look like you're going to be sick. Do you need me to pull over? It's okay if you do. It happens to the best of us."

"I was just thinking about what Ewan did to Mario," she said.

"Oh, that must have been rough." I wasn't really in the mood to get all negative again. We just escaped some serious trouble. We should have been celebrating, not grieving. I thought about Jackson. It had already been a long day and it wasn't even noon!

"The show was sponsored by Snax Max," Felicity said. "They are a corporate food conglomerate that owns a bunch of fast food restaurants. Ewan was eating a Beefy Max Burrito supreme when he snapped."

"That's not what made him sick though."

"How do you know?" She turned to look at me. "No one knows what's causing people to kill and eat each other. How do we know it wasn't contracted through bad food?"

"Man I hope not," I said. "I'd do just about anything right now for a Wetzel's Pretzel."

"Have you ever tried the pepperoni twist?" Benji sat up from the backseat. "They are amazing!"

"Almost worth risking a run through a mall for."

"Not me," Felicity said. "I can't get the image of Ewan biting him out of my head. One minute he was chowing down on that stuff and sipping a gallon of soda. The next he was on stage biting Mario's jugular."

"That's understandable," I said. "I'd probably feel the same way if that had happened to me."

"Turn off up here," she said as we passed the sign announcing Ojai.

"We're not going to Ojai," I said, firmly shaking my head from side to side. "We talked about this. Especially now that we've given away most of our gas. We barely have enough to get to Hueneme."

"If it wasn't for me, we'd be walking right now," she said. "Plus it was your genius idea to hand out our fuel."

"That was the only way to get them to let us go," I loudly protested.

"He was this close to just letting us go. I had it all under control until you butted in to the conversation."

"Don't act like I didn't help."

"I saw your hand on the door," she said. "You were getting ready to pick a fight. We're lucky we're not all dead. If that guy wouldn't have come along and recognized me . . ."

"You mean Scar?" I interrupted.

"If Scar wouldn't have interrupted, we might all be dead on the side of the road now."

"Don't worry," I said. "I am sure they would have kept you for a pet, like you kept Rasputin."

"Let's put it to a vote," Felicity said, ignoring my not so playful jab. "Everyone who thinks we should let me go see my mom and be with my family, especially after I just saved our lives from bloodthirsty bikers, raise your hand."

She raised her own hand. The cocky smile on her face meant only one thing—that Benji had sided with her.

"Come on Benji," I said, adjusting the rearview mirror to see his hand fully extended. "We don't have enough gas for that."

"Fair is fair. She has a point."

Sell out, I thought. *Who's side are you on anyway?*

"Two to one," she said. "Looks like we're heading to Ojai."

"I thought the saying was you can never go home again once you're famous." I turned onto the connecter and took us up and over a bridge toward Ojai. She cheered and Benji joined in.

Little Judas, I thought. *You'd do anything to get her attention.*

Was that a pang of jealousy I was feeling? I couldn't lie. I did like Felicity, but I was trying to figure out if that was because of who she was as a person or if it was because she was famous.

Give it time, a dark little voice in the back of my mind said. *Just give it time.*

"Don't worry," she said. "I know my way around town like the back of my hand. I could guide you there blindfolded. Plus I know an out-of-the-way gas station you can hit up when it's time to go."

We drove the short distance east into town and she guided us along a series of roads toward her mom's place. Since she told me it was up on a hill, I wasn't all that worried. For some reason zombies tended to move with the path of least resistance when left alone. Of course that was before they began to form hordes and knock down walls, so I couldn't be sure I wasn't just giving myself a false sense of security for nothing.

The road up to her mom's place looked like something out of Christopher Robin's wildest fantasies. There was a crooked old tree and a wooden mailbox with her new husband's name on it, SWANSON. I half expected there to be a red balloon tied to it and one of the S's to be painted backwards.

"This is it," she burst out, unable to contain her excitement.

"Did you really grow up here?" Benji asked.

"Yep. My dad lived in Las Vegas, so my sister and I would have to see him twice a month for the first few years after the divorce. Mom gave up everything and moved us out here. When she remarried her new husband moved us in with him out here. It's paradise. I wish I had never left. After I started getting gigs in Hollywood, she got an apartment out there too, on Gower. That place was literally a roach motel." She laughed.

Benji climbed up to hear her story. He was totally spellbound.

"She didn't come to live with you?" I found it hard to believe. The media had always painted her mom to be the cause of all her problems--a money hungry failed actress who pushed one daughter into acting and the other into an early grave. Her little sister moved to Vegas at fourteen to live with her dad and ended up an underage stripper at a biker bar outside Glendale. She went missing for over a month then phoned in from Sturgis to say she was still alive. Two weeks later she was found stabbed to death in a motel in midtown Manhattan. No one knew how she got there. There were needle marks up and down her arms. Felicity was just starting to become a household name. Her sister's death pushed her over the edge. It was all the media would talk about for nearly a year. The crime was never solved.

"After Cassie died, she thought about it," Felicity said. "The media began hounding her, following her around the grocery store. It took a real toll on her marriage. I told her that she and Phil could come live with me. I was leaving to shoot in Mexico and they could stay there while I was gone. I was so excited when she said she would, but then she backed out at the last minute."

"Was that when you shot *Double Trouble*?" Benji asked.

"It was," Felicity said, tearing up.

"What's wrong?" I asked.

"I didn't realize how much I missed her," Felicity said, laughing and fanning her tears away with her hand. "I can't wait to see her."

"Here we go." I drove up the hill. There was a Ford F150 with huge monster truck tires in the driveway and a Subaru next to it in front of a ranch style house. We parked and got out. I grabbed my blade and held it out in front of me, twisting from side to side and leaning over to stretch. I glanced around, searching the trees for signs of people, living or dead. It was eerily quiet but we appeared to be alone.

Thank God for small miracles, I thought.

Benji and Felicity started to walk into the house but I called out to stop them.

"Let me go first," I said. "Just in case."

Felicity looked annoyed but she didn't protest. I walked in and she pointed to the right, toward the master bedroom. Moving along the hallway I could see pictures of her and her sister from when they were kids.

Stay focused, I thought. *There will be time to get the full tour later.*

I hadn't wanted to come to Ojai in the first place. I was damn sure I didn't want to get turned into the living dead for my troubles.

The bedroom door was ajar, so I pulled it back slowly. A dry wind coming in through the open window blew part of the curtains back, making me freeze in place. Then I saw them. On the bed, dressed in their wedding clothes, were an older man and woman. They were perfectly still with their eyes open and just the hint of a smile on their faces. The woman was holding a note in her hand.

No, I thought. *Not another note. Not more tragedy. Not today.*

But it wasn't in my control. Already Felicity was making her way into the room. Deep down inside I wished I could protect her from what she was about to see, but I knew I couldn't. First Jackson and now this. It almost made me want to give her back the pills I'd confiscated at the beach house.

"What's going on?" Her voice faltered. Even as she spoke she knew the answer.

I stepped aside and bowed my head.

"No," she cried. "No!"

"What is it?" Benji asked.

Felicity turned to me.

"Don't let him see this," she said in a hushed tone. "Go out in the living room and wait for me. Please?"

"Of course." I walked to the door and turned Benji around, leading him away.

"Are they dead?" He looked up at me, waiting for an answer he already knew.

"Yeah."

"What are we doing?"

"Giving Felicity some space. It's a lot to take under normal circumstances, much less on the same day as Jax."

"I understand," he said with a note of detached sadness in his voice.

I realized that I was the only one who still had family in our group now. While I had seen more than my fair share of death, I had never seen one of my relatives killed by a zombie or laid out dead. We sat there in silence listening to the wind blow through chimes on the porch and eventually Felicity came out holding the note.

Benji ran over to her and threw his arms around her. She started crying again but she didn't seem as upset as I expected her to be. Perhaps she was just too exhausted to take it all in. She looked at me and held up the note.

"Two weeks ago," she said. "They took sleeping pills and died peacefully holding hands."

"I'm so sorry," I said, rubbing the back of my neck and avoiding eye contact.

"You know the crazy thing is that I had to find them today after I found Jackson this morning. What kind of messed up karma is that?"

"It's totally unfair," I agreed with her, kicking the end of the sofa absentmindedly with my sneaker.

"And how did they know I would come back here?" She wiped fresh tears from her eyes. "The letter is addressed to me. All it says is how much they loved me and how proud of me they are and not to give up hope no matter what. Why should I keep fighting when everyone I love is dead?"

"I don't know," I said. "Maybe they left if for you because you were all they had left?"

"Yeah, and now I'm on my own."

"You've got me," Benji said, wrapping his arms back around her waist. He began to cry. "My family died too. I had to watch them die, even my little sister. It was the worst thing I've ever seen. Every night when I go to bed I can still see her face looking at me, begging for help, right before they began biting her all over."

"I'm so sorry," Felicity said, stroking his hair and looking at me.

I held my hands up as if to say I didn't know where this was coming from. The truth was Benji had never shared that much with me. Sure he told me about what happened with his family, but he was reserved and quiet. Most of the time he just kept to himself. It wasn't until that moment that I realized how bad he'd been hurting inside.

"My first few weeks on the base were the hardest," he said. "But then Xander began to look out for me. He had my back when the other kids teased me or stole from me or tried to beat me up. He's taken care of me, made sure I don't get eaten or left behind or kidnapped by neo Nazi's."

"Neo Nazi's?" Felicity threw me a puzzled look.

"It's a long story."

"We're family now," Benji said, letting go of her and wiping his face. "We're all we got left now. I know that won't bring back your parents, but it's better than nothing."

Felicity leaned over and kissed him softly on the forehead. The look on his face said it all. I thought for a minute he was going to pass out right there.

"Thank you," she said, "little brother."

"What do you want to do?" I asked. "I'd be more than happy to help you bury them in the soft grass of the front yard if you like."

"I think that would be nice. They deserve a proper burial."

Benji and I fetched some shovels from a tool shed out near the garage and set to work while Felicity began to poke around the house for things to take with us. To cool us down, she made fresh lemonade from ripe lemons she picked on a tree in the yard and some sugar she found in the kitchen. There was no ice, so we drank it warm but it still tasted amazing.

Luckily the ground was moist and it took us less than an hour to dig one big hole for her parents to share. Benji was too squeamish to help move the bodies so he went with Felicity to pick wild flowers to line the bottom of the grave. When they had filled all the empty spaces up with colorful poppy flowers, honeysuckle, and larkspur, I set about the task of moving the bodies.

Her mom was light and stiff as a board, which made her easy to move, but her stepfather was already beginning to decay. I had to hold my breath to avoid the putrid smell of decomposition coming off of him. Twice I lost my hold and nearly dropped him, but recovered in time. I set them both on the grass then slowly and carefully pulled them into the grave with me to make sure I didn't farther disturb their corpses. When they were laid out side by side as they had been in their bedroom, I joined their hands together and closed their eyes.

Benji made the sign of the cross over himself as I climbed out.

"Thank you," Felicity said. "Before you bury them I'd like to say a few words."

She proceeded to pay tribute to her mother in loving detail, thanking her for all she had done for her and her sister. Then she lavished praise on her stepfather for his love and support, for taking care of her when she was young, and for caring for her mother and being a faithful companion to the end. When she was done we were all crying.

"You can bury them now," she said.

Benji and I took up shovels and gently filled the hole back up with dirt. When we were done, she fixed a white crucifix to the top of the grave with their names written on it that she'd made while we were digging.

"Do you want to stay here tonight?" I asked. I wasn't sure that it was safe for us. In fact I was fairly certain it wasn't, but I would stand watch all night if I had to in order for her to have one last night with her mom in her childhood home.

"No," she said, wiping away fresh tears.

"Are you sure?" I was doing my best to be supportive. "We can take turns making sure it's safe."

"I've already grabbed a few things that remind me of her. I think it would be worse for me to stay. It's hard just being here now. I can't imagine waking up and not having her here."

"We'll go then," I said, and she shook her head and cried again.

"I'm coming to the base with you," she confided.

"Yes."

"We're sticking together. Like a family."

"You know it," I answered back. "We're gonna need gas though to make it back."

"No problem. I know just the place to get it."

CHAPTER EIGHTEEN

Felicity grabbed the bag of stuff she'd gathered from the house and got back in the Lexus. She turned and handed a small teddy bear to Benji.

"His name is Rasputin," she said. "Scar gave him to me at Comic Con."

"You weren't just making that up?" I stared at her in disbelief.

"I would never lie about that." She gave me a shocked look. "Take the way we came up and go back down the hill, then turn left instead of heading right back to the highway. The Hasslebeck's Chevron station should be down about a quarter of a mile."

We rolled down the hill and headed toward the gas station. I'd like to be able to tell you that I was surprised when we came around the corner in a wooded canyon and rolled smack dab into the middle of an armed road block, but I was starting to get used to it—as much as anyone can get used to having automatic weapons pointed at them. These weren't bikers. They looked like normal people, townsfolk, except they were armed to the teeth and not interested in hiding it. They quickly surrounded all sides of the SUV and began looking in to see who we had inside. A dopey looking guy with ruffled sandy blonde hair and sad puppy dog blue eyes tapped my window with the muzzle of his Uzi. He didn't look much older than me.

"Roll down the window," he ordered. I looked at Felicity and she nodded to me. No point in getting us lit up and killed over a simple request. I complied.

"Yeah," I said. "What's up, man?"

"What are you doing here?" He didn't sound like much of a leader. He sounded, for lack of a better term, slow in the head.

"We were just looking for some petrol. Heard there was a gas station down this way."

"We've got some gas."

"Great." I felt like he was holding something back. "Can we buy some?"

"We'll give you some for free," he said. I checked the mirrors to see that the others were closing in on all sides of our car. They still had their guns up as if they were ready for a fight.

"That would be very cool of you." When he didn't respond I added, "Is there something I'm missing?"

"No," he said, looking nervous. "We're just not used to having strangers wander into our midst, especially so close to Harvest."

"What's harvest?"

"A time of giving thanks and praise to our Lord and savior," he said without batting an eye.

Perfect, I thought. *They are a bunch of brain washed religious fanatics. That's why they're acting so strange.*

"We just want to get some gas and be on our way, if you don't mind. We've still got a long drive ahead of us."

His eyes grew wide as Felicity leaned forward and he caught sight of her.

"Felicity?"

Here we go again, I thought. *Another crazed fan boy.* I knew it had definitely saved our hides the last time around, but it was still annoying. Why did it bother me so much? I couldn't put my finger on it. Here I was working so hard to keep us all safe and get us where we needed to be. I had to fight Tank off and lie our way out of trouble and all she had to do was use her fame. It just didn't seem fair.

"Okay yeah I know," I said. "It's very exciting to meet a celebrity in real life but she's just a person like you or me. Trust me. Spend an hour with her and you'll see she's no different than anyone else."

"Darren?" She leaned over me, growing excited. "What are you still doing here?"

"Are you serious?" I asked in an exasperated tone. "Is there anyone you don't know? Come on!"

"What am I doing here?" He ignored my outburst. It was like I didn't even exist. "I live here, remember? What are you doing here?"

The Uzi was on a strap that hung from his neck. He had reached both his hands in across my chest and was now holding hands with Felicity, staring deeply into her eyes. I was tempted to make a grab for the gun and teach him a lesson in staying alert. A dark, sinister emotion twisted around in the pit of my guts watching him fawn over her. If I hadn't grown up learning to control my emotions I would have thought it was jealousy.

"I came back to see my mom," she said. Tears filled her eyes again.

"How is she?"

"She's . . . She passed."

"I'm sorry to hear that," he said with genuine compassion. "You really shouldn't be here."

"It's getting late," one of the others said. "Soon the sun will set. The Messiah will want to meet our new guests before dinner."

"We weren't really planning on sticking around that long," I said.

A woman with a shotgun at her hip walked right up to the car, pointing it at my face. "We insist. No one enters or leaves this hallowed ground without the blessing of the Messiah."

"Who is the Messiah?" Felicity asked Darren as he pulled his hands back and broke eye contact.

"Only he can reveal himself to outsiders," Darren said.

"I don't like this," she said.

"Me neither," I replied.

"It's going to be fine," Darren said. "The Messiah is all-seeing and wise and compassionate. He will know what's best to do."

"Really, we were just passing through," I said, but they were already pulling open the doors. They held them open and rode half in and half out with their guns trained on us.

"Drive slowly," the woman said. "We will guide you into camp."

Darren seemed to give Felicity a look that said he was sorry, but it was way too late for that. We pulled down the road, passing the Chevron on the way. A little voice in the back of my head told me to fight, but I knew it was useless. They would cut us to shreds if we tried to make a break for it. Whatever was going to happen, we'd just have to ride it out to the bitter end.

No one is taking my sword again, I vowed. *They'll have to pry it from my cold dead hands.*

As we drove, we passed groups of roving armed units on patrol who looked up and watched us drive farther in. I was suddenly really glad I hadn't tried anything stupid. It looked like they had been stocking up on weapons and ammunition for decades. I remembered learning about the massacre at Waco for social studies when I was still in school. This was starting to look a lot like that, but without an end in sight.

"Look over there," Benji said, pointing out the open door.

We all turned our heads. There were camps set up along the sides of the roads. In between them were tents that offered goods and services. It was an outdoor market like something from the Renaissance Faire I'd gone to when I was Benji's age. There was even a guy carrying a large drumstick in his hand and eating it as he walked along. I was so distracted that I almost ran over some people crossing in front of us. A loud thumping on the hood of the SUV brought my attention back to the road.

"Watch where you're going," the woman barked. "Make a left up here and drive all the way up onto the property. Keep it under five miles per hour, and whatever you do don't run over any children."

I turned onto the gravel road and pulled down a wooded lane with children darting in and out of the trees, laughing and playing. When I came out the other side, I pulled up in front of a huge building with several armed guards posted out in front.

"What is this place?" I asked.

"I don't remember it," Felicity said.

"Pull up over there and shut the engine off," the woman ordered.

Everyone who had been riding on the side of the vehicle jumped off and steadied their weapons on us, leaving the doors wide open. I did exactly as she said, without hesitation. We all got out. I strapped my blade on my back again. I was ready to fend off an argument over them disarming me again, but it never came.

Guess they figure one sword won't do much against a hail of hot bullets blasting through me, I thought. It made sense. It would be futile to fight. It wasn't like we just had to get off the property. We had to make it out of town in one piece.

"What now?" I was doing my best to sound as nonthreatening as possible. Under the circumstances I'd say I was handling things pretty well.

"Now," she said with a smile, "you meet our Messiah, Bryan Crowe."

We were led into the building slowly at gun point. There were more young children running around playing tag. They didn't so much as stop and give us a look, which seemed odd, since we were clearly being marched around as prisoners. I would have thought for sure that their curiosity would have gotten the best of them, but no such luck.

"Nice place you've got here," I said, craning my head around to take in the paintings of Biblical stories on the ceilings.

The muzzle of her gun jabbed me in the small of my back. "Keep moving."

She'll kill you for sure if you step one toe out of line, I thought. I'd never been more sure of anything in my life. She had the determination and resolution of a devotee blinded by faith. Chills went down my spine as the realization set fully in that she wouldn't hesitate for a second to murder us if given the order.

Before we knew it, we were standing before a middle aged man with a long beard sitting on an elevated, gold painted throne covered in pillows. Behind him, the wall showed one long mural depicting the last supper through the crucifixion and resurrection.

A pretty teenage girl with a bob cut stood next to him, actually feeding him grapes. He leaned over and whispered in her ear. She turned and looked at us then ran off.

"Welcome," he said, standing up and coming to greet us. "My name is Bryan Crowe and I am a humble servant of God almighty. I have been waiting for you."

Felicity groaned and the girl jabbed her in the back with her gun.

"It's all right Rowena," Bryan said, addressing his fierce female warrior. "Our faith does not require blind obedience from others."

"Glad to hear it," I said, stepping forward and extending my hand. "My name is Xander."

He took my hand in his. His grip was firm and unyielding like metal, but his hands were soft like a girl's. Chances are he wasn't doing a whole lot of hard labor in the promised land.

Probably leaving that for the kids, I thought. *Or prisoners.*

"Welcome," he said with a wide grin. He released my hand and took Felicity's. "And who might you be?"

He leered at her and something inside of me stirred to life, dark and brooding and ready to chop his hand off if he got too friendly with her.

"Felicity." She looked away from him.

"Welcome, child," he beamed, lingering a moment too long before turning his full attention to Benji. He went down on one knee and looked my friend in the eyes, giving him his full, undivided attention.

"How's it going, champ?" His voice was much more relaxed.

"Um," Benji said, looking up at me. I nodded that it was okay to respond to Bryan. "Okay."

"What's your name?"

"I'm Benji."

"Nice to meet you, Benji. I'm Bryan." He sat down in front of my friend. "Hey, do you like playing hide and seek?"

"Yeah." Benji sounded a little confused.

"Well we've got over ten acres of zombie-free land to play on," Bryan said. "Dinner isn't for another hour. Do you want to explore the grounds and play with some of the other kids?"

Benji looked at me again. I wasn't sure what to make of it. All I wanted to do was get out of town, but that looked less and less likely to happen in any hurry. We were almost out of gas and they had what we needed. Not to mention, we were severely outgunned. It might be good for Benji to run around with kids his own age while the adults sorted out the unpleasant details. I shrugged and Benji turned back to Bryan.

"How will I find my way back?"

"Judah will show you," Bryan said. Without another word, a young boy with a mess of chocolate brown hair Benji's age walked over to him, ignoring the rest of us.

"Hey," the boy said, extending his hand to Benji. "I'm Judah."

"I'm Benji." He nervously took the boy's hand.

"It's okay, Benji," Judah said. "You don't have to be afraid. Come on, I'll show you where we grow our crops. We got a working tractor and everything."

"See you at supper, kiddo," Felicity said, stopping Benji

for a moment and kissing him on the head. Judah led Benji outside and I turned on Bryan.

"Okay. Now that the kid's out of the way, let's hear it. What's your deal?"

"I don't know what you mean," Bryan said, looking slightly offended.

"Come off it."

"Your little brother will be fine. Better than fine with Judah as his guide. I would never hurt a child. The Lord said we should be like children if we are to enter into his kingdom."

"What's with the religious compound?" Felicity said, cutting to the heart of the matter. "You've built up a cult following for the end of times and armed yourselves to the teeth, hoping something like this would happen and it did. You've been planning this since long before Z-Day. That about cover it?"

"Are these not the end of days?" Bryan asked with that creepy grin appearing on his face again. "The book of revelations describes the end of times as a period when the dead shall walk the earth because Hell is overflowing and there is no more room for them. Does that sound accurate to you?"

"I don't believe in Hell," I said flatly.

"The fact that you don't believe in it doesn't mean it doesn't exist. If you ceased to believe in electricity because you don't understand how it works, electricity would still exist. For hundreds of years people thought the earth was the center of the physical universe and that the sun rotated around us. It makes sense if you think about it. They were observing it every day with their own two eyes. It was hard to get them to believe otherwise, to teach them to understand that our planet actually rotates around the sun. Did that make it less true, because people didn't want to believe in it?"

"I thought you religious types eschewed science," I challenged.

"We don't," he said, calmly looking between us. "And you're missing the point. Hell is as real as this world, and the end of times as predicted by the divinely inspired book of God is at hand. We are all living witnesses of God's great plan to abolish sin from the earth once and for all and restore this world to the paradise it once was."

"Praise him," Rowena said, making the sign of the cross over herself.

"Sin?" I scoffed. "You mean like kidnapping wayward travelers at gun point?"

"The earth was once a great paradise," Bryan said, ignoring my jab. "A Garden of Eden, until sin entered in the form of the serpent. Man's weakness cost him dearly but the blood of the Lamb atoned for that weakness with his great sacrifice. The scriptures tell us he will come again and cleanse the earth with fire and we will be set free."

Felicity gulped, looking scared.

"Your followers referred to you as the Messiah," I said. "Is that what you've been telling them?"

"It's not for me to say that I am the chosen one," Bryan said, in a well polished routine. "As I told you, I am but a humble servant of the one true God."

"Sounds great," I said. "Like I told your armed guards here, we're just passing through. All we need is a little gas and we'll be on our way."

"I'm afraid that's not going to be possible."

"Why?" I stared him hard in the eyes. "We know you have petrol. We passed the station on the way here."

"You've come at a very special time. We are celebrating a religious holiday we call Harvest. We've spent months getting ready."

"That's great," I said. "Just one more reason to let us get out of your hair."

"You don't understand," Bryan said. "No one can pass through this area without receiving a special blessing. This is hallowed ground. You are standing in the promised land."

"With all due respect," I began in a voice that seemed

anything but respectful—but Felicity cut me off.

"Then give us your blessing and we will be on our way," she countered.

"I will be happy to give you my blessing, child," he said, turning his full attention to her. "At the proper time and place."

"Well how long is that gonna take?" I asked, flabbergasted.

"Don't worry. It won't be long. After the feast and the teaching tonight many will be blessed and baptized as the spirit moves through them. By morning you will feel like a different person."

"Can't you just give us your blessing now?" Felicity asked. "Why can't we leave before the festival?"

"You could," Bryan said calmly. "If you had gas in your car, which you won't. Worldly work is frowned upon during Harvest time, especially after sundown. Besides, everyone is preparing for the great feast tonight. It truly is a special occasion. You'll see."

"Why didn't they just let us barter for some gas and be on our way then?"

"I'm sorry, but it is the law," Bryan said with a touch of genuine regret in his honeyed voice. "All new visitors must be questioned before being allowed to pass. The righteous have many enemies during this period before the Lord comes again. We can't be too careful."

"We're not even adults yet," I argued. "That doesn't make any sense."

"You have killed before," he said, staring directly into my eyes. "You would strike me down right now if I threatened harm to you or your friends. I have no doubt about that."

A chill ran down my back as I felt Rowena's hatred surge toward us.

"You must earn my blessing to leave," he said. "I will be happy to grant it to you tomorrow so that you may be on your way. Until then I'd like you to think of yourselves as my guests. You will be staying with me tonight. I insist."

Listening close by, Rowena looked both shocked and hurt by these words but she recovered quickly.

If that's some kind of big honor he just bestowed on us, I thought, *he can keep it.*

Felicity slipped her hand into mine and gave it a squeeze. She was obviously just as scared by this turn of events as I was.

"Rowena, please show them to my quarters and stay with them," Bryan said. "I will be along after I have a word with Darren."

"As you wish," she said, then turned to us. "Follow me."

We were marched back out at gun point and across the yard to another entrance. On our way out I glanced over my shoulder and caught a glimpse of Darren skulking in and kneeling before Bryan Crowe.

CHAPTER NINETEEN

"So what's the deal with that guy Darren?" I asked, picking at the edges of the hem of my new clothes.

"He was kinda like my first boyfriend," Felicity said.

"You sure know how to pick em."

We were sitting in a large waiting room full of sofas and chairs. There were crosses on the walls and a Bible in the corner, but nothing else. No television, no reading material, nothing to occupy us except ourselves and our own thoughts.

After we were led off to Bryan Crowe's private mansion and guest quarters, we were separated and treated to our own private tour of the immediate grounds. My guide was a kid about a year younger than me named Jonah. He was perfectly brainwashed to give the most banal sort of answer to any question I could come up with. He rattled off the great history of their leader, talking about his trials in the desert and how they mirrored the tales of Christ in the Bible. Jonah told me that Crowe was drawn to this special land by an angel of the Lord, that he settled here and prepared for the end of days as instructed by God. I did my best to follow along, but I was pretty bored after ten minutes. I started asking questions about the way things worked and what they thought the rest of the world was doing, trying to catch Jonah off guard and get him off topic, but he didn't budge.

"You can't trip me up with your worldly questions,"

Jonah patiently explained. "I am a child of God now."

I hated him with an unnatural intensity after that. I half wished a zombie would come along and bite him so I could do the honors of sending him off to his redeemer.

"I see, but aren't we all God's children, no matter what religion we practice?"

He glared at me. I was certain that it was only a matter of time until I was escorted to a mass grave site where troublesome visitors were disposed of. Instead I was taken to a private showering area and left to get clean, despite my numerous protests that I didn't need another shower. I wasn't really comfortable so I just splashed some water on myself and washed my face.

When I got out I found all my clothing gone. Instead, a neat new pile of bright white sheets that had been stitched into garments awaited me with my katana sitting on top.

Smooth move, I thought. *Sneak in and snatch my clothes but leave my weapon. Smarter than you know. I would have torn this place apart to get it back.*

I picked the garments up and held them out in front of me.

"What are we going to, a Klan rally?" I mumbled.

They fit well enough, and since I didn't have any other options I put them on. It felt like I was wearing a cheap Halloween costume.

"Where are my clothes?" I asked when I came out of the bathroom to find Jonah patiently waiting for me.

"Civilian clothing is not appropriate for tonight's festivities," Jonah replied with a smile. "Your street clothes will be returned to you in the morning."

I was tempted to say something smartass like *don't forget to use starch* but I held it in. I just stared at him instead, trying to make the moment as uncomfortable as possible. They were keeping us as prisoners but kept acting like we'd actually chosen this. It was the least they deserved.

Jonah led me to the waiting room where I found Felicity wearing an equally disastrous pair of bed sheets stitched into the shape of an ugly dress. If this had been an episode of *Project Runway*, the designer would have been cruelly excoriated then sent home weeping. I tried not so successfully to stifle back a giggle. Felicity shot me a nasty glance for a warning.

"Hey," I said, turning to Jonah. "When are we going to eat? I am starving and you've separated us from our resources."

"Someone will be along shortly to take you to the feast," Jonah said. "Have a blessed night."

"Oh and you too, buddy," I said, flashing him a fake smile. "Mahalo."

He retreated out of the room, shutting the door behind him. I could hear the lock click into place.

Great, I thought. *Once again I'm locked up like a caged animal. How do I keep getting myself into these situations?*

After some time had passed and we realized we were probably alone, I took up the subject of Darren with her. She hadn't seemed to want to talk about him much, but I had lots of questions. She tried her best to answer my inquiries in single word replies but I wasn't backing down.

"He seems a lot older than you," I said, referring to Darren. "That's all." A little voice in my head reminded me that just a few hours ago I thought Darren looked the same age as me. I promptly invited that little voice to shut the hell up.

"He was a senior in high school and I was still in junior high," Felicity said. "It was before my acting career took off. It feels like forever ago."

"Creepy. What kind of guy goes for a girl that young?"

"He is actually one of the sweetest, most genuine people I've ever met," Felicity fired back, sounding annoyed by my persistent line of questioning. "It's a small town with small town values. There was nothing creepy about it."

"If you say so," I said, trying to fight off my obvious jealousy. "He just seems a little weird."

"Besides," she said, ignoring my taunt, "all we ever did

was hold hands. We never even kissed."

"Never?"

"Not once. Are you satisfied? Can we stop playing Spanish Inquisition now?"

"No one ever expects the Spanish Inquisition," I said in a high falsetto voice, but instead of laughing she just smirked. I was really under her skin today.

Does that mean she wishes she had kissed him? a little voice in the back of my head asked. I shouted it down yet again. I was disgusted with myself. Less than a week ago she didn't exist and all that mattered was getting Benji to the safety of the base. Now I had no idea where Benji was or if he was safe and I was thinking about Felicity way too much for my own good.

"What do you know about this Bryan Crowe guy?" I asked, switching gears. "He is supposed to be the Messiah according to my new best friend, Jonah, but I don't recall the Bible saying anything about Jesus holding people against their will at gunpoint."

"He may not remember me, but I remember him," Felicity said, shaking off a tremor that ran through her. "I was six years old and my friend Caley was having a birthday party. It was a big deal since her family was what we used to call wealthy back then. What?" She had turned to me when I made a face.

"I'm sorry," I said. "It's just hard to think that there was a time in your life when you weren't rich and famous."

"I grew up dirt poor," Felicity protested. "My mom and my sister and I didn't have much after my dad left. We moved out here because it was cheap, and we lived in a rented mobile home for the first year after the divorce. I remember my only toy was a half melted Barbie with no clothes that I found abandoned in the sand lot. My mom cleaned her up and sewed her some new outfits. They weren't much better than what we are wearing now, but they meant the world to me."

"That must have been tough," I said.

"It was," she admitted, looking up and making eye contact with me. "Anyway, most of my grade school class was there. Bryan Crowe showed up to do magic tricks and make balloon animals for all the kids. It was a perfect day with a *piñata* and cake, but it ended strange. There was some commotion and then my mom came to get me and all the kids left at once."

"What happened?"

"One of the kids had gone missing for over half an hour," Felicity said. "They found her out near the stables with Bryan Crowe. Her dress was torn. She was eight."

"So why didn't they put him in jail then and there?"

"They tried, but they didn't have any proof of wrong doing," Felicity said. "The girl didn't have any signs of abuse. She said she went to the stables on her own to look at the horses and he found her there. She said he just talked to her but she couldn't remember about what. She didn't know how her dress got torn. The police questioned the rest of us but nothing ever came of it. That was the end of his career as a kid's party entertainer though."

"I'll bet. I'm sure word got around pretty fast after something like that. I'm surprised that he wasn't at least run out of town."

I expected her to argue about how easy going and permissive Ojai was, but her brow furrowed instead and she looked really upset.

"I started having nightmares about him. I couldn't close my eyes without seeing him waiting for me in the dark in a clown costume. It got really bad. One day I begged my mom to tell me about him. I thought if she made him seem more human to me, I could get past my irrational fear."

"What did she say?"

"At first she wouldn't tell me anything."

"That must have been frustrating," I offered, trying to move the story along. I wanted to know as much about this guy as I could. What were his weaknesses, aside from young girls?

"She told me it wasn't appropriate for kids. But I stuck with it, bugging her the way only a child can and eventually she caved," she said. "She told me that he was a drifter. She said she didn't know where he was originally from, that no one did, but everyone knew he arrived from Vegas as a failed magician. He'd gone there to show his act on the strip and had fallen flat on his face. Shortly after the incident at Caley's party, he reinvented himself again."

"Let me guess," I said, "he became the Chosen One?"

"Pretty much. He set up in the old Jehovah's Witness church and began preaching about peace and love."

"I can't believe anyone would even show up. I'm going out on a limb since I've never seen him pull a rabbit out of his hat, but I'm guessing his second coming routine is only slightly worse than his card tricks."

"Are you kidding?" A fiery spark shone in her eyes as she recalled details from her pre-celebrity childhood. "This is Ojai, land of burnouts and hippies. He had an immediate following. They loved him! He stopped wearing black clothes and trying to look like Cris Angel and started looking more like a Biblical prophet with that ridiculous beard."

"So what happened?"

"He set up a commune in the woods. People came from all over the world and lived there. You would see them dressed in white rags like the ones we're wearing now, coming and going by foot into town. They were always smiling these big creepy smiles, like they were loaded out of their minds."

"Let me guess," I said, "it didn't last. Something went wrong."

"Sort of," she answered. "At first it was quiet up in their commune. Everyone kept expecting something to happen, a sex scandal, a mass suicide, just something . . . but it never did. Eventually we just accepted them. They were another strange part of our crazy little town. Weird but harmless."

"And then?"

"And then the kidnappings began," Felicity said.

"Gee," I blurted out, looking around the room, "why am I not surprised to hear that?"

"No. You've got it wrong. It's the other way around. People began kidnapping his followers."

"Who would want to do that?"

"Friends and family members of his devotees," she explained. "It was in the national news. A rich heiress came to hear him speak one night and refused to leave. She gave everything she owned to him and became a true believer. Her parents were mortified. They hired a team of cult deprogrammers to kidnap her and undo the brainwashing."

"Did this happen a lot or was it just the one incident?"

"That was the tip of the iceberg," she continued "The heiress eventually went back to him. After that, it started happening all the time. Then Nightline did a special on it."

"That's crazy. I'm surprised I've never heard of him before."

"So am I. He was pretty famous for a while. I remember being on location in Mexico and watching a repeat of a program about him on the crime channel on satellite television. It all seems like a strange dream now."

"Or this is," I said. "But I know what you mean. So what happened then?"

"It got to the point where any time you'd see a white van in town you got to wondering if there was a paid team of exit counselors hiding inside," she told me. "Some of the people rescued starting telling stories about devotees being forced to take drugs and about group marriages conducted by the prophet. They said he had several brides."

"So why didn't the government step in and do something?"

"They did," Felicity said. "They came in with armed SWAT and raided the compound. They hauled Bryan off to jail, practically parading him around town like some kind of martyr. The only problem is, they didn't find anything."

"Did someone tip him off they were coming?"

"Maybe. Who knows? All I know is that they questioned his followers and in the end they didn't have anything to hold him on except a few misdemeanor permit violations that got dropped. All it did was make his faithful all the more devoted."

"That's probably when they started arming up," I said.

"Makes sense," she replied. "But that was almost ten years ago. I can't imagine how much artillery they'd have by now."

"Enough to keep us in line. So what do we do?"

"We could fight our way out. "We might not be able to get the SUV back but we could find Benji and head out on foot."

"Don't think it didn't cross my mind," I said. "They would cut us to pieces, starting with that chick Rowena. Plus we have no idea where Benji is or what state he's in. For all we know, they're holding him hostage to get us to behave. I think it's strange he's not here now."

"Well we can't just stay here forever," she argued. "Who knows what he'll do to us, to me?"

I realized for the first time that she was truly scared of him, of what he might try to do to her as a young woman. If he liked young girls ten years ago, chances were his habits hadn't changed much.

"We're going to have to go along with whatever he has planned," I said. "At least for the time being, until we can figure out an escape plan. Try to blend in, I guess."

"Xander," she said with big pleading eyes. "I can't."

"I'm not saying you should offer yourself to him," I said quickly. "That's not what I meant at all. I'm just suggesting we start to give him the impression that he is winning us over to his freaky religion long enough to figure out how we are getting the hell out of here."

"That's like playing with fire," she cautioned. "You know that right? A guy like Bryan Crowe can't be reasoned with. You can't cut a deal with him. In the end, all Bryan cares about is twisting and distorting reality until it fits the way he wants the world to be — his own."

Before we could argue, the door was opened and Rowena came in toting her automatic weapon.

"It's time," she spat in disgust at the sight of us. "Get up and get moving."

CHAPTER TWENTY

We were marched out back across the main entrance again. I noticed right away that our vehicle was gone. *Great*, I thought. Any chance of jumping in and escaping was now long gone. I knew it wouldn't be that easy but still it sucked to have my suspicions confirmed.

Rowena led us to a large outdoor area with cooking pits. There were six banquet style tables nearby that looked like they had been hewn out of large trees then sanded down and made into tables by a master craftsman. The ground was comprised of soft, dusty brown dirt with not a single rock or pine needle to catch your foot on. It was as level as the tables. The sun had set and at first the only light I could make out was coming from the pits. Then, as my eyes adjusted, I saw that there were low level lights on all the trees and structures. I squinted, trying to make out what they were when I heard Bryan's ominous voice wash over me like a bucket of ice water.

"Bioluminescence," he said. "It's a natural, chemical reaction similar to the kind found in fireflies, only we use a special kind of concentrated bacteria that we cultivate ourselves. It's called Luciferase, ironically enough. It's taken from Satan's original name when he was an angel—Lucifer, which means light bearer. He was the most beloved of all the angels once upon a time. Then things changed. I see you are dressed for a night of festivities."

He stepped forward into the light to greet us.

"Where is Benji?" I asked gruffly. My rudeness didn't throw him off a bit. He was in good spirits.

"He is around. He's been playing a fierce game of capture the flag with the other kids. They've really taken to him."

"Benji has that effect on people," I said. "He's a great kid."

"I agree. Come now, join me at my table as my honored guests."

Rowena fell back as we willingly followed him to the middle table and sat down. There were six young girls seated with him. I looked to Felicity to see that her features had hardened. She glared at Bryan. Before we could say anything, he let out a laugh that seemed to set Felicity more on edge.

"I can see from the disapproving look on your face that some introductions are in order," Bryan said. "These are my wives."

"All of them?" I asked, unable to help myself. They were all around our age or younger.

"I am very blessed," he said with false modesty. He gestured around the table in a circle, naming each girl as he went. "This is Annabelle, Syriah, Leah, Tara, Beatrice, and Victoria. Say hello girls."

"Hello," they replied dutifully in unison like some kind of sideshow attraction.

"Isn't it against the law to have more than one wife?" I asked. "No offense."

"I am glad you asked." Bryan smiled. "It is against man's law but not God's law. In the Old Testament we see many instances of polygamy. Moses had two wives, at least. Abraham had three known wives. Then there is the case of King Solomon who had seven hundred wives and three hundred concubines, and he was considered one of the wisest men to have ever walked the face of the earth!"

"How many wives does one man need?" Felicity fumed.

"I would say the perfect number is seven." He winked at her. "It's a holy number."

"Seriously though," I interjected. "Why do you need all these wives?"

"It is a responsibility and a privilege. I am blessed by God almighty who said we may take as many wives as we can comfortably maintain. Verily he tells us to go forth and be fruitful and multiply."

"Amen," said Leah, leaning over and kissing him on the mouth. She couldn't be older than fifteen.

He could be her grandfather, I thought, grossed out by the sight. I did my best to hide my feelings.

"It's time for the toast of the feast," Bryan said, standing up.

I could see now that we were surrounded by devotees on all sides, watching our every move. Chefs stood by the fires with meats that looked like skewered rabbits and vegetables, waiting for the order. Another group of helpers moved from table to table filling glasses. Bryan already had a large, ornate bottle of his own red wine open. He poured a generous helping into the chalice in front of him and held it up.

"Brothers and sisters," he began in a loud, booming voice that echoed out across the valley beyond the banquet area. "Tonight we join together to celebrate our great good fortune in being gathered as one family in the final days of our Lord and Savior. Praise God! Hallelujah!"

"Hallelujah!" A deafening chorus of hundreds joined in raising their glasses.

"As we come together in this special time of Harvest, let us not forget those blessed souls we have lost, those that have gone before us into the arms of the Lord." Bryan bowed his head. "We will see them again in the promised land soon enough."

A wave of *amens* crashed over us again.

"May the blood of the Lamb cleanse us of our sins and bring us peace." He put the chalice to his lips and tipped it back, taking a strong gulp of wine before passing it to us.

"No thanks," Felicity said, pushing it away.

"It's important," he pleaded in a soothing voice. "It's part of our customs. Harvest lasts from sundown through the rise of the full moon. It begins with a drink of the blood of the Lamb, symbolizing the sacrifice that Jesus Christ made for us on the cross which washed away our sins. You see? You have to drink."

"Fine," she relented. "I'll drink if it will shut you up already. To Jesus." She tilted her head back and took a big swig. She set the cup back down on the table. "There. You happy?"

"I am happy for you," he corrected. "You don't know this since you are new but when you finish drinking you are to pass the cup to the person on your right. Then they drink. We repeat this until the offering is gone."

"If you say so," she said saucily. "I just hope we eat soon because I am not good at handling my liquor. I haven't had a drink since rehab."

She passed the cup to me and I took a sip. It was red wine but it tasted overly sweet, as if someone had added sugar to hide something else.

Don't be paranoid, I told myself. *You saw him drink out of it. If they wanted to kill you they could have taken you out a million different ways by now. All they'd have to do is march you to the tree line and gun you down, not secretly poison you.*

I took a full swig and passed it to my right, to Syriah. She took a good sip and passed it on.

I could smell the meat had been put on the fires. It smelled good. Within ten minutes the cup had gone around several times and the bottle was empty. We were all laughing and smiling. I couldn't feel my face. Although I wasn't used to drinking, I knew this wasn't from being drunk alone. I was right. There was some kind of drug in the wine. I felt happiness bursting in my chest and flowing through every part of me. Whatever it was, it felt good. I had no fear anymore — not of death or zombies or cult members holding us hostage. Feelings of love and peace and happiness washed over me again and again. Anything seemed possible. For a minute I thought I might be able to fly.

Pretty soon everything seemed to be running together. Food was brought to the table and we ate, but I don't know what it was. Then the world began to spin and spin. People got up and danced and took off their clothing. I stood up and began searching for Benji. The last thing I recall was turning to see Felicity staring at one of the bio-luminescent lights on the trees and laughing over and over.

The next morning I woke up in an empty bedroom with a dull headache. The white of the walls seemed to be seeping into me and making me nauseous. I climbed out of bed and the whole room seemed to spin. The first thing I noticed was that I was naked. The next thing I noticed was that my normal clothing was left in a pile next to the bed.

Did I take off my clothes last night in front of everyone? I wondered, but I sure hoped not. What if Felicity had seen me naked? That would be super embarrassing!

I quickly put on my clothing then searched the pocket and found that the pills I had snatched from the bathroom at Jackson's place were long gone. I had forgotten to mention them to Felicity so I couldn't say anything. For a minute I wondered if that was what they fed us the night before, but then I realized they had made Felicity seem really calm. Whatever was in the wine we drank had the opposite effect. For all I knew it was ecstasy and angel dust.

Panic came over me as I realized I didn't have my sword. The last place I recalled having it was at the dinner feast where I had set it on the table. Frantically I searched around the room. Relief washed over me as I found it propped against the wall in the corner. I checked the blade to make sure it was still clean then slid it over my shoulder and walked out.

In the living room I found a glass of water and two aspirin with a note telling me to meet up with them for breakfast when I felt better. I popped the sour white pills into my mouth and gulped down the liquid like a thirsty dog. My stomach felt like a gurgling pit of acid.

I threw open the door and stepped outside. The cool air felt good but the sun seemed to be burning a hole through my head. I began to hope the aspirin would kick in fast.

Jonah approached me with a kind smile. "How are you feeling today, brother?"

"I'm all right," I said, trying to belie the pounding headache that was setting in.

"You sure seemed to be having fun last night," he said with a smile.

"Funny," I replied. "I can't remember much of it."

"That's how it is when the spirit of the Lord takes over you."

"Or when the drugs in the wine kick in," I said. He laughed as if I was kidding but I just stared at him.

"All right then. I've been waiting for you. It's my honor to take you on a tour of the grounds, after breakfast that is."

"I'm gonna skip breakfast if you don't mind," I said as the nausea returned. "Just some bottled water would be nice."

"Done."

"Where is Benji?"

"I don't know about your friend, Benji," Jonah said. "He spent the night with the other kids. They have their own cabin across the way. Children tend to keep different hours than adults and we've found it's best for all if they are kept separate."

"And Felicity?"

"She got up about an hour ago. She went to see Bryan and I believe she is now on a tour with Darren."

"Great," I said with a fake smile. "That is just perfect."

"I am glad you are pleased," Jonah said with a genuine smile. It was obvious he really believed in all this religious stuff and was happy to be one of Bryan's minions. "Shall we go then?"

"Lead the way," I replied with a flourish of my hands.

The tour actually turned out to be pretty cool, against all odds. They were a highly skilled, self sufficient group of people who knew how to build, how to trap and hunt and fish and live off the land. They understood science and medicine. They were creative and smart and generally kind, if only just a little creepy. Everywhere we went they sang the praises of their messiah and wished us a happy Harvest.

The aspirin kicked in soon enough and my headache began to fade as my body returned to normal. I drank two large bottles of water Jonah provided for me and ate a stick of rabbit jerky he'd carefully wrapped in a strip of tan cloth for the tour. To his credit, Jonah never once gave in to my taunts or teasing or sarcastic remarks. Against my better judgment I began to like him. It was hard *not* to like the guy. He was just too nice!

He showed me a water purifying station they had set up and talked about their failed attempts to create a small power plant.

"We just don't have enough fuel to power it. We'd need coal or gasoline or something strong, and in the end it wouldn't be worth it for what we could generate and store. For now, we've found other ways around the problem."

"Like bioluminescence?"

"Exactly," he replied. "Or as we like to call it — God's electricity."

A group of kids across the way ran screaming into the woods. I thought I caught sight of Benji from behind, disappearing off in the high brush.

"Too bad you can't harness the energy of all those kids," I said. "You'd have more than enough to power the whole of California."

"That's the truth."

I looked up and saw Felicity off in the distance with Darren, talking.

"What's over there?" I pointed in their direction.

"The pits," he said. "I'm not sure you're ready to see

them."

"Nonsense. I've made leaps and bounds since this morning. I'm practically converted to your way of life." I smiled.

He looked pensive but relented, probably realizing that I wouldn't give in without a fight. "Try to keep an open mind," he cautioned as he led the way.

Darren looked up and saw us coming. He had a frown on his face as he talked to Felicity. She had her back to us so I couldn't tell what she was thinking. Jonah smiled and waved to them and Darren waved back.

When we got close to the spot where they were standing, I began to smell a faint scent of death and decay. Then I heard the low moaning. Instantly my hand went to my sword in defense. Jonah calmly put his hand on my shoulder.

"It's okay," he said soothingly. "We are safe."

We reached them and I looked past Felicity to see what she was staring down at. There was a natural ravine set into the side of the hill that had been dug out and covered over with metal bars. Inside were upwards of a hundred zombies milling about. Undead men, women, and children shuffled back and forth moaning and groaning. Occasionally one would lift its head, sniff the air, then snap with its rotten teeth in our direction.

"What the hell is that?" I was starting to lose my cool.

"Those are people," Jonah replied. "Just like you or me, only they are suffering."

"Those are zombies," I countered. "They are dead, infected people."

"Yes. Exactly."

"So why are you keeping them penned up like that?"

"I knew he wouldn't understand," Darren said to Felicity.

"I'm not sure I do either," Felicity replied, turning and taking me by the hand. "Why don't you explain to us both again?"

Darren looked angrily at me. I tried my best to fight back the smile blossoming on my face.

"Okay then," he said, regaining his composure. "We believe that the living dead are people just like the rest of us who have committed terrible sins and are now paying the price for their transgressions."

"That's pretty cold, man," I said, but he stopped me.

"Let me finish. This is going to take a really long time if you keep interrupting every time you don't understand something rather than just saving your questions for the end. Got it?"

"I'm good," I said, puffing up my chest and pulling Felicity slightly closer to me.

"We have nothing but the greatest compassion for them. That's why we care for them."

"By keeping them penned up like animals?"

"Are you going to let me tell this story or not?"

I shook my head and Felicity squeezed my hand.

"Go on," I said through clenched teeth.

"We don't believe in killing people unless we have to, for self-defense," he said. "These poor souls aren't hurting anyone in there. We believe they are the dead that are referred to in the final book of the Bible, Revelations. We believe that when Christ returns to walk the earth he will be able to heal them, just as he did with the lepers of Galilee."

"He shall raise them up just as he did with poor Lazarus," Jonah said, "who had been dead for four days and returned to life as Christ commanded."

"That's right," Darren said. "So until then we do our best to care for them and keep them out of harm's way." He stopped and stared at me, crossing his arms and waiting for me to say something harsh.

"What if they get out--" Felicity asked.

"It's never happened," Darren said before she could finish her sentence, shaking his head in disapproval. "Not once in all the time we've kept them here."

"We are blessed with some very talented brothers and

sisters," Jonah said with a pleasant smile. "We like to believe the Lord is watching out for us."

"What about the children?" I asked.

"What about them?" Darren cocked his eyebrow in surprise.

"They seem to run free all the time. It's like *Lord of the Flies* out here. You know the kinds of trouble young kids can get into unsupervised. What if they were to fall in?"

"Like I said," Darren repeated. "It's never happened. Our kids may be young and free spirited, but they are smart enough to know when something is dangerous and avoid it." He turned and shot me a challenging stare.

"What?" I asked defensively.

"I'm waiting for some insensitive comment. You seem to get such a kick out of spitting on our faith."

"Sorry. I never considered keeping them penned up like this. I've spent the majority of my time since the outbreak either killing them or running from them. I never saw them in this light before. I couldn't afford to be compassionate. I was fighting for my life and the lives of the people I cared about. This is just blowing my mind."

"I guess I have had more time to adjust to it," Darren said, softening at my confession. "I come up here every day."

"Every day?" Felicity looked at him.

"Without fail."

"Wow," I replied. "Why are you so committed to them?"

"You see the woman with the ponytail?" He pointed to a zombie in dirty, sack like clothes not unlike the ones we'd worn the night before.

"Yeah."

"That's my wife, Nicole."

Felicity leaned in and stared hard.

"Do you mean Nicole Boschard?"

"I do." Darren fought back tears. His overreaction was starting to make a lot more sense. "We were married right after I got out of high school. We were trying to start a family when the outbreak happened. I can remember how afraid she used to be watching the news reports. It wasn't until she accepted Jesus into her heart that she came to know peace. It doesn't seem fair that she ended up here."

"The Lord works in mysterious ways, brother," Jonah said, putting his hand on Darren's shoulder. Darren shook him off. "Let's not relive this again now in front of our guests. Come away and let them talk among themselves while you regain your composure."

Darren looked like he might punch a hole through Jonah's face for a minute, but in the end he relented and they walked off a distance.

"That was . . ."

"Awkward." Felicity finished my sentence.

"These people are crazy. Keeping zombies caged up like this and all the God talk. I can't wait to get out of here."

"You seemed to be enjoying yourself last night," she said, looking up at me with a smile.

"I don't know how to say this, so I am just going to come right out and ask." My voice shook. "I don't remember anything from last night. I am pretty sure we were drugged."

"Me too. I'd say it was ecstasy or GHB from what I remember of my very short club days. So what's your question?"

"I woke up with no clothes," I said. "Did I get naked in front of everyone?"

She laughed at me. "Don't worry. Almost everyone was naked. I didn't see too much." She gave me a wink.

"Wow. This is embarrassing."

"I'm pretty sure that's the least of our worries."

"What is it now?"

"You mean aside from being held captive on a creepy religious compound?"

"Right," I said.

She stopped laughing and got serious. "Bryan asked me to join his harem." She looked down at her hands.

"When? Last night after he drugged us out?"

"No. He was a perfect host last night, aside from slipping us drugs. I think he was trying to be on his best behavior."

"So when did he ask you to join his tribe of child brides then?" I noticed that my fists had clenched up in anger.

"This morning at breakfast. He asked if he could speak to me. I thought he was going to talk about Benji, but the next thing I knew he was telling me how beautiful I was, how God had a special plan for me. He said that God told him I should be his seventh sacred vessel or something like that."

"I ought to cut his lousy head off," I said as an ugly jolt of hatred surged through me. "Who does he think he is?!"

"He thinks he's the Messiah!" She laughed a little at my overreaction. "Calm down, Xander. It's not like I said yes."

"What did you tell him?"

"I told him I was flattered." She sighed, taking both my hands and twisting back and forth. Her cheeks flushed. "But that I didn't feel in my heart that I belonged here. I told him I had feelings for someone else."

"Yeah? Who's that?" I was starting to lose all control. Usually I could just tell myself to calm down and things went back to normal. Ever since I had met this girl my emotions were all over the map. Now she was going to tell me that she was in love with her junior high crush Darren again and I was going to blow my top.

That's why he gave her the tour this morning, I thought. *They are sneaking away to confess their love for each other! He probably even wanted to get his wife's blessing to take a new girlfriend. These people are sick and twisted!*

Before I could get any more worked up, the unimaginable happened—Felicity leaned over and gently kissed me on the lips. Her lips were so soft and I could feel the slightest hint of her warm breath as she leaned in and pressed them to mine. For a moment it felt like the ground dropped out from under my feet. We were floating together in a bubble of light, far away from the cares of this messed up world. There was no Bryan Crowe, no zombies, only pure happiness and bliss that went on forever.

She pulled back first and stared nervously at me with her sea green eyes.

"Does that answer your question?" Her voice had a slight tremble in it.

It blew my mind that a celebrity like Felicity Jane could be worried in any way that I would reject her. In that moment she was totally vulnerable.

"It answers a lot of my questions about life," I said with an impish grin.

She punched me playfully in the shoulder and bit her lip. I laughed. She took me by the hand again and we walked down to Jonah and Darren. I felt more confident than I can ever remember feeling in my life. Darren, on the other hand, looked sick to his stomach. His face looked pale and he avoided making eye contact the rest of the way back to camp. Jonah was just as oblivious as he had always been; blissfully unaware that anything had changed when, as far as I was concerned, everything in the whole world had just changed back up on that hill.

CHAPTER TWENTY ONE

Bryan and Benji were waiting for us when we got back. They looked almost like a father and his son talking about the birds and the bees on a camping trip. Bryan rubbed Benji's head, messing up his hair, and they both laughed. Smiles lit up both their faces when they saw us coming in.

"There they are," Bryan said. "How are you feeling this morning?"

"Great," I said, meaning it for the first time I could remember.

"Fantastic . . . and you?" Bryan eyed Felicity with an unspoken intensity that made her squirm.

She gripped my hand tight. "I'm fine," she said as pleasantly as she could manage.

"So," he sounded like a used car salesman getting ready to wrap up a sale, "you've seen our lands, come to know our people and our way of life . . . what do you think?"

"It's really amazing," I said. "I admire the way you've managed to put all this together and keep everyone content."

An unexpected smile flashed across his face, while Felicity turned and gawked at me in shock.

"That's wonderful to hear." He burst with glee. "The others will be so pleased to know you're staying with us. You're going to love it here. I can get you set up in your own dwelling by the end of the festival and then we just have to find you a job."

I held up my hand to stop him. "That's not necessary. We're not staying. I need to get to my brother and let him know I'm okay. I appreciate your hospitality and ask for your blessing to leave."

Bryan stared at us with a smile frozen on his face. He held his silence as if he was thinking hard—right up to the cusp of the exchange being truly awkward. "Does he speak for you as well?" He turned his full attention to Felicity, who seemed to almost wither under his glare.

"Yes. I'm not staying here. I'm with Xander."

Suddenly, Darren turned and stormed off toward the road. I followed him with my eyes but the rest of the group just ignored him.

"Of course," Bryan said, the fake note of sympathy returning to his voice. "I understand. I give you both my blessing. As of last night you may consider yourselves honorary members of our church. Please feel free to return any time you like and visit."

This is too easy, I thought. *There has to be a catch. It's almost like he's trying to get us to leave but I can't figure out why.*

"Okay then," I said. "Now if we can just have our vehicle back, we'll be on our way."

"Jonah," Bryan said. "Would you please bring their car around?"

Jonah wordlessly jumped to obey his command, running off toward the tree line. We all sat there for a while in awkward silence trying not to look at each other.

"What have you been up to?" I said to Benji to try to lighten the mood.

"I've been having the most amazing time."

"That's great," I replied, feeling glad that Bryan had kept his word about not hurting children, other than the ones he illegally married.

"I've been playing in the woods and made all sorts of new friends. It's wonderful here."

Bryan smirked at his words, cocking his head toward us

in an *I told you so* look.

"I'm glad you've been having fun," I said.

"I've been learning a lot too."

"Like what?" Felicity asked.

"Did you know that my family is alive and well right now in heaven? It's true. I'm going to get to see them all again when Jesus comes back to lead the armies of the righteous against the children of the damned."

It was like something from a horror movie come to life. They'd used the kids against us to turn Benji's head and fill it full of religious nonsense. They were manipulating him with the death of his family. I glared at Bryan, who returned my burning gaze without shame or remorse. How could they do this to children? How could they fill him with fairy tales about the death of his family, then use that hope to make him do what they wanted?

That's the real sin, I thought. *Giving Benji false hope to use him against us as a weapon.*

Bryan seemed so resolute in his faith. That's what made it all work. I realized as he held my stare for an uncanny length of time that his real power was that he didn't just say these things to his followers, he truly believed them. In his mind not only did God speak to him but he guided him to this place and kept him and his followers safe from the end of the world.

"Grab your stuff, Benji," I said. "We're going."

Bryan Crowe didn't offer a word.

"No. I'm staying here."

My head spun around in shock and anger. "Are you kidding me right now?"

"I like it here. There are plenty of other kids my age and we get to play together, and best of all the zombies can't hurt me anymore."

"These people are strangers. How do you know they will protect you?"

"You were a stranger once too," he protested. "And you took care of me."

"That's right," I practically shouted. "I did. I've watched out for you since those kids picked on you at Vandenberg and I still am looking out for you. It's my job to keep you safe."

"This is where I belong now. It's safe for me here. At last I don't have to worry."

"You said we were family now," Felicity said softly, kneeling down to his level and brushing the hair out of his eyes. "You sure you don't want to stay with your family?"

"All of these people are one big family too," Benji said, getting a little overexcited. "Just like we are. Xander has to go to find his brother, but you could stay here with me. Maybe when Xander is done fighting he could come back and live here with us."

"That sounds like a wonderful plan," Bryan interjected.

"No," Felicity said, looking up and into Bryan's eyes. "I can't stay here."

"Why not?" Benji was practically pleading with her.

"You're just going to have to take my word on it, little man," Felicity said, kissing him on the head. "It's not safe for me or Xander here anymore."

"Enough," Bryan said in a firm tone. "The child has decided to stay of his own free will. You must respect his decision."

I turned to look at Felicity and she shrugged.

"Are you sure this is what you want?" I asked Benji, and he nodded that it was. "Okay then. I guess this is where we part ways."

I walked over to Bryan. He puffed out his chest as I approached and several of his guards readied their weapons just in case I started a fight.

"Please take good care of him."

"You have my word," he replied. "His soul is in my care now."

"I will be back to check on him. If anything is out of place, you'll have to answer to me."

"There is no need for threats here," Bryan simpered.

"Particularly on this holy day. I've already told you that you are welcome to visit whenever you like." He looked over to Felicity and she scowled at him in contempt. "Both of you."

"You can count on it," I said.

Jonah pulled up in our Lexus and stopped, getting out. He signaled to Bryan, who turned back to us.

"A full tank of gas as promised," he said. "I give you my blessing and wish you peace and love in the Lord's name as you head on your way. Amen."

The entire congregation behind us sang out a matching chorus of *amens* that practically shook the leaves from the trees. I couldn't believe we were really going to leave Benji behind, that this was actually happening. There was nothing I could do about it. I climbed into the Lexus and shut the door. Felicity kissed Benji goodbye one last time then joined me.

We pulled out slowly onto the road heading out of town. Felicity made a quick sweep of the vehicle to check for our belongings. They were all there, including the bear she had given Benji named Rasputin. She held it in her lap as we drove and didn't say anything. A tear escaped her eye and she quickly wiped it away. I pretended not to notice as I was dealing with my own feelings as well.

The tents on the side of the road were abandoned now. The roads were virtually empty of people as we made our way out of town.

I turned to Felicity. "Don't you think it's weird that Darren ran off like that?"

"I thought you didn't like him," she said, not looking at me.

"I can't honestly say that I do."

"Maybe it was just too painful for him to say goodbye. Or maybe Bryan wouldn't let him come. Maybe after he heard about Bryan trying to convince me to be his sacred seventh bride he was afraid he might flip out on him . . . or on you. For all we know, he could be locked up in cult jail right now somewhere back there."

"That's true," I said taking her words in. "Did we do the right thing back there, leaving Benji behind?"

"I don't know." She sighed. "He said it's what he wanted but he's just a kid. He doesn't understand how dangerous those people can be. It's like he's blinded by their sense of community."

"He lost his entire family right before his eyes. I can understand the appeal of wanting to believe they are in heaven and that he is going to see them again one day, of wanting a loving, supportive family that repeats that message over and over again. That's pretty irresistible stuff."

"But why do they want him?" she asked. "Why go to such effort for just one kid?"

"I don't know. I guess it's just what cults do. They recruit people and convert them. It's their only function really if you think about it. Spread the message."

"Like a virus."

We drove for a while longer in silence until we reached the end of the winding canyons that led to a straight stretch back to the 101 Freeway. I was just getting ready to punch it when, without warning, a man came running out onto the highway in front of us, waving his arms. I hit the brakes and the Lexus came to a halt, skidding past and nearly clipping him. A few inches to the left and he would have been tagged by the tail end of the SUV.

"What the hell was that?" Felicity screamed.

"I don't know," I said, then amended my statement. "A man waving his arms. He looked normal, you know, as in alive."

Felicity looked in her side mirror.

"It's him. It's Darren."

"Jesus." I gasped. "He scared the hell out of me. Why did he do that?"

She was out of the car before I was finished talking. She ran up to him and shoved him hard in the chest. I unbuckled my seat belt, threw open the door, and hurried over to join them.

"What was that for?" She looked angry as she shoved him again. "You trying to get us killed? Huh?! Or are you just trying to kill yourself by taking the coward's way out?"

"I had to stop you," he panted, scared and out of breath. "I couldn't let you leave."

"Why's that?" My blade was unsheathed in my hand, reflecting the fading sun light. I hadn't noticed taking it out. Must have been force of habit.

"Your friend, Benji."

"What about him?" Felicity demanded. If she still had feelings for this guy they were fading fast.

"They are going to sacrifice him. That's why they wanted him to stay."

"Start explaining fast," I threatened, my hand gripping my sword harder.

"The Harvest festival," he said, gulping down air with his hands on his knees and a terrified look on his face.

"We know," Felicity said. "We were both drugged then baptized last night, remember?"

"But they left Benji alone because he's just a kid," I said.

"Wrong," Darren finally straightened up as he spoke. "It's because he's an outsider, a stranger no one will miss. Do you remember those zombie pits I showed you this morning?"

"Where you wife is." Felicity shook her head.

"What about them?" I asked.

"Bryan doesn't believe in killing zombies. He says they are the damned but that we should have mercy on them."

"You kinda covered all this earlier," I said impatiently. "Get to the part where they want to hurt our friend before I cut you in half for almost running us off the road." I took a step toward him and he held up his hand to fend me off.

"Hold on. My wife wasn't just attacked by a zombie at our house on Z-day and rounded up. She was sacrificed during a Harvest celebration to them. An offering is selected and placed in the pits for them to feast on."

"That's horrible." Felicity gasped, covering her mouth

with her hands.

"Bryan says it's God's will and that when Christ comes back he will redeem them. The others believe it helps keep us safe from zombie attacks, but I know what it's really about."

"What's that?" I loosened my grip on my weapon. He was obviously in a great deal of emotional pain thinking about his wife as he spoke.

"Control," he said. "Keeping us in line. You see, the whole process is supposed to be a lottery. All our names go into a jar and he selects. God guides him to the sinner who must be cleansed, or that's what he told us. We all know it's not true."

"That's why he wanted us to stay," Felicity said. "We're sinners in their eyes."

"Precisely," Darren said. "Nobody is attached to you. No one is going to miss you. They'll just assume you're paying for your earthly transgressions. That way Bryan gets to keep his facade up and no one steps out of line. He does this four times a year and almost every time it's been an outsider. The last time, he kept a couple of hikers he found and locked them in his house for three weeks."

"Who was his first victim?" I asked, curiosity getting the better of me.

"Town sheriff," Darren said.

"Figures. Get him out of the way. So why didn't he choose me? I'm obviously the sinner in this group. Half of those people would probably cheer to see me get eaten. Why pick a kid?"

"Less of a fight, I suppose." Darren shrugged. "It's not the first time this has happened. They make him feel special and welcome, like he belongs, then once you are out of the way, they give him the bad news. By then it's too late. They are probably telling him right now. From what I've seen they don't like to wait."

"I told him I was coming back," I said. "How did he plan on explaining Benji's transformation?"

"He wouldn't have to," Darren said. "He'd just make up a story that Benji had gone off in search of you and you'd never be the wiser. Like I said, he's thought of everything."

"What time is the Harvest sacrifice?" Felicity asked in a panic. "They can't kill him right away can they? We've got to go back and save him!"

"When the full moon reaches its peak," Darren said. "Like I said, they've probably already begun preparing him. There is a purification ritual for the offering that involves prayer and a sedative. They want him as docile as possible when the time comes."

"If they give him anything like what they slipped us last night he won't even know what's happening," I said.

"Then we have to go now!" Felicity's voice cracked in desperation. "Get in. You're coming with us."

Darren didn't hesitate. We all ran back to the Lexus and swung it around, heading back into town.

"You're going to have to forgive me for asking this," I began, "but why are you helping us again?"

"I will never forget the look in my wife's eyes," Darren said, lost in thought. "She wasn't afraid anymore. It's like she wasn't even there. She was already one of them. Every day I go down to the pits to see her, hoping for a sign of life in those dead eyes. Something, anything, that tells me she remembers me. I keep hoping that he is right, that she is with the Lord and that he can bring her back on Judgment Day, but I know now that's just a bedtime story they tell the small children. She's not coming back, not to her old life, not to the world of sin. I can't let that happen to another person. I can't bear that weight on my conscience."

"Why did he choose your wife?" I wasn't trying to be insensitive, but I wasn't sure I understood. I wanted to know everything I could before I faced him again.

"To keep me under control. I asked too many questions, challenged him. You see, I didn't think it was right that he had all those young brides. My wife didn't either. She got me riled up and I began to enjoy putting him on the spot in front of the others. I think I embarrassed him over it one too many times."

"And here I figured he didn't care what anyone thought," I said sarcastically.

"After her Harvest I stopped asking questions. I've blindly obeyed him until you came back into my life. I thought he was the Messiah, sent to save us all, but now I can see I was just a fool who wanted something to believe in."

Felicity kindly patted him on the arm and he hung his head.

I raced back as fast as I could without flipping the SUV in the narrow canyon curves. By the time I came around the corner, I could see a large crowd had gathered.

Darren was right, I thought.

Bryan wasn't wasting any time at all. We'd been gone less than thirty minutes and his diabolical plan was already well under way.

I drove the SUV right up and through the large crowd. People moved out of our way like drugged sheep as we approached the inner circle where Crowe was. I wondered if they were still feeling the effects of last night's revelry or if they had been freshly dosed again.

It makes sense, I thought. *It's not normal to kill a child. The only way he can get them to go along with it is to keep them loaded on the blood of the Lamb, whatever that concoction is. That way no one else's conscience gets in the way. Too bad he hadn't given a double dose to Darren. Maybe he was planning on drugging him too. Maybe that's why he ran away.*

"The cleansing ritual has already begun," Darren said, pointing to a small figure at Crowe's side.

Sure enough it was Benji, dressed in white robes, swaying back and forth. I slammed the car in park and jumped out with my sword ready to taste blood. Instantly a ring of armed guards surrounded Bryan. He didn't seem the least bit concerned.

So that's why they sent us out on a tour of the promised land earlier, I thought. *They were getting us out of the way while they prepared the sacrificial ritual.*

They could have slipped Benji something before we got back so he'd be ready. Bryan knew we wouldn't stay. He knew that one way or another I would leave. He'd been playing us since the moment we arrived, knowing he could pull Benji away from us. He was truly evil down to the core.

"What are you doing here?" Bryan glanced up and saw Darren slinking out of the car. "Ah, I see. Judas has brought you back to spread discord like a serpent in the garden."

"Let him go," I shouted, "or so help me I will cut your head off where you stand and throw your corpse to the zombies."

"You wouldn't make it three steps in my direction." He laughed. "You are in my world now. Mind your manners or I will make things more difficult for you than you can imagine."

"Benji! Benji get over here right now," Felicity called out to him, but he didn't move. I could see his eyes were large and nearly solid black. It was no use. They had already administered the sedative. He was so drugged out he didn't even know what was happening.

"It's too late for your friend," Bryan said. "He's already been cleansed and had his soul sent to God above. He was a very brave little boy. He will be missed, but we will see him again when the Lord returns. Amen."

The chorus of each loud, echoing amen was almost deafening. Were they mad? They were willing to kill an innocent kid to appease some false prophet? I wheeled around to see that many in the crowd had the same drugged look on their faces that Benji had. They weren't crazy, or not entirely. They were high.

"What did you give him?" I asked, fearing that he might be poisoned beyond saving.

"He drank from the blood of the Lamb," Bryan said. "His soul is now clean as the fresh white snow and at peace. He is ready for the Lord to receive him. When the moon reaches the peak of the sky, he will enter into the kingdom of heaven and take his place beside God at the throne."

"The hell he will," Felicity said, fighting her way through them then holding Benji. She looked frantic.

"You promised to take care of him," I shouted. "You lied to us in front of all these people just so you could do your sick ritual!"

"I know it appears that way, but you are wrong. It's been decided," Bryan boomed. "Just as Abraham was told by God to sacrifice his only son, just as God himself gave up his only child to save the sinful world, so too now must we offer up this child to protect ourselves from the children of the damned. It is out of my hands. There is no other way but his way. God's will be done."

"We're not going to let you take our friend and throw him into a pit of flesh eating zombies, pal."

"I don't see how you can stop me," he said in a smaller voice, so only the immediate circle could hear. "You are outnumbered in every way imaginable and we have the might of the one true God on our side."

"You will pay for this. If it is the last thing I do."

"If you are suggesting violence, again I assure you it will be the last thing that you do. Know that I am ready to die for my beliefs. I have nothing to hide from my God. Can you say that?"

"Nothing to hide?" I roared. "Except the murder of innocent people and your harem of child brides you mean?"

"This is pointless. Arguing with the damned about God's sacred laws is like pouring clean water into a dirty cup and expecting it to remain pure. You are obviously sent of the devil to disrupt a sacred ritual during a holy celebration. Either you leave immediately and never return or I will be forced to take matters into my own hands."

"It's against spiritual law to spill blood on this day," Darren shouted, stepping up to Bryan. "You said it yourself. Only they who are worthy to be received into the kingdom of God shall have their blood spilled on this sacred day."

"What's the policy on freeing the sacrifice and letting him leave with the people who love him?" Felicity hugged Benji to her.

"Once a sacrifice has been selected the ritual must proceed," Darren said.

"There," Bryan interrupted. "From the mouths of apostates come truths even he can't deny."

"However," Darren continued, "A volunteer may come forward to take their place. I didn't learn about that until after you took my wife from me. If I had known, I would be in that pit right now instead of her."

"She was chosen by God," Bryan hissed. "You should be so lucky."

"Then I volunteer," Felicity shouted.

Darren, Crowe, and I all spun around to her at the same time. In fact, she had the whole crowds' full attention.

"There has never been a volunteer before," Bryan mumbled, shocked by her words. "Do you fully understand what you are committing to, young lady?"

"I do. I will not just stand by while you kill him. He's my family now, whether he likes it or not."

"Fine. Release him and take her to the cleansing room to be prepared."

The guards immediately seized her.

"No!" I shouted, pushing my way forward.

"As for you," Bryan said, "you are to take him and leave at once. The devil and his minions are not welcome here. This is your final warning, or so help me God I will strike you down and make it another first during this sacred day."

"Darren," I shouted. "Do something!"

Darren looked sick to his stomach as he watched Felicity being pulled away. He seemed crippled with fear and unable to move. My mind began to race, trying to think of a way to save her. Every approach I considered seemed futile. Bryan Crowe was right. We were outnumbered. There was only one way to win her back. I would have to take her place.

I knew I could take on zombies in hand-to-hand combat, but not if I was drugged out. Maybe if I tried hard enough I could overcome the poison, or manage to spit it out. Either way, I had to do something. I couldn't just let them take Felicity away and kill her. I opened my mouth to speak but the words came out of Darren's lips instead of mine.

"I volunteer," he said. "I will take her place in the pit."

Bryan groaned. This was turning into much more of a hassle than he had imagined.

I was almost close enough to him now to make a move, but I knew his devoted followers would gladly take the impact of my blade in order to lay down their lives for their savior.

"No," Felicity said. "I can't let you."

"Are you sure?" Bryan asked, looking almost bored by now. "You won't be able to change your mind when she is gone, you know. Think about what you are doing, Darren."

"I should have done it long ago. I belong in the pit with my wife."

"Let her go," Bryan said, practically rolling his eyes.

Felicity ran forward and hugged Darren. "You are so brave. So amazingly, wonderfully, brave and stupid."

"It's the right thing to do," Darren said. "I knew what he was planning the minute you pulled into town. I should have said something before. I'm not brave. I'm a coward."

She silenced him with a long kiss that hushed the crowd. A twinge of jealousy shot through me at the sight, but I pushed it back.

The guy is sacrificing his life for her, I thought, *for all of us. The least he deserves is a goodbye kiss from his first love.*

Darren pulled back and smiled.

"I will never forget you," she said, staring into his eyes.

"I never did forget you. I love you. I always have and I always will."

"I love you too." A fresh round of tears burst out of her eyes. She hugged him tightly as he turned to me.

"Take good care of her," he said. "I want you all to have

a long, healthy life filled with happiness and joy. I'm paying the ultimate price for it."

"I will," I said, my mouth going dry at his words. "I promise."

"Time to go now." He pulled away from Felicity. "Don't worry. I won't feel a thing. I won't even know it happened."

Two guards led Darren off through the crowd to wherever Bryan did his purification ritual. I turned and glared at him.

"Well?" He glared back. "You got what you wanted. What are you waiting for?"

"Nothing," I spat.

Felicity grabbed Benji and led him to the car. I got behind the wheel and slowly began to back up and out of the crowd. They parted for us, leaving a wide circle to flip the car around. The last thing I saw as I looked back was Bryan's shark-like eyes glaring at us in utter contempt as we pulled away.

Felicity rode in the back with Benji, who looked very ill. He was sweating out the toxins of whatever they had given him. Even though it was warm in the car, he violently shivered every few seconds from head to toe.

"It's okay now," she cooed. "You are safe. Everything is going to be okay."

I pulled off the dirt road and back onto the highway out of town. I slammed my foot down to the floor and the car rapidly accelerated. Felicity didn't say a thing. If anyone decided to jump out in front of our car now, they were getting run over. One way or another I was getting the hell out of this town for good.

CHAPTER TWENTY TWO

The drive back to the 101 Freeway seemed far bumpier than the ride in. A cloud of black smoke rose off in the distance in the direction we were heading, and I hoped it wouldn't be something that was gonna slow us down. I wanted to get to the base as soon as I could and have Benji looked at by medics. He seemed to be coming around some as we drove on, but I couldn't be sure how much they'd given him or how it was affecting his circulation.

Felicity cradled his head in her lap and silently cried. I wasn't about to try to comfort her after what had just happened. What could I say? I just felt lucky to have escaped with my friends and my life. That unexpected confession and kiss we shared up on the ridge was still floating around the edge of my consciousness, but it was slightly tainted now by everything else that had happened.

Benji let out a moan and writhed around. Felicity looked up at me with concern.

"Hang in there, buddy," I said. "We'll be there soon."

We connected onto the 101 and headed south without incident. As we drove through the remains of Ventura, I couldn't help but think how much it looked like a Hollywood movie set for the end of the world. Like the kind you might see on a back lot tour of Universal Studios — only there were real dead bodies everywhere. Smashed cars littered the road. There were so many I had to slow down to maneuver through them. At one point I had to push a car out of the way with my front bumper.

Benji sat up. "What's happening?" He looked groggy, but otherwise okay.

"We're passing through what's left of Ventura," I said. "Just pushing some scrap metal out of the road to get through. How you feeling?"

"My head hurts." He moaned. "And I am really thirsty."

"That sounds about right. We've got plenty of water. Go ahead and crack open a bottle."

Felicity was already on it. She reached back behind the seat and brought out a couple of water bottles, unscrewing the lid of one and handing it to him. Benji gulped it down as fast as he could and moved on to a second bottle.

"What's the last thing you remember?" Felicity asked.

"I'm not sure. It was all like a dream."

"Try to think," I urged him on. "Did they give you something?"

"That's just it. I don't remember taking anything. One minute I was watching you drive off, and the next thing I knew everyone was gathering around Bryan and me and crying and praying. I started to feel kinda funny, like my head wasn't really attached to my body. My heart felt full of love, like it could burst out of my chest, you know? For a moment I thought maybe I had caught the holy spirit they are always talking about."

"They must have slipped it to you before we left," I butted in.

"Go on," Felicity cooed. "What happened then?"

"I can only remember parts. I was in a big white room. They kept giving me some kind of sour grape juice to drink while I was changing into these." He gestured to his homemade sacrificial outfit.

"How much did you drink, buddy?" I needed to know he wasn't going to fall over and die on us. Even though he was talking, he still looked pretty sick.

"Not much," he said. "It tasted funny. They kept telling me to drink but I'd only take small sips."

"What else did they tell you?"

"They said I was going to a place where there was no more pain or suffering. I remember that because they said my family would be waiting for me there. One of the girls was singing some hymn and crying, but it didn't seem weird. Her tears were glistening on her face like she was an angel. That's the last thing I remember, other than waking up here. What happened?"

"They were going to kill you," Felicity said. "They wanted to sacrifice you to the zombies for some religious ceremony. They were trying to get us out of the way so we wouldn't interfere."

That seemed to sober him up a bit. He sat up and stared at her.

"What happened? How did I escape?"

"She saved your life," I said. "Felicity offered to take your place. She was ready to die for you, but in the end they settled for one of their own instead."

Benji turned and gaped at Felicity.

"Why?"

"Because," she said. "We're family now. I couldn't let them hurt my little brother."

"I am really glad we met you," he said.

"Me too, kiddo."

She kissed him on the forehead again. Benji looked past me out the front windshield. He pointed off in the distance.

"What is that?"

"I don't know," I said. "Looks like some kind of fire."

We came around the corner and the Pacific Ocean burst into view. The Ventura pier was completely on fire. I didn't even know how that was possible. It was eerily beautiful in a post-apocalyptic way. We marveled at it in silent wonder.

Just past the pier we ran into a full flock of zombies ambling across the freeway in search of food. They looked like a herd of cows that had wandered from a field to block traffic, but in this case they most likely wandered onto the interstate to find and eat drivers in stalled cars.

"Lock the doors," I yelled.

"They are locked," Felicity hollered back.

"Good." I calmed down. "Then buckle up and hold on. We may have to hit a few to get past."

"Be careful," she cautioned.

I didn't want to slow down but I knew from firsthand experience that speeding up could be disastrous. The zombies would not get out of the way. We were going to have to hit them to get through. The last thing we needed was to be stalled out in a zombie horde with no way to escape.

"What's the plan here?" Felicity asked.

"Drive straight through," I said, nudging the car forward.

Instantly they were on us. The zombies surrounded all sides of the car and began beating their fists against the windows. Either this batch of the dead were smarter than the rest or they were starting to learn to work together. The car rocked back and forth and Benji began to freak out.

"I don't want to die!" he screamed at the top of his lungs.

"We're not going to die out here," I said, giving the car some gas and running down a couple of flesh hungry monsters in the process. "Just relax."

The words were barely out of my mouth when a big man in a tattered blue Mammoth Mountain hoodie punched through the window and grabbed Benji by the arm. We all screamed at the same time. There was shattered glass all over the backseat. I tried to turn around and hit the man but my seat belt kept me locked in place.

Now that would be an ironic way to die, I thought. *Trapped in a car by a seat belt. I thought these things were supposed to save lives.*

Felicity began beating the man in the head as he tried to pull his weight up and into the car to get a bite of either of them. I hit the seat belt release and swung around, punching the man square on the top of the head and driving him out of the car.

"Get us the hell out of here!" Felicity screamed.

I slid back down in the driver's seat and hit the gas. We accelerated hard and ran over several zombies in a row. They made loud thumping sounds as their upper torsos slammed into the hood, in one case denting it. I could feel the tires going over the ones we'd hit, like large and gruesome speed bumps. Up ahead to the left there was a break in the horde. I turned the wheel and floored it that way. A woman's arm hit the side of the windshield, causing it to crack into a brilliant spider web of broken glass.

We were free again. The road ahead was not obstructed. I looked in the rearview mirror, expecting to see a line of carnage we'd cut across the horde. Instead they had just reformed and began slowly lumbering after us.

"Is everyone okay?" I asked. "Anyone bit or injured?"

"We're fine," Felicity said in a shaky voice. "That was close."

"What about you Benji?"

"I'm fine," he said. "He grabbed me but he didn't get a chance to bite me. Man, he smelled horrible. I can still smell it."

"Good. I'm glad we're all in one piece."

"That was rough," Felicity admitted.

"You look like you sobered up a bit," I said to Benji.

"Yeah. I'm just hungry now."

"Don't worry. It looks like we're almost in Oxnard now. We'll stop up here in a bit and make some of that space-age grub that we brought with us from Jackson's place. I'm personally looking forward to trying some exotic cuisine."

"So close to the base?" Felicity seemed shocked by my plan.

"They'll take everything once we get there," Benji explained. "At Vandenberg the only thing they left me were my comics."

"That's right," I said in my best old timers panhandler

impression I could muster. "And I've been dreaming about them there fancy pancakes since yesterday."

Felicity and Benji's laughter was cut short by the sound of several hard thuds hitting the side of the car.

"What the hell was that?" Felicity managed to get the question out just as the answer came.

Several men dressed like rogue warriors from a Mad Max movie came running out onto the highway, pointing weapons at us and firing. They hit the side of the car again. The air was filled with the sound of metal pinging on metal and then the passenger side window shattered and sprayed me with glass. I shook my head to free the loose shards from my hair.

"Get down!" I hollered.

A man with a bright pink Mohawk, wearing dusty outdated military gear, ran out in front of the car. In his hands he carried a bow and arrow. He raised them up and took aim directly at me. There was no time to swerve and I worried I might flip the car. I slid down in my seat and punched the gas pedal hard. I could hear the man's legs crack as the front of the Lexus slammed into him. He screamed in agony and flew over the top of the car, but I didn't stop.

Steam poured up from the radiator. The temperature gauge began to rise. The check engine light went on. Worst of all, the fuel gauge began to fall. I didn't know if we were really leaking gas or if we'd just damaged the sensor in some way. Either way, it looked like we were going to have to abandon the car sooner than I thought.

"Damn," I yelled. "We're not gonna make it. We were so close!" I punched the steering wheel in anger.

"Who are those people?" Felicity asked.

"I don't know," I said, feeling the panic rise up in me. "But I am guessing they're not friendly."

"What are we gonna do?" Benji asked.

"I've got to get us off the freeway. We're leaking fuel and we need to find cover in case they track us."

"Won't the zombie horde take them out?" Felicity asked.

"We can't count on that, but I sure hope so."

I saw a place in the road where it came level with the city streets and I jumped the barrier, popping the back left tire in the process.

"Hold on," I screamed as the car shot like a bullet over the succulent covered divider and onto the asphalt. Sparks flew out from the back of the Lexus like Fourth of July fireworks as the rim hit the ground.

"I thought you said we were leaking gas," Felicity shouted over the sound of rushing wind coming through the smashed windows.

"I'm pretty sure we are," I said, doing my best to keep the car under control as I rammed up and over another curb and into a mall parking lot.

"Oh my God," Felicity wailed.

"What?"

"The car is on fire!"

I looked in the rearview mirror but couldn't see it. My first thought was that we were going to explode, like when a car is hit in the movies. I slammed on the brakes and the car skidded to a stop, wrapping around the concrete base of a light fixture near the entrance to Macy's. I turned around to find Felicity and Benji huddled together in the back, waiting for the explosion.

"Don't just sit there," I shouted. "Get out now!"

They yanked open the door on the side that wasn't smashed into a pole and scurried out. I threw mine open, grabbed my katana, and bolted.

My head hurt and I was feeling slightly disoriented and dizzy. Something warm and sticky ran down my face. I reached up and discovered it stung when I touched the top of my head. I stared at my hand when I saw it was covered with blood.

You must have smashed your head into the windshield in the accident, I thought. *It's not going to kill you but whoever those people are might. Plus there could be zombies out here. You've got to stay calm and find cover. Whatever you do, you have to stay awake and not panic.*

My little motivational pep talk was working. I motioned for Felicity and Benji to join me.

Felicity held her hands over her mouth when she saw me.

"Are you okay?"

"I'm fine," I lied. "It's just a scratch. We've got to keep moving."

"What about the car?" Benji asked. "All our supplies are in there."

"The car is done. It's just a matter of minutes before it goes up in flames, leading those people to us and probably another horde of zombies as well."

"What are we supposed to do?" Felicity asked. "We can't just go on foot."

"For now, it's our only option," I argued. "We're pretty close now to the base. I say we cut across the mall and head toward the coast. We can use it as a guide to make sure we stay on course. If we keep walking, we'll reach Hueneme before sundown."

"You want to go in there?" Felicity asked. "How do we know it's not crawling with zombies?"

"We don't. It's just that out here in plain sight we're sitting ducks for whoever those crazy maniacs are that attacked us."

"Are you sure you're okay?" Felicity asked, touching my face. "I'm not sure you're supposed to move after an accident like that. You might have a concussion."

"I think it's okay as long as I don't go to sleep right away."

She leaned in and kissed me.

"Guys," Benji said. "I think I see someone coming."

I looked past Felicity to see a cluster of men in the distance walking on the highway. These weren't zombies. They were hunters, coming to get us and have their revenge for their fallen comrade, no doubt.

"Let's move." I drew my sword.

Benji practically sprinted past me and Felicity followed him.

There was tenderness in my right ankle as well. I didn't notice it until I began the walk up the mostly empty parking lot toward the front entrance.

Please let the doors be open, I thought. If they were operated by electricity, or locked up and we had to go the long way round, we were goners for sure.

Benji reached the front first and waited for me. A pane of glass had been removed cleanly from the store window, letting us freely step in. I poked my head inside, half expecting to get it chomped by a hungry zombie, but the store was empty of people as far as I could see.

"Stick together." I turned to Benji. "Whatever happens, I don't want you running off unless I say so. Got it?"

"I got it, boss man."

We climbed in, sliding past a rack of dresses as I glanced back toward the abandoned Lexus. The cluster of hunters was getting closer. They were definitely coming for us.

CHAPTER TWENTY THREE

We made our way through the department store, walking up a frozen escalator and out into the main part of the mall, without spotting a single zombie. As far as I could tell the place hadn't been infested with the dead. There were none of the telltale signs--no blood, no human remains strewn about, no smell of rotting death and decay. It seemed totally impossible, but the mall was clean. The stores were all open, but shrouded in darkness.

Above us a clear panel skylight allowed rays of the sun to illuminate our path. Birds flapped around over our heads, going back and forth between stores on the second level. My stomach growled as we marched past the food court toward an exit on the other side of the mall, passing a Wetzel's Pretzel.

That's just what I needed to see, I thought. *I'm freaking starving.* I'd have killed a hundred zombies for a pretzel right then and there and stacked the bodies into neat piles for our not so friendly new friends.

"Can't we stop and check to see if there is anything edible?" Benji was as hungry as I was. Maybe more since he'd just come down from drinking the blood of the Lamb.

"There's no electricity," I said. "Which means the food's all spoiled anyway. Besides, if we did find anything we'd have to prepare it. We've got hunters on our trail. We don't have time to stop and cook."

"The smell would lead them right to us," Felicity added in a soft voice.

"She's right," I said. "Our best hope is to head to the coast like I said and hope we lose them along the way. For now we've got to at least stay ahead of them."

"We can't go forever without eating," Benji pouted.

What's wrong with this kid, I thought? *We're being hunted down like wild animals and he is crying about missing his juice box at snack time?*

Benji was usually pretty easy going. I chalked it up to the trauma of the accident and being grabbed by that big zombie. That would be enough to freak anyone out. Still, I hoped he would get it together and not slow us down. Everyone needed to stay focused if we were going to make it out alive and together.

"We'll find food along the way," I said.

"What if we don't?"

"We will. Worst case scenario, we eat at the base. Now stop arguing and hurry up."

Benji scowled at me. I had become the mean parent. I guess someone had to play the role but that didn't mean I had to be happy about it.

"Come on," I said. "I don't want to argue about this all day."

I heard a high pitch whistle hum through the air to my left side.

"Xander?" Felicity's voice sounded off, like she was fighting back tears. I turned in surprise to see an arrow sticking out of her right arm.

"What the hell?"

I walked over and looked at it. It had pierced all the way through the skin under the bone and out the other side. Bright red drops of blood dripped from the barbed tip. I heard another whistle zing right past me before I could comprehend what had happened to her. The second arrow skidded off the shiny stone floor next to me, clattering across the tiles. I looked off in the direction the weapon had come from to see one of the hunters stringing up a third arrow. He smiled at us with black teeth.

"What do we do?" Felicity looked at me with big pleading eyes.

"Run," I yelled, drawing my sword and holding it out in front of me. Benji and Felicity turned and bolted for the sliding doors at the end of the mall.

The third arrow whirred directly toward my head. I brought my blade up as I ducked and knocked it into a planter between the Orange Julius and Hot Dog on a Stick.

The bowman crouched down to reload just as his buddies came tearing in from the darkness of the department store with their guns drawn.

Arrows are one thing, I thought, *but there is no way I'm gonna be able to dodge a bullet.*

I turned and ran toward the exit as fast as I could. The sound of gun shots rang out like loud thunder. I didn't stop. I couldn't. My lungs burned as I pumped my legs up and down as fast as they would take me until I reached the others.

Benji and Felicity were trying desperately to pry open the heavy glass doors, but with no luck. I joined in on Benji's side, managing to get them open about an inch. Felicity let out a shrill cry of pain and let go, clutching her wounded arm.

I looked back toward our enemies. They were advancing with their weapons drawn. We were trapped! They fired again and the bullets hit the glass to the left of us. Felicity quivered in fear and slumped down to the floor.

"Are you hit?" I asked, but she didn't answer. "I said, are you hit?" She shook her head no, unable to speak. She was quivering from head to toe.

She's probably going into shock, I thought, *from the wound the arrow made. Hell, it's still sticking out of her!*

They were less than a hundred feet away now. At this range, their aim was sure to improve.

"We're going to die in here," Benji cried. "Do

something!"

I turned back to the doors and began to pull with everything I had in me. Benji joined me and the door began to slowly roll back. I could feel all the muscles in my arms and chest burning.

Don't stop, I told myself. *They are depending on you. All of our lives count on it. Pull harder!*

I gave out a cry and yanked the doors open a bit more. My arms felt like stretched rubber left out in the hot sun. The muscles were giving out and I was losing my grip.

Another shot rang out and hit the glass mere inches from my head. *I am not going to die like this. I can't! Not after everything we have been through. Not without saying goodbye to Moto.*

I stepped between the doors, propping my legs against one side with my back against the other. The doors came open, but the pain in my back and legs was almost unbearable.

"Go," I yelled in a hoarse voice. "Go NOW!"

Felicity crawled through and Benji followed her.

I turned to see them standing on the sidewalk staring at me.

"Come on," Benji yelled, trying to pull me through with both hands.

I gave the doors one last push and fell through. A chorus of gunfire erupted from inside the mall as the hunters screamed and wailed at our escape. Several of the shots made it out through the small crack before the doors closed and fully shielded us.

Miraculously, we weren't hit. My whole body ached and I panted like a wounded animal as I stood back up on trembling, unsteady legs. The hunters pounded on the glass but didn't try to pull the doors open.

"That's odd," I said. "Why aren't they following us?"

Benji frantically tugged at my arm. I turned around to see the reason why we'd been left alone. A small crowd of about a hundred zombies had begun to wander toward us from across the parking lot. The familiar sound of their unearthly moans and horrible stench reached me at the same time. I fought back my desire to vomit as a breeze sent a wave of decomposing stench over us.

"This is bad," Felicity said. "We're trapped. What do we do?"

"Get behind me," I said, holding up my blade. "We're going to cut a path to freedom."

"That's insane," Benji cried.

"We'll never make it," Felicity added.

"We've got no other choice," I replied, letting out a war cry and charging at the ones closest to us. With a flash of my blade I took off a fat zombie's head, kicking his rotting body over. It felt like stepping in putty, but I didn't slow down. Without missing a beat, I brought the sword back across my body to the right with all the force I could manage and took off another zombie's head with a clean sweep. The rest of the zombie horde didn't seem to notice my bloodthirsty rampage. They just stepped over their fallen friends and kept coming at us like the mindless killing machines they were.

Swinging in a wild circle, I sliced my way through another, then punched a thin zombie out of my way before freeing my blade from the last victims chest. Dark coagulated blood oozed from the tip of my sword like an oily film of dead pulp. I shook it off and drove the weapon back through the neck of a screeching woman who lunged for me, nearly knocking me over. There were more of them than I had realized. They were reaching me too fast and I was taking too long to kill them. Benji and Felicity were right. This wasn't going to work. There was no way I was going to be able to fight them all off.

"Xander look out," Felicity cried as a thickly built male zombie snapped at me teeth first like a rabid dog.

I leaned back just out of his bite radius and felt the horrible chill of his cold breath on my face. He looked like he had been a body builder before being turned, and I was dismayed to discover that he still had the strength of one as he gripped me by the throat and began to squeeze the life out of me, raising me completely off the ground with my feet kicking at the air. I beat my left fist helplessly into his chest to no avail as stars popped in my field of vision.

Felicity screamed at the top of her lungs. I prayed the rest of the horde hadn't already moved past me and gotten to them. My right arm flailed wildly with my sword still in hand, but I wasn't able to make a dent in the monster even by hacking chunks of flesh from his back. He pulled me forward toward his open mouth, preparing to tear off the front of my face.

In a last ditch effort I jerked my right arm upward, lodging the sword into his head. I felt his grip loosen but he didn't relent. He was still making every effort to eat me alive. With all the strength I had left in my already sore muscles, I forced the end of the sword handle down until the blade slowly sliced up and through his brain, removing half of his head and exposing rotten gray matter and more oily black blood in the process. He let me go and fell over with an unsatisfying grunt. I fell to one knee, gingerly touching my neck and gulping in air as fast as I could. I was dizzy but I forced myself back to my feet to continue to fight.

"Come on!" I screamed. "Is that all you've got?" Adrenaline pumped through me as I stood back up. I was ready to die fighting but I was going to take down every last one of these creatures before I did.

"Xander, look," Felicity said as she pointed to the middle of the horde.

A flash of light drew my vision off to the right and I turned to see the strangest thing I'd ever witnessed in my whole life. The zombies turned back on a man who was walking among them. He calmly swung two objects that seemed to be made entirely out of reflected light in a blur around his body. The horde seemed so captivated by him, they had forgotten all about us.

His face was painted like an Indian warrior and he had

several crows feathers tucked into his hair. His expression was a mask of calm resolve. He wore a thin layer of chainmail over his upper torso and head and protective metal armor from the waist down to his metallic boots. Light reflected off his mirror polished armor as well as whatever he was using for weapons, giving him the impression that he was glowing almost from head to toe.

I thought of the pictures Moto had once shown me of Shaolin warrior monks.

How is he doing that? I wondered to myself. *It's like he's somehow able to communicate with them.*

The zombies would turn to attack him then stumble back, looking confused and disoriented. Whoever he was, he calmly moved through them like he was taking a stroll through the park on a lazy Sunday afternoon. He might as well have been walking on water as far as I was concerned. He was headed right for us but I didn't feel any fear. Instead, an indescribable calm began to settle over me at the sight of him, like for the first time in forever everything was going to be all right.

"On your right," Benji called out.

I turned to look at him, confused by everything that was happening as I felt a sharp pain shoot through my right side. Something cold clamped down onto my skin. Glancing down I saw a small zombie boy in a blue and yellow striped shirt had latched his dirty mouth onto my stomach. With a sharp strike from my elbow I dislodged him, then swung around and took his head clean off. I watched the expression go blank on his kid zombie face as his lifeless head rolled to a stop at the curb and his small corpse fell over flat.

My hand shook as I touched the wound and saw bright red blood forming. I'd been bitten! I heard Felicity yelling something at me but I couldn't make out what it was. There was a loud ringing in my ears and I could feel my heart beating hard in my chest. I started to feel woozy. My legs wobbled beneath me as they gave way. The last thing I remembered was the ground rushing up to meet me and then seeing a big burst of light.

***

When I opened my eyes again, I was lying on my back looking up at the inside of a canvass tent with a hole that went straight up into the sky. The brown skinned man with the bird feathers in his hair and black paint on his face worked over a fire nearby, boiling water.

After rolling my head to the side, I found my sword lying next to his two huge shiny knives. My reflection was clearly visible in them. I could tell I was in deep trouble with a single glance. My skin was already turning a yellowish green to match the bile rising up from my stomach, and my forehead was beaded with feverish sweat as my body tried to fight off the killer infection. I touched my side where I had been bitten and winced with pain.

"Awake to the dream of reality," the man said with a smile.

"Who are you?"

"I'm called many things by many different people. It all depends on how they see me or what they need from me."

"I don't need anything from you." I tried to sit up but fell over in agony.

"We all need something from each other. Life is by its very nature interdependent. You can call me Simon if you like. You've more than earned the right.

"Where am I?"

"Paradise City."

"I thought we were in Oxnard."

"That's what it used to be called," he explained. "Before things fell apart. There isn't much that remains as it once used to be." He had a cryptic way of talking, as if everything he said was a riddle or Zen koan waiting to be unraveled. My head throbbed and I tried not to think about it.

"Who were those people hunting us?" I was already starting to feel feverish.

"Cannibals. They would have eaten you all if they could

have caught you. Turned your organs into soup and your flesh into strips of jerky."

"Just like zombies," I said, attempting an ironic smile.

"Worse. Zombies don't have free will, while the cannibals know exactly what they are doing and just don't care. There aren't many people left out here. Almost everybody is a zombie. Cannibals track passing traffic on the freeway to trap fresh victims. I saw your car hit that pole in the parking lot from my little hill up here and knew you were in big trouble, so I headed down. I figured if you had any sense at all you'd cut through the mall and head west."

Despite my state I took his words as the compliment they were intended to be. It felt good to know I'd been right, even if it had cost me my life. None of that mattered as long as the others were safe.

Panic shot through me as I realized I didn't know what had become of them. *What if the zombies had eaten them?* I couldn't go to my grave without knowing, and judging from the way I felt I knew I didn't have long until I changed.

"Where are my friends?" I asked, confused. I tried to sit up but didn't have the strength. It felt like a boulder had been dropped on my chest.

"They are outside, waiting," he said. "You were very brave. You saved their lives."

"I was very stupid. I'm paying the price for it now." The realization that I was going to become one of those flesh eating monsters wasn't fully kicking in. It was just more than I could handle at the moment.

"I don't think so," he countered. "Your brother will be very proud of you."

"How do you know my brother?" I lifted my head, straining to look at him.

"Moto is a friend. That's more than I can say for the rest of his tribe. He will be pleased to learn his little brother has become a fierce warrior. He's been looking for you since news reached him about Vandenberg. He left me a walkie to contact him if you came this way. He said you would make it. That you were strong and would find your way to the base. Turns out he was right."

"It's too late," I said. "I've been bitten."

"Don't worry," Simon said. "He will be here soon. He was very excited to hear you were still alive."

"I'm dying." I fought to stay awake. "By the time he gets here he'll more than likely have to chop off my head."

"I wouldn't be so sure. Things are not always as they appear in this world. Nor are they otherwise."

"I saw you," I said, ignoring his brain twister. "You were walking right through a crowd of zombies but they moved out of your way. It was a miracle, like parting water with your bare hands. How did you do that?"

"It's a long story," he said with a pleasant smile that made me feel calm and at ease. "The short answer is by controlling my breathing. I've spent years learning how to lower my heart rate through meditation. It helps me to move calmly among them without drawing attention to myself. Usually I don't have to raise my weapons at all. Today required I move with greater speed than normal, hence the light display. Forgive me if it seemed vain. It was not without purpose, I assure you."

"I thought zombies were attracted to movement," I said.

"If that is true, then why don't they attack each other?"

"I don't know. I always assumed they came after us because we smelled alive, like food."

"They are driven by hunger. Like all predators, they use their senses to search out victims. Most people panic when they see them, causing their heart rates to skyrocket and their skin to sweat. Just like a dog can smell fear, so too can the undead sense our repulsion of them. Add to that the fact that most people scream or wave their arms and run around like chickens with their heads cut off, and it's no wonder they zero in on us as if they had heat seeking technology."

"So you're saying if I stood perfectly still in the middle of a zombie horde I wouldn't have been bitten?"

I thought about Joel and Tom's story of hiding under the

dead soldiers as the zombies passed by them.

"I can't say that for sure," he admitted. "What I can tell you is that I have been walking with them in a trance-like state on many occasions and have not been attacked."

"How do you remain calm when you know they can turn on you at any moment and rip you to shreds? How is that possible?"

"You have to learn to change the way you see the world. When you view them with compassion, your fear is transformed into sympathy. These were people once, just like you and me. They had hopes and dreams, families, loved ones. Just like you and me they wanted more happiness and less suffering in their lives. They had plans for the future. Now they are eternally damned to wander the earth with a terrible hunger that cannot be fulfilled, reviled as monsters. It's heartbreaking in every way imaginable."

"I'm glad you are so sympathetic," I said. "Considering I will shortly be one of them. But I still think you should cut my head off the minute I change. I don't want to be responsible for killing anyone."

"You're going to be just fine." He opened his hand and revealed two blue pills. "Your friend Felicity told me to give you these. She said she took them from your pocket in Ojai. She told me to tell you not to be mad at her."

So she stole the pills back from me! I wasn't mad at her. A pang of sadness shot through me knowing that I would never get to kiss her again, that the moment we shared up on the hill was the best we would ever have together.

I raised my head and he placed them in my mouth. He took a bottle of water from the ground and placed it to my lips. It felt cool and refreshing. I gulped down as much as I could.

"How is she?" I asked. "How is her arm?"

"I managed to take the arrow out and clean the wound," he told me. "She's going to be just fine. The shaft went almost clean through. She is very lucky it only hit her arm."

The pain in my body was growing. It spread across my

entire chest, radiating out from the wound in my side and even ran down my legs. I panted steadily to relieve some of the agony, trying to breathe it away.

"I'm going to need you to listen to me," Simon said. "An antidote is on its way, but for now we're going to want to slow down the spread of the virus. The pills will help calm you but I want you to work on your breathing with me. Got it?"

"Yes," I managed. The pain was growing exponentially now. I could feel it in my toes and finger tips.

"Remember what I told you about controlling my heart rate with meditation?"

I nodded in reply, too sick to answer. My throat felt dry like hot sand at the beach.

"We're going to slow yours down now too. I want you to close your eyes but concentrate on the sound of my voice."

I closed my eyes without argument.

"That's good. Now I want you to focus on your breath as it moves in and out of your body. Don't try to control it. Just become aware of it. When thoughts arise, resist the temptation to follow them. Instead, gently push them aside and return your concentration to the breath."

I did as he said and immediately began to relax. The pain was still there, but I wasn't fighting against it now so its effect on me didn't seem as overwhelming.

"Think of your mind as a vast blue sky without end and your thoughts like white, fluffy clouds. They don't come from anywhere and they don't go anywhere. When the causes and conditions are right, clouds appear. Don't follow the clouds but return to the calm, peaceful blue of your mind."

He kept talking in a soothing voice that lured me deeper into a state of total relaxation, but I stopped focusing on the meaning of what he was saying. A calm rose in me, overriding the pain that was consuming my entire body. I surrendered to it completely and let it take me where it wanted me to go. I felt my spirit mix with the blue of my mind, like water poured into water as everything I knew faded away into emptiness.

CHAPTER TWENTY FOUR

For a while I wandered, dead and disembodied, through a collage of memories from my childhood. I saw Mrs. Sanders, my kind third grade teacher, watering flowers in her garden. She stopped to wave as I went by. She looked the same as she did when I was a kid. The fact that she had been dead over a decade gave me further conviction that I had passed away.

So this is heaven, I thought. *Strange. I expected something else, like clouds or angels playing harps or Morgan Freeman in a white suit telling me he was proud of me.* Instead I was drifting past a river of soothing memories filled with people I had once known and loved who had passed before me. More than anything I wanted to stop and talk to them, to find out what they knew, not just about this afterlife but about what had happened in the place that I had come from. What I wanted didn't really seem to matter.

The river slowly pulled me onward, past my best childhood friend Doug's mom Cindy, who had died of leukemia, and Sally, the girl I asked to prom who later died in a car accident while texting, and Jim, my brother's friend who had been killed in action in Afghanistan. I saw the Parker twins off in the distance, chasing after fallen soldiers I'd known at the base. Joel ignored me but Tom turned from over a hundred feet away and smiled. He waved then darted off.

What about your mother? I thought to myself. *Where is she?* No sooner did I think it than her smiling face appeared.

"Oh son," she said, her voice like ringing crystal wind chimes. "I am so proud of you. I love you so much."

"I love you too, Mom," I managed before she melted away. "I miss you so much."

The whole world became a blur of shifting blue shapes: hexagons and trapezoids and rectangles formed and crashed into one another in a dizzying array of fractal patterns, like a kaleidoscope. My mind tried desperately to attach itself to these forms, but it disconnected as the colors came together and crashed apart like waves in a turbulent storm. I could hear voices gathered around me but I couldn't make out the words they were saying. Every now and then a sentence would get through.

"You're going to feel a pinch and then the burning will stop," someone said as a sharp pain shot through me followed by hard pressure. Almost immediately I felt a soothing sensation like being bathed in cold ice water. I began to shiver all over.

"Try to relax," Simon said, his words transforming into a living jelly that wriggled across my skin and made me laugh. Warmth returned to my bodiless form like a ray of sunlight penetrating my heart. I felt like I was falling through a vast and endless blue sky, but I wasn't afraid. Nothing mattered anymore.

Then the ground came rushing up toward me and I landed in a soft foam of sand. A ripple ran off from where I touched down, in every direction as far as the eye could see. I was in a desert and my body was normal again.

"Where am I?" The words came out of my skin like an exhaled breath.

"Nowhere," the sky answered back.

"Everywhere," the echo replied.

Round red bubbles began to form at my feet from out of the sand. I leaned over and picked one up. It looked like a shiny red pool table ball. I put it in my mouth and felt its smoothness on my tongue. It tasted like chlorine and bubble gum and Tuesday afternoons. I didn't know how that was even possible.

"The world is nothing more than a child's dream," a voice said. It seemed to come from all around me at once, from the sky and the cactus and the bubbles popping at my feet.

"How do I get home?" I asked.

"Everywhere is possible if you desire it enough," the voice sang, revealing a shimmering trail in the sand that seemed to lead off to the horizon. I put down the red bubble ball and began to follow the trail, feeling light and calm. "Every when is possible too."

I walked for what seemed like days, coming across an old chair at one point, a singing grandfather clock, and a book with no words that spoke in riddles when you cracked it open. Each time I reached the ridge of a sand dune, I was back where I had started.

Days passed. When I was hungry, delicious food appeared. When I was thirsty, the sky parted and poured sweet juice into my open mouth. I never saw another soul. I just kept walking and talking to myself and the voice in the sky.

Finally, after what felt like months, the desert began to fade away behind me, sand whooshing past in fluffy white blurs, leaving clean white walls. I sat up and stared at my brother Moto dressed in his military gear. He was as real and solid as anything I had ever seen, smiling down at me with kind brown eyes.

"Welcome back, solider," he said.

CHAPTER TWENTY FIVE

"This is a dream," I said. "It has to be. I'm dead."

"No," he said, nodding his head side-to-side but still smiling. "You're not. Sorry to be the one to break the bad news to you. You're going to be just fine."

"I was bitten by a zombie." I shook my head in disbelief. "You don't come back from that. Do you?"

I reached down and pulled up my shirt, finding I had gauze taped to my ribs. I ripped it back, not expecting to be as painful as it was. It made me wince and close my eyes as I let out a gasp. When the pain subsided, I took a good look at the wound. A crescent shape bite mark the size of a small child's mouth perforated the flesh of my abdomen just below my rib cage, but it had scabbed all the way over. To the casual observer it might have looked like I got tangled up in something, or was peppered with broken shards of glass in a fight.

"You see?" Moto pointed to the wound. "It's almost healed already."

Despite my mind arguing that it wasn't possible, the evidence showed he was right. The injury was now nothing more than a tiny island chain of hardened blood ringed by puffy, pink flesh. It appeared to be no more life threatening than a cat scratch.

"In no time at all you'll be as good as new," Moto assured me. "Which is first-rate! I've got a lot to tell you.

Gotta get you caught up to speed."

"How is this possible?" I was still having a hard time wrapping my head around the fact that I wasn't one of the living dead.

"Apache radioed to us," my brother told me. "We got there as fast as we could."

"He said you'd been looking for me?"

"I sent choppers up to Vandenberg after I found out. There were no survivors. None of the deceased matched your description. I knew you'd make it out. I believed it in the pit of my stomach. It's been all that's kept me going since. The thought of seeing you again. You have no idea how happy I was to hear from Apache."

I thought about the black helicopters that passed over us when we were on the road to New Lompoc. How different would things have been if Benji and I had stayed near the base?

"He told me that you had been asleep for about five minutes," Moto continued. "We administered the antidote before moving you so we wouldn't lose any time."

"Did you just say *antidote*?" My head was spinning. "Does that mean that the outbreak was caused by a virus?"

"Yes. We know that now for sure. We even know who created it. It was one of our guys, not some terrorist attack like we originally suspected. What we don't know is how it got out. We are still working on that."

So much for Felicity's fast food theory, I thought. Not that I would be having Arby's any time in the near future, the way things were going.

"So there is a cure for it?"

"Yes and no," he said, looking around the room nervously. He glanced up and over my head, holding his gaze on something for several seconds before returning them to me. "It's complicated."

I turned and saw he was looking at a camera with a red flashing light on top. I had been so out of it, I hadn't seen that there were several cameras recording our conversation.

"If there is a cure then why are there still zombies?" I wasn't trying to be difficult or ungrateful. I really wanted to understand. "Why can't we just give a dose to everyone that's been infected and end this whole nightmare?"

Moto sighed and rubbed his temples. "First of all, there wouldn't be enough of the antidote to save everyone. It's not easy to make. Many of the ingredients were hard to come by before Z-Day. Now they are virtually impossible to get."

"Like what?"

"Spider venom for one," Moto said. "One of the side effects of a bite from a brown recluse is that the tissue around the wound dies. Doctors have to cut the dead skin and tissue away from the wound, and a lot of times people end up needing plastic surgery to cover the nasty looking scar. The way in which the healthy cells go necrotic is similar to the way the zombie virus functions, in part. There are a lot of parallels. So we figured out how to isolate the chemical that does that and reverse engineer it as part of the antidote. The problem is that it requires plenty of actual spider venom—or an equally rare synthetic compound that takes weeks to yield small batches of under absolutely perfect lab conditions."

"Let me get this straight," I said, "you're saying that I'm gonna be like Spiderman now?"

Benji is going to be so jealous, I thought.

"Will I have super human strength and be able to swing through the air and shoot webs to slow bad guys down?"

"Not that I've ever seen," he said. "But you've always had a supernatural ability to annoy people. Looks like you've retained it. That should come in handy around the base. Really help you win new friends over."

Moto grinned from ear to ear as he teased me. Things were getting back to normal in some small way. It felt good to have my brother back, even if he was reminding me of what a bossy know-it-all he usually was.

"And you've kept your killer sense of humor," I fired back.

"That's just one part of the recipe," Moto finished his explanation. "There are a ton of very complicated steps that go into creating the cocktail. The vast majority of the ingredients are as dangerous to use as they are to locate or whip up."

"I lost all track of time and space," I said. "It's weird, because I am sitting here talking to you but I don't even feel like the same person that I was before. The truth is that if the walls melted right now and you sprouted butterfly wings and began singing opera, I wouldn't be all that surprised."

I half expected him to argue that I had been through a traumatic experience, but instead the smile slid off his face and his demeanor grew darkly serious.

"One of the other ingredients is Ibogaine," he said. "It's a powerful natural hallucinogenic derived from a root. It's banned in the United States, or it used to be, but you can easily get it in Mexico, if you don't get butchered by surviving cartel members or devoured by hordes of zombies with over a million corpses in them."

"So it makes you trip out?" That would account for the wild visions and out of body experiences I had undergone.

"Shamans used to take it," Moto said. "It's about a hundred times more powerful than LSD or mushrooms. They were giving it to junkies the last I heard because the trip was so heavy it scared them off ever using drugs again, that's if they lived through it. The dose you received was cleaner and more balanced than just eating the plant version, but it was also much stronger."

"How long does it last?"

"Usually not more than a couple of days. We were starting to get worried about you."

"How long have I been out?"

"Seven days."

Seven days? Is he kidding? How could I be high and locked in a room for a whole week and not know about it?

"I'd like to argue with you but I kind of lost track of time where I was," I said. "Am I still on it now?"

I turned my hand over in front of my face several times and waved it in the air. Moto laughed at me.

"No," he said. "You'd know. You were pretty incoherent when you were juiced up."

I looked around the room again at all the cameras. They'd been monitoring me like a lab rat. I knew it was a small price to pay for not being a mindless zombie, but it still made me uncomfortable. I didn't want to sound ungrateful so I kept my thoughts to myself.

"Will I feel any side effects?"

"It's possible," he said. "A few people reported feeling mild aftershocks after being given the antidote—like flash backs, but nothing serious. Walls breathing, people melting, losing track of time, that kind of thing."

"Oh," I said. "So nothing too scary like people around me transforming into flesh eating demons that want to kill me . . . or delusions of grandeur."

"No more than normal for you," he said, raising his finger to his temple and making a cuckoo bird gesture. "You've always been a little Loony Tunes, if you know what I mean."

"How did I get here?" I asked, ignoring his taunt.

"You were strapped down and transported in an armored Humvee. You were too close to consider air lifting. We only have one chopper and our fuel supplies are limited. Apache caught us up to speed on your condition and your friends filled in the blanks."

"Apache?" I shook my head more. "He told his name was Simon."

"Really?" Moto couldn't hide his amusement. "We never could get him to tell us his name. Not even to me in private. We took to calling him The Apache because he lived in a teepee and talked like a crazy Indian. It's like the guy speaks in riddles or something."

I smiled as I remembered thinking the exact same thing. I'd almost forgotten along the way what it was like to have real family that I grew up with. It made the end of the world that much easier, knowing he was with me.

"It's amazing what people will open up and tell you when you are about to die," I said sarcastically.

"I know what you mean," he said. "Believe it or not I've been where you are right now."

"What?"

My mind reeled. My brother had been bitten by a zombie? He'd had to go through all of this alone? It was more than my brain could comprehend.

"I'll tell you all about it later," he said, "or at least as much as I am allowed to tell you. In case you haven't noticed, we're not alone."

"Who is watching us?"

"I asked the general for permission to debrief you," he said. "He's been kind enough to give us some leeway considering the unusual circumstances around your discovery. He said only a Macnamara would try to kill a horde of zombies with a toothpick carnival sword to defend his two pals, more or less. I'm paraphrasing. Basically, I think you impressed him."

"So what aren't you telling me?"

I knew my brother's 'poker tells' from growing up with him. He was definitely keeping something from me, and it was big.

"Let's just start with what I *can* tell you," he said. "You are not allowed to tell anyone about being bitten by a zombie or about receiving an antidote. That's the big one. It's not as hard as it sounds though. No one in the outside world would believe you and no one here has the clearance to ask about it."

"What about the civilians on base?"

"Good question." He patted me on the shoulder. "It brings me to my next debriefing point. There are no civilians at Port Hueneme. If civilians were allowed, I would have brought you here from the start. The only non-military personal here are doctors and the wives of enlisted men. This is an advanced military base, the last one on the west coast. If you decide to remain here, you will need to enlist. Otherwise, you will be shipped to a controlled civilian population area, most likely the clean zone out near Las Vegas."

"I'm not old enough to enlist. I'm only sixteen."

"Age is no longer a consideration for those who wish to serve their country," he explained, sounding like a recruiting commercial. "America needs all the able-bodied trained soldiers it can get to fight this war."

"I don't want to be separated from you again. Will I get to stay here?"

"The general has assured me that if you are so inclined, I will be allowed to personally oversee your training. You're already temporarily assigned to my unit, just in case."

"I'm in," I said without hesitation.

Moto smiled, but there was sadness in his eyes. "Glad to hear it, soldier. I assured them that you would react this way. It's gonna make things a whole lot easier for a lot of jumpy people. Now the first thing we got to do is get you changed out of those hospital scrubs and into a proper uniform. After that, we're gonna shave off those curly locks of yours." He ran his fingers through my hair and messed it up. "If you need a moment to say goodbye to your Justin Beiber fever hairdo, I'll understand."

"What did you guys do with Benji?"

"You'll be happy to know that your little friend gladly enlisted the minute we got him back to camp and gave him a hot meal and a shower. He's been assigned a non-combat job working in the canteen. He's eager to see you, so he'll be glad to know you're up and moving around."

"He was there," I said. "He saw me get bit. What am I supposed to tell him?"

"It's not a problem," Moto said. "Benji is a soldier now. He's been debriefed, just like you. If the subject comes up, all you have to say is that the incident is classified and you're not allowed to talk about it."

"Oh," I said lamely. It was going to take a bit to get used

to this new way of life as a soldier.

"Aren't you forgetting about somebody?" Moto wore that knowing grin that drove me crazy when we were kids. It was the same look he gave me when Darla, the girl who lived across the way from us back home, brought me a Valentine's card one year.

"Felicity Jane," I said. It all seemed like a dream that I had been involved with a celebrity I'd met along the way. Then again, flesh eating zombies had taken over the world, so everything seemed kinda like a dream.

"Don't be shy," Moto said. "She's a great girl."

"Is she still here?"

"She is. They tried to send her away to a clean zone when she refused to enlist, but she said she wasn't leaving until she saw you. Apparently you made quite an impression on her."

"What am I supposed to tell her?"

"Tell her the truth. Tell her you are not allowed to talk about it and all that matters is that you are here now, alive and well. She'll understand."

"Are they going to make her leave?"

"Under normal circumstances they would for sure," he said. "As I said, this is an active military base. Strictly speaking there are no civilians here, aside from doctors and research assistants. I think we both know she's no ordinary girl."

"So you're saying that they are looking the other way and letting her stay because she was a celebrity?"

"I'm not saying that," he said, gesturing to the cameras again to remind me we were being watched.

"Then what are you saying?"

I could feel myself bristling at the suggestion that they were giving her special treatment because of who she was. I didn't like the thought of people treating her like a trained monkey that was there to amuse them. She was a real person, and she deserved to be treated with dignity and respect. I could feel the blood pounding in my ears as my desire to protect her at all costs began to override my logic and reason. I didn't even know what I was getting upset about.

"I'm saying that the higher-ups have decided for the time being that she is good for the troops' morale," he said. "You should be grateful. If she was just some girl you'd met on the road she'd be in the desert right now, probably working on a farm."

"When can I see her?"

"Just as soon as we've put you through the enlistment process and sworn you in. In addition to your enrollment application, there is some extra paperwork they are going to want you to sign as well, mostly going over what we've talked about here and how you can't repeat any of it without their permission."

"What are we waiting for?" I began looking for the exit to the padded white room. I wanted to see Felicity as fast as I could. Moto stopped me and gave me a bear hug that lifted me clear off my feet. I could feel a pinch in my side where the wound was, but I didn't complain.

"Glad to have you back, little brother."

"Glad to be back in one piece."

He gave me another big hug that nearly crushed the wind out of me, but I didn't fight him. For the first time in a very long time, I felt like everything was finally going to be okay again.

CHAPTER TWENTY SIX

"So they've had a cure all this time and they don't want anyone else to know about it?"

Felicity couldn't stop rubbing my freshly shaved head. It felt good at first, but after about ten minutes it was starting to get on my nerves. She hadn't stopped touching me since she caught sight of me crossing the base with Moto, on the way to get a batch of immunization shots. She'd been talking to a group of spellbound soldiers and stopped mid-sentence, jumping up and racing to throw herself into my arms. I had to practically pry her off the front of me, and when I did she showered me with kisses. Not that I minded, to be honest. I just didn't expect her affection to last this long. I'd never saved a girl's life before by trying to sacrifice myself. I didn't know how long the effect lasted.

"Keep your voice down," I whispered, looking around to make sure we weren't being watched more than usual. "They warned me that I'm not allowed to tell anyone, even you."

"But I was there," she protested. "How did they expect to hide that from me?"

"I'm just letting you know what they said. They made me sign a stack of paperwork saying I wouldn't talk about it. You'd have thought that there were camera units waiting outside to interview me or something. It was weird. Then the general congratulated me personally and gave me a medal of valor."

I absentmindedly ran my fingers over the small medal pinned to the chest of my clean new uniform.

"What are they going to do? Arrest you?" She turned and wrapped her arms around me, putting her head on my shoulder.

"They could," I said, nodding at some passing marines who couldn't take their eyes off Felicity. "Technically speaking, they own me now. They can do whatever they want to me if I break the rules."

"Moto would never allow it." She shook her head.

We were sitting out near the mechanical generators, staring at the electric fence in the distance. Felicity had offered to give me a tour of the base after I got my shots and Moto had thought it was a good idea. He'd dashed off in a hurry, then caught up with us a few minutes later and gave me back my katana.

"Now that you are a soldier you can have this back," he said. "We'll get you a gun later as well but for now just make sure you don't lose this again."

The blade was shiny and clean. I could tell by its pristine condition that he'd spent time sharpening and oiling it while I was locked down in the loony bin. I turned the blade over in my hands.

After that, we'd gone to see Benji in the canteen. He'd practically jumped over the counter to greet us, giving me a big hug then standing back and saluting me when his superior officer chastised him.

"Look what I found," he said in an excited, breathless voice as he held up a new comic book. "It's the Justice League."

"Glad to see nothing's changed," I teased him.

He didn't try to ask me about the incident with Simon the Apache at the mall, and I was glad not to have to lie to him. Felicity on the other hand kept bringing it up until I cracked. One look in her sea foam eyes and I knew there was nothing I could keep from her. For the first time in my life I was in love.

"Moto doesn't have as much power as you think," I said.

"What does that mean?"

"It means that he's not going to be able to keep them from shipping you off to Vegas when the general gets tired of you distracting his men with all your charms."

"I'm not distracting them," she protested.

"Really?" I pointed off in the distance where a bunch of soldiers that had been sitting and watching us quickly turned and pretended to be working again. "Are you sure about that?"

"I can help out around here too, you know," she pouted. "If that's how it's going to be then I will enlist like you did. Is that what you want?"

"No. Honestly I don't. There is no guarantee that they'd let you stay here at this base even if you did join up. You'd be completely at their mercy. In all likelihood, they'd send you off to the clean zone to supervise civilians and we'd be right back where we started."

"I don't want to leave you," she purred, leaning over and planting a kiss on my cheek that I could feel through my whole body. In the distance I heard one of the men whistle.

"There is another way," I said sheepishly, the words turning to sand in my mouth.

"What is it?"

"We could get married," I offered, unable to look at her. "If you were my wife then they would have to let you stay with me here. They wouldn't be able to separate us."

I turned and faced her. She looked like she was fighting back tears.

Cat's out of the bag, I thought. *No going back now.*

"Listen," I said, "I know we are both young but the world has changed. People used to get married at our age back when life was shorter, younger even. I can't imagine losing you again. I don't want to be separated. It's the only way."

My heart beat hard in my chest. I hadn't felt this afraid

taking on a zombie horde. It felt like an eternity without words. I wished I had died for real as I waited for her response. For a moment I thought the embarrassment of her impending rejection might just do the trick and finish me off.

"Are you serious?"

I looked her dead in the eyes. I couldn't read her reaction. Her gaze was intense and unblinking as it met mine.

"Yes," I said. "I am. I don't know what it is about you, but you've been under my skin from the minute you threatened to kill me with a shotgun. What can I say? I love you, Felicity Jane. Will you marry me?"

I didn't have to wait long for her reply this time. She threw her arms around my neck again and began crying on me. She squeezed me tight and then pulled back and kissed my neck over and over.

"So is that a yes?"

"Yes! Yes! A thousand times yes!"

I felt a wave of relief wash over me. Felicity pulled back and I kissed her hard on the mouth. It was amazing. I couldn't wait to be able to tell Moto. The base had a working chapel. We'd have the ceremony there with a small group of my brother's friends, the general perhaps, and Benji, of course. Felicity could get a job on the base and we'd see each other at night after I was done with my training and rounds. Things weren't so bad after all. Everything was finally going to be okay.

I leaned in and kissed her again, feeling that amazing sensation of time standing still as our lips touched for a thrilling few seconds. Loud air sirens wailed and pulled us from our perfect moment. They echoed off every side of the base. Standing up, we could see what looked like a huge dust cloud in the distance heading straight our way. After a moment it became clear that there were thousands of people out in the distance moving toward the base at a slow, steady pace.

"Is that what I think it is?" There was a note of wonder and awe in her voice as she spoke.

"Yep," I said matter-of-factly. "It's a massive zombie horde. The biggest I've ever seen."

"What do we do now?"

"Now," I said, reaching out and taking her hand in mine so that our fingers laced together, "we fight." I held my blade in my free hand and watched in awe as the first wave of the dead crashed through the electric fence and began slowly pressing forward in our direction.

-THE END-

ACKNOWLEDGEMENTS

First and foremost I would like to thank my loving and supportive wife, Angie. Without her constant encouragement, this book wouldn't be possible.

Thanks also to Troy Fuss, Don Salerno, Ani Arakelyan, and my hardworking editors, Patricia Bains-Jordan and Louise Bohmer. Last but not least thanks to Jacob Kier and Permuted Press for taking a chance on me.

The majority of this book was written while listening to *Appetite for Destruction* by Guns & Roses. Rewrites and edits were done to Metallica, Marilyn Manson, and (believe it or not) Bob Marley.

Look for the next book in the series coming in 2014 from Permuted Press!

Join the Horde on Facebook!
facebook.com/ZombieAttackRiseOfTheHorde

For more of my work and to keep in touch with me visit http://devansagliani.com.

Follow me on Twitter @DevanSagliani

PERMUTED PRESS

14
BY PETER CLINES

Padlocked doors. Strange light fixtures. Mutant cockroaches. There are some odd things about Nate's new apartment. Every room in this old brownstone has a mystery. Mysteries that stretch back over a hundred years. Some of them are in plain sight. Some are behind locked doors. And all together these mysteries could mean the end of Nate and his friends. Or the end of everything...

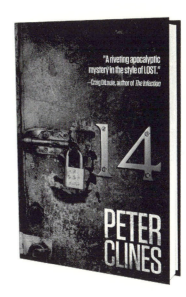

— PERMUTEDPRESS.COM —

BREW
BY BILL BRADDOCK

Ever been to a big college town on a football Saturday night? Loud drunks glut the streets, swaggering about in roaring, leering, laughing packs, like sailors on shore leave. These nights crackle with a dark energy born of incongruity; for beneath all that smiling and singing sprawls a bedrock of malice.

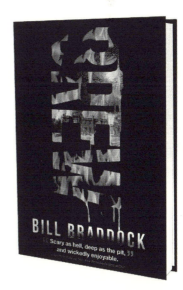

PERMUTED PRESS

PERMUTED PRESS

THE INFECTION
BY CRAIG DiLOUIE

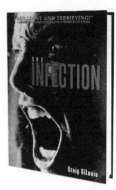

The world is rocked as one in five people collapse screaming before falling into a coma. Three days later, the Infected awake with a single purpose: spread the Infection. A small group—a cop, teacher, student, reverend—team up with a military crew to survive. But at a refugee camp what's left of the government will ask them to accept a dangerous mission back into the very heart of Infection.

--- PERMUTEDPRESS.COM ---

THE KILLING FLOOR
BY CRAIG DiLOUIE

The mystery virus struck down millions. Three days later, its victims awoke with a single violent purpose: spread the Infection. Ray Young, survivor of a fight to save a refugee camp from hordes of Infected, awakes from a coma to learn he has also survived Infection. Ray is not immune. Instead, he has been transformed into a superweapon that could end the world … or save it.

--- PERMUTEDPRESS.COM ---

THE INFECTION BOX SET
BY CRAIG DiLOUIE

Two full #1 bestselling apocalyptic thrillers for one low price! Includes the full novels THE INFECTION and THE KILLING FLOOR. A mysterious virus suddenly strikes down millions. Three days later, its victims awake with a single purpose: spread the Infection. As the world lurches toward the apocalypse, some of the Infected continue to change, transforming into horrific monsters.

PERMUTED PRESS

PERMUTED PRESS

BLOOD SOAKED & CONTAGIOUS
BY JAMES CRAWFORD

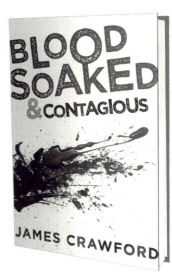

I am not going to complain to you about my life.

We've got zombies. They are not the brainless, rotting creatures we'd been led to expect. Unfortunately for us, they're just as smart as they were before they died, very fast, much stronger than you or me, and possess no internal editor at all.

Claws. Did I mention claws?

PERMUTEDPRESS.COM

BLOOD SOAKED & INVADED
BY JAMES CRAWFORD

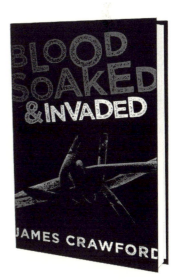

Zombies were bad enough, but now we're being invaded from all sides. Up to our necks in blood, body parts, and unanswerable questions...

...As soon as the realization hit me, I lost my cool. I curled into the fetal position in a pile of blood, offal, and body parts, and froze there. What in the Hell was I becoming that killing was entertaining and satisfying?

PERMUTED PRESS

PERMUTED PRESS

DOMAIN OF THE DEAD
BY IAIN MCKINNON

The world is dead, devoured by a plague of reanimated corpses. Barricaded inside a warehouse with dwindling food, a group of survivors faces two possible deaths: creeping starvation, or the undead outside. In their darkest hour hope appears in the form of a helicopter approaching the city... but is it the salvation the survivors have been waiting for?

— PERMUTEDPRESS.COM —

REMAINS OF THE DEAD
BY IAIN MCKINNON

The world is dead. Cahz and his squad of veteran soldiers are tasked with flying into abandoned cities and retrieving zombies for scientific study. Then the unbelievable happens. After years of encountering nothing but the undead, the team discovers a handful of survivors in a fortified warehouse with dwindling supplies.

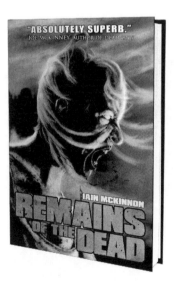

PERMUTED PRESS

PERMUTED PRESS

AMONG THE LIVING
BY TIMOTHY W. LONG

The dead walk. Now the real battle for Seattle has begun. Lester has a new clientele, the kind that requires him to deal lead instead of drugs. Mike suspects a conspiracy lies behind the chaos. Kate has a dark secret: she's a budding young serial killer. These survivors, along with others, are drawn together in their quest to find the truth behind the spreading apocalypse.

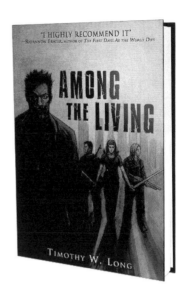

— PERMUTEDPRESS.COM —

AMONG THE DEAD
BY TIMOTHY W. LONG

Seattle is under siege by masses of living dead, and the military struggles to prevent the virus from spreading outside the city. Kate is tired of sitting around. When she learns that a rescue mission is heading back into the chaos, she jumps at the chance to tag along and put her unique skill set and, more importantly, swords to use.

PERMUTED PRESS

PERMUTED PRESS

ROADS LESS TRAVELED: THE PLAN
BY C. DULANEY

Ask yourself this: If the dead rise tomorrow, are you ready? Do you have a plan? Kasey, a strong-willed loner, has something she calls The Zombie Plan. But every plan has its weaknesses, and a freight train of tragedy is bearing down on Kasey and her friends. In the darkness that follows, Kasey's Plan slowly unravels: friends lost, family taken, their stronghold reduced to ashes.

— PERMUTEDPRESS.COM —

MURPHY'S LAW
(ROADS LESS TRAVELED BOOK 2)
BY C. DULANEY

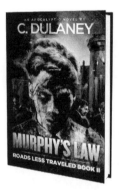

Kasey and the gang were held together by a set of rules, their Zombie Plan. It kept them alive through the beginning of the End. But when the chaos faded, they became careless, and Murphy's Law decided to pay a long-overdue visit. Now the group is broken and scattered with no refuge in sight. Those remaining must make their way across West Virginia in search of those who were stolen from them.

— PERMUTEDPRESS.COM —

SHADES OF GRAY
(ROADS LESS TRAVELED BOOK 3)
BY C. DULANEY

Kasey and the gang have come full circle through the crumbling world. Working for the National Guard, they realize old friends and fellow survivors are disappearing. When the missing start to reappear as walking corpses, the group sets out on another journey to discover the truth. Their answers wait in the West Virginia Command Center.

PERMUTED PRESS

PERMUTED PRESS

NEW ZED ORDER: SURVIVE
BY TODD SPRAGUE

The dead have risen, and they are hungry. In Vermont, John Mason and his beautiful young wife Sara believe that family can survive anything. When the apocalypse arrives they pack food, clothing, and weapons, then hit the road seeking refuge in the mountains of John's youth. There they, together with family, friends, and neighbors, build a stronghold against the encroaching mass of the dead.

PERMUTEDPRESS.COM

THE JUNKIE QUATRAIN
BY PETER CLINES

Six months ago, the world ended. The Baugh Contagion swept across the planet. Its victims were left twitching, adrenalized cannibals that quickly became know as Junkies. THE JUNKIE QUATRAIN is four tales of survival, and four types of post-apocalypse story. Because the end of the world means different things for different people. Loss. Opportunity. Hope. Or maybe just another day on the job.

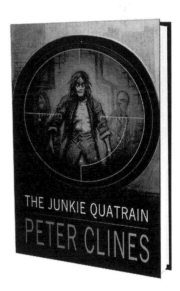

PERMUTED PRESS

PERMUTED PRESS

THE UNDEAD SITUATION
BY ELOISE J. KNAPP

The dead are rising. People are dying. Civilization is collapsing. But Cyrus V. Sinclair couldn't care less; he's a sociopath. Amidst the chaos, Cyrus sits with little more emotion than one of the walking corpses… until he meets up with other inconvenient survivors who cramp his style and force him to re-evaluate his outlook on life. It's Armageddon, and things will definitely get messy.

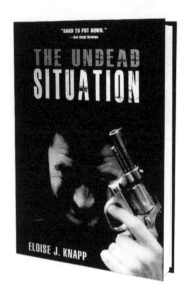

— PERMUTEDPRESS.COM —

THE UNDEAD HAZE
(THE UNDEAD SITUATION BOOK 2)
BY ELOISE J. KNAPP

When remorse drives Cyrus to abandon his hidden compound he doesn't realize what new dangers lurk in the undead world. He knows he must wade through the vilest remains of humanity and hordes of zombies to settle scores and find the one person who might understand him. But this time, it won't be so easy. Zombies and unpleasant survivors aren't the only thing Cyrus has to worry about.

PERMUTED PRESS

PERMUTED PRESS

DEAD LIVING
BY GLENN BULLION

It didn't take long for the world to die. And it didn't take long, either, for the dead to rise. Aaron was born on the day the world ended. Kept in seclusion, his family teaches him the basics. How to read and write. How to survive. Then Aaron makes a shocking discovery. The undead, who desire nothing but flesh, ignore him. It's as if he's invisible to them.

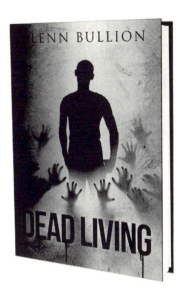

---PERMUTEDPRESS.COM---

AUTOBIOGRAPHY of a WEREWOLF HUNTER
BY BRIAN P. EASTON

After his mother is butchered by a werewolf, Sylvester James is taken in by a Cheyenne mystic. The boy trains to be a werewolf hunter, learning to block out pain, stalk, fight, and kill. As Sylvester sacrifices himself to the hunt, his hatred has become a monster all its own. As he follows his vendetta into the outlands of the occult, he learns it takes more than silver bullets to kill a werewolf.

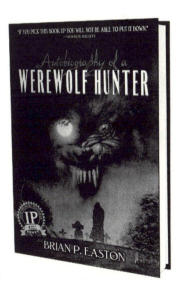

PERMUTED PRESS

PERMUTED PRESS

INFECTION:
ALASKAN UNDEAD APOCALYPSE
BY SEAN SCHUBERT

Anchorage, Alaska: gateway to serene wilderness of The Last Frontier. No stranger to struggle, the city on the edge of the world is about to become even more isolated. When a plague strikes, Anchorage becomes a deadly trap for its citizens. The only two land routes out of the city are cut, forcing people to fight or die as the infection spreads.

— PERMUTEDPRESS.COM —

CONTAINMENT
(ALASKAN UNDEAD APOCALYPSE BOOK 2)
BY SEAN SCHUBERT

Running. Hiding. Surviving. Anchorage, once Alaska's largest city, has fallen. Now a threatening maze of death, the city is firmly in the cold grip of a growing zombie horde. Neil Jordan and Dr. Caldwell lead a small band of desperate survivors through the maelstrom. The group has one last hope: that this nightmare has been contained, and there still exists a sane world free of infection.

PERMUTED PRESS

PERMUTED PRESS

MAD SWINE: THE BEGINNING
BY STEVEN PAJAK

People refer to the infected as "zombies," but that's not what they really are. Zombie implies the infected have died and reanimated. The thing is, they didn't die. They're just not human anymore. As the infection spreads and crazed hordes--dubbed "Mad Swine"--take over the cities, the residents of Randall Oaks find themselves locked in a desperate struggle to survive in the new world.

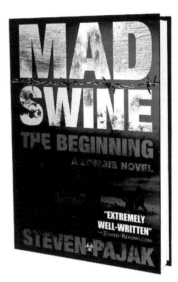

— PERMUTEDPRESS.COM —

MAD SWINE: DEAD WINTER
BY STEVEN PAJAK

Three months after the beginning of the Mad Swine outbreak, the residents of Randall Oaks have reached their breaking point. After surviving the initial outbreak and a war waged with their neighboring community, Providence, their supplies are severely close to depletion. With hostile neighbors at their flanks and hordes of infected outside their walls, they have become prisoners within their own community.

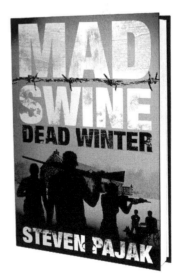

PERMUTED PRESS

PERMUTED PRESS

DEAD TIDE
BY STEPHEN A. NORTH

THE WORLD IS ENDING. BUT THERE ARE SURVIVORS. Nick Talaski is a hard-bitten, angry cop. Graham is a newly divorced cab driver. Bronte is a Gulf War veteran hunting his brother's killer. Janicea is a woman consumed by unflinching hate. Trish is a gentleman's club dancer. Morgan is a morgue janitor. The dead have risen and the citizens of St. Petersburg and Pinellas Park are trapped. The survivors are scattered, and options are few. And not all monsters are created by a bite. Some still have a mind of their own…

— PERMUTEDPRESS.COM —

DEAD TIDE RISING
BY STEPHEN A. NORTH

The sequel to Dead Tide continues the carnage in Pinellas Park near St. Pete, Florida. Follow all of the characters from the first book, Dead Tide, as they fight for survival in a world destroyed by the zombie apocalypse.

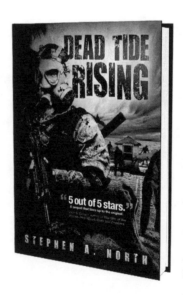

PERMUTED PRESS

PERMUTED PRESS

RISE
BY GARETH WOOD

Within hours of succumbing to a plague, millions of dead rise to attack the living. Brian Williams flees the city with his sister Sarah. Banded with other survivors, the group remains desperately outnumbered and under-armed. With no food and little fuel, they must fight their way to safety. RISE is the story of the extreme measures a family will take to survive a trek across a country gone mad.

— PERMUTEDPRESS.COM —

AGE OF THE DEAD
BY GARETH WOOD

A year has passed since the dead rose, and the citizens of Cold Lake are out of hope. Food and weapons are nearly impossible to find, and the dead are everywhere. In desperation Brian Williams leads a salvage team into the mountains. But outside the small safe zones the world is a foreign place. Williams and his team must use all of their skills to survive in the wilderness ruled by the dead.

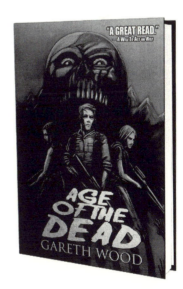

PERMUTED PRESS

PERMUTED PRESS

DEAD MEAT
BY PATRICK & CHRIS WILLIAMS

The city of River's Edge has been quarantined due to a rodent borne rabies outbreak. But it quickly becomes clear to the citizens that the infection is something much, much worse than rabies... The townsfolk are attacked and fed upon by packs of the living dead. Gavin and Benny attempt to survive the chaos in River's Edge while making their way north in search of sanctuary.

PERMUTEDPRESS.COM

ROTTER WORLD
BY SCOTT M. BAKER

Eight months ago vampires released the Revenant Virus on humanity. Both species were nearly wiped out. The creator of the virus claims there is a vaccine that will make humans and vampires immune to the virus, but it's located in a secure underground facility five hundred miles away. To retrieve the vaccine, a raiding party of humans and vampires must travel down the devastated East Coast.

PERMUTED PRESS

PERMUTED PRESS

THE BECOMING
BY JESSICA MEIGS

The Michaluk Virus has escaped the CDC, and its effects are widespread and devastating. Most of the population of the southeastern United States have become homicidal cannibals. As society rapidly crumbles under the hordes of infected, three people--Ethan, a Memphis police officer; Cade, his best friend; and Brandt, a lieutenant in the US Marines--band together against the oncoming crush of death.

— PERMUTEDPRESS.COM —

THE BECOMING: GROUND ZERO (BOOK 2)
BY JESSICA MEIGS

After the Michaluk Virus decimated the southeast, Ethan and his companions became like family. But the arrival of a mysterious woman forces them to flee from the infected, and the cohesion the group cultivated is shattered. As members of the group succumb to the escalating dangers on their path, new alliances form, new loves develop, and old friendships crumble.

— PERMUTEDPRESS.COM —

THE BECOMING: REVELATIONS (BOOK 3)
BY JESSICA MEIGS

In a world ruled by the dead, Brandt Evans is floundering. Leadership of their dysfunctional group wasn't something he asked for or wanted. Their problems are numerous: Remy Angellette is grief-stricken and suicidal, Gray Carter is distant and reclusive, and Cade Alton is near death. And things only get worse.

PERMUTED PRESS

PERMUTED PRESS

PAVLOV'S DOGS
BY D.L. SNELL & THOM BRANNAN

WEREWOLVES Dr. Crispin has engineered the saviors of mankind: soldiers capable of transforming into beasts. ZOMBIES Ken and Jorge get caught in a traffic jam on their way home from work. It's the first sign of a major outbreak. ARMAGEDDON Should Dr. Crisping send the Dogs out into the zombie apocalypse to rescue survivors? Or should they hoard their resources and post the Dogs as island guards?

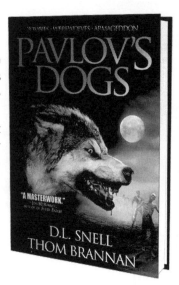

— PERMUTEDPRESS.COM —

THE OMEGA DOG
BY D.L. SNELL & THOM BRANNAN

Twisting and turning through hordes of zombies, cartel territory, Mayan ruins, and the things that now inhabit them, a group of survivors must travel to save one man's family from a nightmarish third world gone to hell. But this time, even best friends have deadly secrets, and even allies can't be trusted - as a father's only hope of getting his kids out alive is the very thing that's hunting him down.

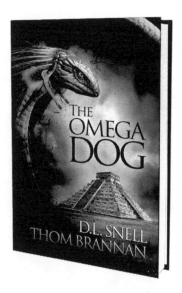

PERMUTED PRESS

NOW AVAILABLE IN EBOOK!

LONG VOYAGE BACK
BY LUKE RHINEHART

When the bombs came, only the lucky escaped. In the horror that followed, only the strong would survive. The voyage of the trimaran Vagabond began as a pleasure cruise on the Chesapeake Bay. Then came the War Alert ... the unholy glow on the horizon ... the terrifying reports of nuclear destruction. In the days that followed, it became clear just how much chaos was still to come.

—— PERMUTEDPRESS.COM ——

QUARANTINED
BY JOE MCKINNEY

The citizens of San Antonio, Texas are threatened with extermination by a terrifying outbreak of the flu. Quarantined by the military to contain the virus, the city is in a desperate struggle to survive. Inside the quarantine walls, Detective Lily Harris finds herself caught up in a conspiracy intent on hiding the news from the world and fighting a population threatening to boil over into revolt.

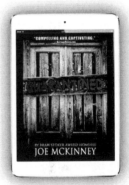

—— PERMUTEDPRESS.COM ——

THE DESERT
BY BRYON MORRIGAN

Give up trying to leave. There's no way out. Those are the final words in a journal left by the last apparent survivor of a platoon that disappear in Iraq. Years later, two soldiers realize that what happened to the "Lost Platoon" is now happening to them. Now they must confront the horrifying creatures responsible for their misfortune, or risk the same fate as that of the soldiers before them.

NOW AVAILABLE IN EBOOK!

Made in the USA
San Bernardino, CA
10 December 2013